The

The Scattering

Lauri Kubuitsile

Published in 2016 by Penguin Random House South Africa (Pty) Ltd

Company Reg No 1953/000441/07

Estuaries No 4, Oxbow Crescent, Century Avenue, Century City, 7441, South Africa

PO Box 1144, Cape Town, 8000, South Africa

www.penguinbooks.co.za

First edition, first printing 2016

1 3 5 7 9 8 6 4 2

ISBN 978-1-4859-0307-9 (Print)

ISBN 978-1-4859-0343-7 (ePub)

ISBN 978-1-4859-0344-4 (PDF)

Cover design by Michiel Botha

Cover photography courtesy of Sam DCruz/Shutterstock (dune)
and starto8/Shutterstock (tea pot)

Author photograph by Thato Ntshabele

Text design by Chérie Collins

Set in 12 on 16 pt Granjon

Printed and bound by Novus Print, a Novus Holdings company

For Ponche

Tsau, Bechuanaland
December 1907

It's not easy coming back from the dead, Tjipuka thinks, lying on her bed looking at her sleeping husband, Ruhapo. Somewhere in that dead time things got lost, things changed. What she thought she knew so well, the things engraved on her heart, were not true any more, but she knew it was wrong to say that out loud. Many people lost everyone after the scattering, so she and Ruhapo were lucky, lucky to have found each other again. Lucky – and she should not make people angry, make the ancestors who had protected them angry, by questioning the parts of her husband that now seemed strange, that now seemed wrong.

So Tjipuka pretends everything is right, as it should be, as she remembers, but she knows it is not. They both do. Things are different, and when she gets the chance, she tries to pick through the pieces to find her husband, the husband she thinks she remembers, to assure herself that he is there. She sifts and sorts the bits that are familiar, and separates them from the bits she's forgotten or were never there before. She wonders what to do with these bits, the bits that belong to a stranger. They make her uncertain about everything else.

Being dead made a lot of things uncertain.

She holds Ruhapo's hands and runs her eyes over them. His hands are her hands, familiar and remembered. The long fingers and square knuckles are the ones she knows. These hands are the ones that made love to her so long ago, and that held their son with such solid love and unreserved joy. These are her hands.

Her eyes glide upward. The wrists are hers too, with their slight dip near the wrist bone. She knows these. She could find them in a crowd of strangers, even years from now, and know she had found her husband. They are the real parts, the parts that survived.

She accepts that they have both risen from the dead and that such a momentous event should affect a person. Tjipuka knows she is changed – why shouldn't Ruhapo be changed too? But still she searches for him, searches for the remembered bits, the loved bits amid the ruins.

She runs her finger along his forearm. He sleeps on. She stops at the inside of his elbow, the soft wrinkled skin; she bends her head and kisses it lightly. She knows this spot. It is one of her favourites. She lingers on it, rubbing her finger lightly back and forth. It reminds her of their life before the scattering, before the blood and the cruelty, before the loss.

Her finger continues over the muscle of his upper arm. It excites her, this muscle she knows so well, tight and ready. It buzzes under the skin with his energy, his masculinity, and she feels it reverberate through her. It is a feeling she's familiar with. This was not lost along the way; she's thankful for that.

Then she holds his shoulder. She feels weak when she does; she wants to fall into him, to give everything to him to carry on those strong, wide shoulders. She knows he can do it. He will not complain. But she won't submit to that weakness – it would not be fair. She knows neither one of them is ready for that. She is not ready to give in, to trust him to bear the load for her. Nor is he ready to accept the burden, free of resentment, free of regrets.

She leans forward again to smell the tender, vulnerable skin in the dip of his collarbone. It is grass and cows. It is sweat and soap. It smells of her. This place is familiar, just as it always was.

All of these places – the fingers, the wrist, the inside of his elbow, the crook of his neck – are soft lies where she could hide forever if she believed in lies. They are the easy places, the familiar, the known. The unchanged. The places where all is calm and kind. The places where love is certain. The places where the husband she lost on Ohamakari lives, where he comes to her and they know each other again. She wants to stay right there with him, as if time had not moved ahead. As if they had never been dead and risen again.

But she cannot. She is always one who wants the truth; it is one of the many burdens she carries. She cannot live in a lie even when she knows how raw and painful the alternative is.

She looks at Ruhapo's sleeping face, not restful even then. But there lies the truth of it all. The truth is in his face. She suspects it is in her face too, but she doesn't know that for sure. She suspects he does and turns away from her so as not to see it.

She wants to close her eyes to his face. Not to look at it. Not to be reminded that nothing is familiar there. It is all a façade, a cruel trick. But she will not turn away. She wants to read the worst of what is there. If she can take the worst, the most horrible, the unimaginable, then she'll be fine. But she must find it; she must plumb it to its depths to be sure she has seen all of it. She must search and search until she can face everything.

His nose looks the same – his wide nose, a nose that she has known since childhood. Unchanged, it tries to carry the entire story of his face, to hide the unfamiliar. But it can't.

His mouth is a failure too. The one she knew had vulnerable edges. Vulnerable to a smile when not intended. It would push in from the sides when he feigned being angry with her. The smile would insist on having its way. That was the mouth that she knew. This mouth, the one he came back from the dead with, has no vulnerability. That was lost in the heat and blood, in the cruelty. No one can blame it. Still, it is unfamiliar. It is someone else's mouth placed on her man. That error, that mistake, makes her uncertain of everything else. What is true and what is false? What can be trusted? Where is the man she loves? Is he his familiar wrist or this stranger's mouth? He cannot be both.

Then there is the lost tilt of his head. When she first saw him clearly, when they were just children, he asked her what she was doing wandering in the bush. When she said she was looking for the castle of the queen, he tilted his head. For her, that came to define him. A tilt of his head meant interest in everything he had yet to know. He was always asking, always curious, wanting to know the next thing, and, once he knew that, wanting the answer a step beyond – the journey to the answer always beginning with the tilt of his head.

She never told him – and likely never would now, it would be too cruel, she thinks – but she fell in love with him with that first tilt of his head. But now it is gone. She sometimes thinks it means her love for him is gone as well. She tells herself that it can't be. Her love is too big to disappear with a tilt of the head.

The tilt has been lost with so many other things – lost in the trampled grass, wet with blood, littered with bodies. In the trees decorated with corpses. In the crying babies and the too-quiet mothers. She doesn't blame him. He's learned enough now. He doesn't ask any more questions, because he doesn't want any more answers. There is no longer any fun in being curious. They all have learned enough. They don't want to know anything else. The answers are known now; they are painful and they are horrible.

Worst of all, though, in that strange unfamiliar face, are the eyes, thankfully closed as she stares at him sleeping. The eyes she knew, the eyes she felt she owned and kept safe in the deep folds of her heart, those eyes were not like these. They were not judging eyes. Those were soft and inviting – accepting and forgiving and loving and caring. A look from those eyes would solve everything for her. Nothing would harm her when she could look into those eyes.

But those eyes are gone. Now only a sleek black wall looks back at her. No one gets in any more, especially not her. She knows why. To live under certain circumstances, parts of you must die. She knows this. She made those choices too. They all did. But what did it mean then? Were they still the same people? Would they ever be again?

She hates him sometimes for his eyes. She wants to beat him and shout and demand he let her in. Not the others, just her. Is it asking too much? Have they not suffered enough?

She hates his shut-off eyes, his untilted head, his hard, unyielding mouth. Let the man who owns these things come and fetch them, she wants to scream. Take these strange pieces away. She isn't sure she can love a man with these bits of a stranger about him. But how can she tell him, stop being you? Stop being this man who you are now? She knows it is unreasonable, but she knows she cannot live in a lie either. He once said he loved that about her, but now he offers tender lies and awful truths, and she can accept neither. How will they ever survive? How will they find their way past all of this? How will any of them find their way past all of this?

Sometimes she thinks they never will. Sometimes she tells herself that she has no option but to love this stranger, and that Ruhapo has no choice but to love the stranger in her as well.

Tjipuka

I

Okahandja, German South-West Africa
February 1894

When she woke that morning, Tjipuka had only one thing on her mind – to collect the queen's castle. In the night, she'd dreamed of holding her hidden treasure and could think of nothing except being free to feel it in her hands. She'd managed to escape her mother's plans for her, to clean the big iron cooking pots, and had only just dug her treasure out of its hiding place in the bush when she heard a noise. Looking up, she saw a boy herding a stray red calf with a stick, coming far too near to where she was hiding.

Tjipuka crouched in the cool, solid shade of the thorn bush and watched him as he passed. She knew stillness, and she tried her best to be the duiker, to melt into her surroundings, to disappear. She was sure he could not see her, but then he stopped.

'What's that?' Ruhapo, the boy, said, his head tilted. She knew then she'd been discovered, but stayed where she was and made no sound. Tjipuka sat holding her treasure, ignoring the boy. She watched a big green praying mantis eat a moth nearly its own size. Sitting still allowed her to discover such things that moving about and making noise hid from most people. She wasn't happy that this boy had disturbed her. And now the praying mantis had flown off too. She hoped that if she didn't speak he would go away. She didn't like boys much and this boy, with his busy arms and legs, made her nervous. She didn't want him seeing her treasure.

Despite her wishes, he bent his head down and tucked it under the canopy of the thorn bush. He looked down at what was in her hand, an egg-shaped object made of intricate brown wax linked like lace, the walls so thin that the light shone through. She held it carefully, but was looking somewhere else.

'What's that?' he asked again.

She spoke to the air to her left, her head turned away so as not to encourage him. 'It's the queen's castle.'

'Let me hold it.'

He held out his hands, but she made no movement, barely acknow-ledging he was there at all.

'I'll be careful, as careful as holding a new calf. I promise. I know how to be careful, I'm good at careful. I just want to hold it and I'll give it right back. I swear I won't break it. Let me hold it.'

Tjipuka looked him up and down. He seemed sincere and she had to admit that this boy did have kind eyes. Honest and sincere, trustworthy eyes. Maybe he was speaking the truth. And he seemed interested in what she had found, which was more than she could say for most people. Her mother shouted at her when she brought home her collections from the bush, saying they made the house dirty.

Her father, always busy with the cattle or with the holy fire he was responsible for as a chief and priest, smiled and pretended to listen, but heard nothing. He'd pat her on the head and say, 'That's nice, Tjipuka.'

It was only Novengi, her best friend, who cared about the things that mattered to Tjipuka. The mysteries in the bush, mysteries like the termite queen's castle. And now this odd, pushy boy.

She gave it to him, but watched him carefully. Perhaps he was not like all the other boys. She watched him as he rolled the royal chamber around in his hands to look at it from every angle. He held it with the respect it deserved, and she appreciated that.

'It's beautiful.'

'It needs to be. A queen deserves to live only in a beautiful house,' Tjipuka said. She usually preferred to be quiet, but, for reasons she didn't quite understand, she wanted this boy to understand things correctly. She wanted him to understand why she thought the way she did.

She'd dug in the termite mound for many days to find the queen's royal chamber. She'd read about it in a book she'd found at the mission station, and wanted to know if it was true – if it was true that the termite queen lived in a beautiful egg hidden deep underground. She'd been looking for some time, months, digging up one termite mound after another, but she'd only been successful two days ago. She'd dug for almost a week on that mound, as far down into the ground as the termite mound had risen above it. She'd spent hours digging, but she didn't mind; she liked being alone in the bush, she understood the bush. She loved its music and its moods. They were easy to understand. It was people she was fearful of, each one so different, each behaving in odd ways that couldn't be understood, ways that had no proper, rational motivation. Unlike nature. Everything in nature was done for a purpose. This Tjipuka found comforting. It was just a matter of understanding the purpose, the reason behind the things she saw in nature, and then it made sense.

She knew people could not be understood. A person killed another – not for food or even because the other person attacked them. They might kill for another reason, one that made no sense at all even when they explained their motivation. A person might smile and then say the most hurtful thing. An animal never did that. Animals would warn you that they were angry, that pain was coming. A hyena might raise its fur, a wildebeest might scratch the ground, an elephant might spread its ears. They never tricked you. All you needed to do was to understand. But you could study humans your whole life, and even another one again, and you'd never understand them – they would never make sense.

Tjipuka had searched and searched for the termite queen. Finally she'd found the big white queen inside her beautiful wax home surrounded by her workers. Tjipuka had apologised for stealing the egg, and had then put them all carefully back into the termite mound and taken the beautiful house for herself. She'd hidden it in a hole nearby. She certainly couldn't take it home where her mother might find it and throw it away; it was far too valuable.

Though she pretended otherwise, Tjipuka knew this boy. He was the son of Ruhapo. Johannes was the boy's school name, Johannes Ruhapo, though most people just called him Ruhapo. The missionaries always gave the children new names because the Otjiherero names were too difficult for their German tongues. Her friend Novengi knew this boy better than Tjipuka, though. Novengi kept track of all of the boys. She wanted to understand them, even though Tjipuka knew it was a waste of time.

'I'll not be marrying a fool,' Novengi vowed – her reason for the close study. Marriages were arranged by their families, but no one would persuade Novengi to marry someone she did not want to. Even her parents knew not to get involved in such an unwinnable fight. In any case, Novengi was already in love with the too-serious Kahaka; even her uncles had heard of it. This was how Novengi knew Ruhapo. Kahaka and Ruhapo were often together – friends, Tjipuka thought.

This boy, Ruhapo, went to the mission school in Otjimbingwe with Kahaka. Tjipuka and Novengi had also gone there, but only long enough to learn to read and write and do a few sums. Tjipuka didn't like the strict rules of the missionaries. The rules were so arbitrary and hard to follow. Why sit still? What did that matter? Did you learn more if you were still? Tjipuka didn't. Why read a book you were not interested in? Who cared what fifty-two divided by six was? It all made no sense to her.

As the youngest at home, and the favourite of her father, Tjipuka was never punished, especially not with a stick. But the missionaries were keen on sticks of all kinds. They had thin ones to slap hard on a small hand, thicker ones to whip across a bent-over back.

One school holiday, Tjipuka came home to Okahandja and an-
nounced that she would not go back to the Christians. Novengi soon
followed, even though she'd been the brightest in their class. She could
not be apart from Tjipuka. They'd learned to read and write from the
missionaries; the rest they'd do on their own.

Now, Tjipuka looked at Ruhapo. She could see he'd grown too tall
for his body, only dangly arms and legs at the moment, but one day
soon he'd fill out and he'd be a strong, fit man. His family had moved
to Okahandja only a few years before. She'd heard stories from her
own father about how they'd lived near Gobabis, in the south, and how
the German settlers had taken their cattle and their land. They were
told that the chief, Samuel Maharero, had signed a paper that gave the
Germans the right to do it; the chief's sons had even helped to push
Ruhapo's father and the other Herero off the land.

When Tjipuka's father said this, he shook his head sadly. He didn't always agree with the decisions of Samuel Maharero, but the Germans had
decided he would be the leader of Hereroland and the people there, their
paramount chief, and there was little that could be done about that now.

The elder Ruhapo had already built his herd larger than the herds of
most of the men he'd found when he arrived in Okahandja. Johannes
was his only son. Novengi told her he was a quick-tempered boy, always
ready to fight if annoyed, though a leader among the other boys. Where
he went, others followed. Even the serious Kahaka respected Ruhapo.
When he spoke, they listened.

Tjipuka liked a person who went where others feared to go. She
respected a person like that; she wished she could be more that way.
Novengi was like that, never afraid of anything. Once a teacher at the
mission school beat Tjipuka with a ruler on the hand and Tjipuka
started to cry. The teacher ordered her to put out her hand again for
another slap. But then Novengi stepped forward and held out her hand.
'Beat me instead.'

The teacher saw the hard look in Novengi's eyes and knew she could
not win in a battle with this determined girl. She brought the ruler down

on her small hand once and with little force, then turned back to the front of the class, leaving Novengi to blow on Tjipuka's hand to make it better and to rub her own on her dress before sitting down again.

Novengi was brave and calm. She feared no one. Tjipuka was timid and wished she and Novengi could live alone, away from all the complicated and confusing people. She wished they could build themselves their own wax egg like the termites and live deep underground where no one could trouble them. She liked to be alone – if not alone, then with Novengi.

But, for some reason, she felt safe with this boy Ruhapo, though she would never let him know it. Not yet anyway. She watched him roll the termite queen's house in his hands, looking at it from every angle, letting the sun shine through its delicate walls, turning them a very pale grey like the sky at dawn. He was trying to learn its secrets and Tjipuka liked that.

His head stayed tilted in that odd way he had. 'Who lives in here with the termite queen?'

'She lives with the workers, who are for her only, and a tiny king. She's big and fat and white. As long as my finger. The workers feed her and take care of her. They even move her around. She hasn't any legs at all. They have to take perfect care of her. They must keep her happy all of the time.'

'Where did you find this?' he asked.

'In the centre of the mound. It's not easy to find. Only certain people are able to find it. You must be very committed.'

'I'm committed,' he said, his mind concentrating on the egg.

She knew he would go and try to find one for himself. She could see that in his face. He was a boy who wanted to understand things completely. He also knew enough to listen if others knew more than he did, so he could learn. Tjipuka liked that about him too. Boys usually liked to hear themselves talk and had little interest in what she had to say. She liked a boy who listened, who thought she had something important to say too.

Keeping his promise, he carefully handed the wax egg back to her, a cheeky smile forming at the edge of his lips. 'Why's a chief's daughter digging in termite mounds? That doesn't seem like such a royal thing to be doing.'

'Why is a mission-school boy moving about the bush? I thought you have books to read. Letters to write.'

He smiled at her flared temper.

Someone called from a distance. Ruhapo looked at Tjipuka, eyes sparkling. 'I must go. But Tjipuka, daughter of Mutati, remember this day. One day you'll be my wife. I'll build you a house made of wax, fit for a queen. I'll make sure I learn how to keep a queen happy too. You'll see ... one day, you'll see I'm telling you the truth.'

'What do you know of wives? Your uncle will pick one for you and you will say nothing,' Tjipuka said, annoyed at his impertinence.

'You don't know me. I need a special wife. A wife who will fill my heart. A wife like you.'

He ran off in the direction from which the voice came, not waiting to hear her answer to his arrogant words.

Tjipuka sat rolling the queen's egg in her hands. Who did this boy think he was, saying such things to her? She could build her own house of wax if she wanted, she didn't need him. She had no intention of marrying anyone.

After a while, though, when the anger had seeped from her mind and she could hear the birds singing in the trees again, she wondered if Ruhapo might be right. Would this determined boy one day be her husband? She had to admit he was different from other boys. Different in good ways, in understandable ways. This was a boy she thought she might be able to give her attention to. And she might not mind too much living in her termite castle with him.

2

Okahandja, German South-West Africa
January 1903

They lay on their bed, the one her father had bought them for their wedding, in a hut she'd built with the other women in the Ruhapo family onganda. They had a small portion of land at the edge of the compound, near her mother-in-law's house.

Tjipuka loved the hut with its simple construction. And she loved the bed with a proper mattress and a carved wooden headboard where beautiful, ornate birds and vines tangled around one another. She kept the plot around the hut tidy and clean. She'd bought a velvet blanket for their bed and an embroidered bedspread in blue and yellow. Despite what she thought she'd always known about herself, she liked being a married woman. She liked making a home for Ruhapo and herself.

Ruhapo ran his hand down her skin and she lay back, her eyes closed, listening to her body. His hand smoothed over her breast, down her flat stomach, and then he let it rest between her legs. Everywhere it passed it left a trail of excitement behind like a warm, golden thread. Tjipuka smiled up at him.

'You're the most beautiful woman in the world.'

'You shouldn't say things you don't know are true. Have you met every woman in the world?' Tjipuka teased.

'I don't need to.' He kissed her, and slowly moved his hand in the place where it was resting. Tjipuka sighed. 'I'll love you for eternity,' he said. 'You're my queen and all I want is to make you happy.'

Tjipuka looked at him. His face was so serious, so determined, that she didn't laugh, though she felt it rising in her throat. He did everything with such conviction and passion, always completely sure that his path was the right one. It made her feel safe, though she thought him slightly reckless. She wondered how he managed such determination when so much was unknown. She tried to believe in his way of thinking. Her nature told her to not trust any direction, to pull apart and examine even the tiniest part of everything. Ruhapo made decisions in a flash, and they were always right because he had chosen them. She tried her best to have faith in him and to think like he did. It made life much easier. It made her happier too, and she had to admit she had never been this happy before.

She felt afraid sometimes for the happiness she felt. She knew she'd always been lucky, but maybe this was too much. Maybe the ancestors would punish her for having too much, for loving Ruhapo too much, for him loving her too much. She tried not to think like that; she tried to push such thoughts away and just enjoy, living like Ruhapo, not like herself.

'You're my husband, you're meant to love me,' she said after some time.

He kissed her and laughed. 'You love me too. I know you do, don't say it. I don't mind because I know it.' He lay back and pulled her into his arms. 'We'll have a special life, you and I. I'll get as rich as the richest German settler. I will have the most beautiful cows in the whole of Hereroland. People will come to me, the master cattleman. They'll be in awe of my herd. And of you. You will be the envy of all women. We'll have children, lots and lots of children. Lots of beautiful, healthy children. They'll be brilliant. They'll go overseas to school like Shepherd did. You know about Shepherd?' She nodded. She knew about Shepherd, who'd gone to Britain for university and had come back and worked

23

as a secretary for Samuel Maharero. But when the Germans had taken over the country instead of the British, Shepherd had moved to Bechuanaland. He was famous for his brilliance. 'Our children will come back from university and teach us all that they learned.' He stopped speaking and looked at his wife. 'Why do you look at me like that?'

'Like what?'

'Like you don't believe me.'

'You're a dreamer.'

'Maybe, but my dreams come true, don't they? Did I not say you would be my wife that day I found a bush woman sitting in the dirt playing with termites? Did I not tell you? And here you are.'

She could see he was annoyed at her for not believing him, but still he couldn't stop a smile from forming at the edge of his mouth. He was susceptible to her, always.

She climbed on top of him, her breasts pressing against his wide chest. 'Yes, you are right, Johannes Ruhapo. You are a special man, a dreamer whose dreams come true. A prophet. Perhaps you're a powerful witch.'

'A witch? A witch, you say? I'll show you what a powerful witch I am.'

He flipped her onto her back and rose above her, laughing. Soon they were together, he deep inside of her – she was lost in him and he in her. She knew he was right. She knew she would love him for eternity and another one if there would be such a thing, but she would not say it out loud. It was bad luck to do so. This was the man the ancestors had chosen for her. It had been written down. Their destiny was decided.

That day, months later, Ruhapo woke early. Someone from his regiment knocked at the door of the hut before the eastern sky lightened. Ruhapo went to the door. They spoke in whispers and the man disappeared.

'What is it? What's happened?' Tjipuka asked from the bed where she lay, still half-asleep. She was pregnant with their first child and felt tired and lazy most of the time.

'I need to go,' Ruhapo said as he pulled on his trousers. 'There's trouble. It's Zürn. Zürn and his soldiers.'

Tjipuka sat up, awake now. Zürn was the head of the German contingent in Okahandja. 'What has he done now?'

'They've disturbed the graves. A boy saw them taking skulls.'

'Of the dead?' Tjipuka asked. How could that be? No one would desecrate the graves of the dead.

'Yes. They sell them in Germany ... for a lot of money. To come to Okahandja, to dig up our ancestors ... it's too much now. They push us and push us, but it's too much now.' He was breathing hard; Tjipuka could see his anger was bubbling at the surface. She hoped he would calm down before he got to the other men.

The people were at breaking point already. Their chief, Samuel Maharero, was handing over more and more land to the settlers. Taking land from his own people to get money for himself. Then there was the rape and murder of a Herero woman by a German man, a woman from a royal family, just like Tjipuka. He raped the woman while her baby lay next to her, raped her then slit her throat. Leutwein, the German colonial governor, refused to allow the Herero to try the man in their courts; instead he went to the colonial courts and was given prison time, which he never served. And now they were stealing from Herero graves? It was as if they wanted to force the Herero to fight. It was as if they were leaving them no option but war.

Tjipuka got out of bed and grabbed Ruhapo's hand as he tried to leave. 'Please, act carefully. Don't lead others to unsafe places. I know that you're angry, but please, be careful. Speak carefully, be mindful of your words.'

Ruhapo pulled his hand from hers. 'What would you like us to do? Must we cower at the Germans' feet as Maharero does? Beg for the scraps they choose to give us? Sit by as they rape and kill our women and take our land? Am I to be Leutwein's dog? What do you want me to do, Tjipuka?'

'I want you to help me raise this child. I want you to grow old with me. I want you to keep your promise.'

His anger fell away and he pulled her to him. 'I keep all of my promises. I said I'll take care of you and love you forever. Do you think a cowardly, greedy German soldier will keep me from that?'

He kissed her and disappeared into the chilly morning.

'Don't be afraid,' Novengi said. 'Doing nothing is what will cause us harm. We need to act. We need to act now.' They sat on a cloth in the shade, waiting for Ruhapo and the others to return.

Novengi, now a married woman too, sided with Ruhapo and her husband, Kahaka; she believed it was time to act. 'It'll be fine. We'll fight a short battle, just enough to let Zürn and Leutwein know we're serious. It'll be over. The Germans will negotiate. An agreement will be found.'

'Do you think so? Do you really believe that, Novengi?'

'I know it.' She laid her elegant hand on Tjipuka's. 'It will be nothing.'

Maveipi, Novengi's daughter, climbed onto Tjipuka's lap. She rubbed Tjipuka's swollen stomach. 'When is my sister coming?' she asked.

Tjipuka held Maveipi's face in her hands and kissed each of her cheeks. 'Soon, very soon. But what will you do if he's a brother?'

'I'll love him too. But make him a sister.' The two women laughed.

Before Maveipi called Novengi mama, she spoke it first to Tjipuka. She was a beautiful girl, so like her parents, tall and brave. She was older than her five years in so many ways. Tjipuka wished she would have a daughter just like Maveipi, though the prophet had told her she carried a boy. Maybe she'd have a girl the next pregnancy.

'Will you let me hold the baby when it comes?' Maveipi asked.

'Of course, how does a sister not hold her brother?' Tjipuka turned to Novengi. 'And you? When will you bring us another child?'

'When all of this is over, I hope.' She sipped her tea and looked out at the quivering hot air from the shady spot where they sat. Maveipi stuck her small hand into the pocket of Novengi's apron. 'What do you want in there?'

'The present,' she whispered, though loud enough for Tjipuka to hear. Novengi smiled at her friend.

Maveipi found what she was looking for and held out her hand to Tjipuka. On it lay a tiny mouse skull. Tjipuka picked it up carefully. 'This is lovely. Where did you find it?'

'Near the well. I thought you'd like it.' Maveipi smiled, proud of her find.

Tjipuka looked at the tiny teeth and delicate bones of the skull. How had it died, she wondered. There were all sorts of dramas playing out un-noticed by people – mighty battles between a mouse and an owl, a snake and a weasel. This tiny find reminded her of that. Life and death always on the line and never paid any attention. She wondered what else we never noticed. It reminded her of the depth and magic of the world. She sat back smiling, holding her present, thankfully forgetting for a moment what the men might be deciding about the people's future.

Novengi stood up. 'We need to go.'

'Where?' Tjipuka asked, surprised. She'd thought they were spend-ing the day together.

'I want to go to the meeting. It's taking long. I want to know what they're discussing.' Novengi's patience, already in short supply, was finished.

'Let me come with you,' Tjipuka said.

'No,' Novengi said firmly. 'No. You stay here and rest. It will upset you, you know how you are. I'll come back when it's over. I'll tell you everything.'

'Leave Maveipi then,' Tjipuka said.

Novengi considered it, but then shook her head. 'No. I think she's old enough to understand what's going on. I want her there. She must understand such things. You rest. Read your books, find a safe place for your mouse skull. I'll come back soon. I'll tell you everything.'

Novengi kissed Tjipuka on the cheek and left. Tjipuka lay on her cloth under the wide camel thorn tree near the sacred cattle kraal and pushed her mouse skull around in her palm. After a while, she dozed, listening to the music of the cattle, the grunts and moos and shifting of their heavy bodies.

She woke up after some time, she didn't know how long. She stuck the skull in her pocket, collected her milking bucket and walked through the empty homestead to the other kraal with the family's cattle.

She wondered about the meeting. Her mind ran where it always did, to thoughts of the murdered woman, her tiny child left to cry next to his mother's dead body. She ran her hand over the bulge of her own stomach. She could feel her baby move. It would not be long before they met, and once they did, she would keep him safe, even if being safe required the Herero nation to go to war. It was a parent's responsibility to her child, the most basic of all – to protect the child from harm. Lately it seemed harm was everywhere.

She sat down and placed her pail under the cow, then grabbed the warm udders and began pulling the milk out. Lost in thought, she didn't hear the person come up next to her until he was near. Startled, she turned quickly, nearly tipping the milk into the dirt.

'Waueza! You're like a leopard, so quiet,' she said angrily. Why was he there? He was always around, never where he was supposed to be.

Waueza was one of Ruhapo's regiment members. Not his favourite, nor Tjipuka's. Novengi called him 'Hyena' for the way he walked with his shoulders hunched and his head down. His family was wealthy, and when they were growing up he had ideas that he would marry Tjipuka, but she had no interest in a lazy boy like him, one who always took the easy way. Her family never even considered him as a suitable husband.

'Why are you not at the meeting? Don't you care what happens to us?' she asked him.

'People are excited about nothing. The Germans will take care of their own. Maharero is right, use the Germans, get what you can from them. Play their game and don't anger them. If we start making problems it will only lead to much worse for us. And what will we gain? The whites always win. Waste of time.' He flicked his hand as if it was all noise about nothing.

'So you prefer to sit and let them kill us?' she asked, annoyed.

'Am I dead?' He laughed, thinking his witticism funny. Then he reached for her arm. She could smell alcohol on his breath. 'Come, let's go. I want you to see something.'

'I need to milk the cows.' She pulled her arm away. He took it again. She hated the way he bossed people around, especially women. As if the entire world was at his beckoning.

'It will only take a minute,' he insisted.

It was best to give in, to look at what he wanted to show her, and then he'd be on his way and she'd be rid of him. She'd save more time that way. She got up and let him lead her back towards the houses. She was surprised when he opened the door to their hut, the one for her and Ruhapo. He went inside and tried to pull her in after him.

'What do you want in there?' she asked.

He kept quiet and held her arm tighter. He tried to pull her into the hut, but she fought him. She clawed at his face with her hands, but he was tall and strong, and he was winning. She didn't want to give him the satisfaction of hearing her scream, but she had no choice. She screamed with all her might, hoping someone else in the homestead had stayed behind too. Someone sleeping quietly, who could hear her screams.

He pushed her onto the bed. She struggled up and pushed him back against the wall, screaming the entire time. When she was almost out the door, he pulled her back, slapping her and shoving her hard onto the bed. 'Lie down,' he hissed.

Tjipuka became scared for her baby. She continued screaming, but fought no more. He was wild now – he might harm her child and she couldn't allow that. Everyone was at the meeting. Was there *anyone* out there? Just when she accepted that no one was coming, that this thing was going to happen, the open door darkened and Ruhapo was there.

He picked Waueza up with two hands and lifted him off his feet, throwing him out of the hut. Outside, he kicked at him with his hard boots. When Waueza tried to stand, Ruhapo punched him and he fell back to the ground. Waueza lay there, the sand around him first dotted, then pooled, with blood. A crowd formed around them, but no one stopped the fight. The battle had been looming for some time – Waueza always hovering on the fringes, always looking at what he could not have. Ruhapo breathed hard and sweat poured from him as he continued to beat Waueza. Only when Waueza was unconscious did Kahaka step forward and put his hand on Ruhapo's shoulder. 'Enough.'

Ruhapo moved back, away from the bloodied Waueza. From nowhere, Novengi pushed through the crowd. She ran up to Waueza on the ground and spat on him. 'Rubbish! You are nothing but rubbish!' She turned to Tjipuka and took her in her arms. 'Are you all right?'

'I'm fine,' Tjipuka mumbled into her friend's shoulder.

But she was not fine. Everything seemed unstable. There were no longer any rules to anything. The world was not turning properly; the ancestors were ill at ease. She no longer knew where the safe place was to take a step – the world wavered in every direction. Tjipuka sensed that this was just a sign of worse to come. It would be a long while until it all settled down and things came right again. She feared for their future, she feared for what had been started. It felt like a wild thing let loose.

Ruhapo walked to Tjipuka's side. Novengi stepped back. He carefully took Tjipuka's hand and led her into the hut. For a few moments, Tjipuka believed that Ruhapo could make everything right again, could stop the world's shaking. For a moment, she let her mind relax and accept what she knew was not true. She ignored the earth's trembling below her and let Ruhapo hold everything steady with his soothing words and careful touch. The lie of his calm voice and firm hands allowed her mind to rest for a few moments and, against her character, she ignored the crumbling under her feet.

She remembered the tiny mouse skull in her pocket, her present from Maveipi. She reached in her pocket but it was not there. She turned back from Ruhapo.

'What is it?' he asked.

She walked to the doorway. A few people still stood looking at Waueza on the ground, no one stepping forward to help him. Tjipuka looked for the little skull this way and that. It became vital that she find it. Then she saw it, on the ground at the doorway, crushed into a hundred pieces.

3
Okahandja, German South-West Africa
January 1904

They lay in the dark, the baby Saul asleep next to Tjipuka. Ruhapo held her from behind and they both looked at their perfect son.

He whispered, 'Tomorrow is the day. Everything will start tomorrow.'

Tjipuka sat up and turned to him. 'Tomorrow? So soon?'

'Yes, the Germans are in the south. The Nama are causing trouble, and the governor and all of the troops are there. Tomorrow is the best time, to attack when they are all away. We will take Okahandja tomorrow. From there we go from farm to farm until our land is ours again.'

She could hear excitement in his voice and it scared her. He was too confident – it was all too easy.

'Are we ready? Do you really think we are ready for this?'

'We have guns, not enough but many. The big problem is ammunition. The plan is to take the farms. They're easier. Later, if we get to Windhoek, there's the ammunitions store. We'll have everything then. We'll batter these Germans to dust. There's no turning back now. It has started.'

'Maybe we should run,' Tjipuka said. 'Others have run to the British, to Bechuanaland. They say we can find a place there. Maybe we should go. We'll take the cattle. Me, you and Saul. I can talk to Novengi. You can convince Kahaka. We could all go. We'll be fine. The Herero there are fine, you know that. They've been given land by the chief of the Batawana, he's a good man. He promised to protect us if we go to him. There's peace and the British are better, better than the Germans.'

'Run?' Ruhapo laughed. 'I wasn't built for running. I'll fight my battles as I always have. Must we let the Germans take all that the Herero own, while we run away to the British like cowards? Have they not taken enough? I would rather die, my blood watering this land, this land of the Herero, our land, than let them take anything else. I'll never run, Tjipuka.'

She crawled into his arms and he held her, but she didn't feel safe there any more. Ruhapo was so sure that all would go well. She tried to push the doubts from her mind and replace them with his assurances. She wanted to believe what he said, but everything was wrong. Ever since Waueza had attacked her, she felt knocked off-kilter. Each step needed consideration. She feared moving, she feared taking any action, she sensed danger on all sides. Ruhapo tried his best to show her that she was imagining things, but his words only chased the fear away for a short time. Her world used to be kind, it used to be simple. Everything was complicated now. And there was their son, Saul, to protect. Some days she only wanted to stay in their hut, lock the door and never leave.

Saul niggled and she reached out and pulled him to them. She nestled him between her and Ruhapo, putting her breast in his mouth. Ruhapo was right. They would fight. They would win. The Germans would be gone. Everything would be fine. It would be just like Ruhapo said. She repeated it until she believed it. It would be just like Ruhapo said.

Tjipuka waited at the Ruhapo homestead. Some of the women had gone with the men to fight too, or encourage them. She waited with Saul and Maveipi. Novengi had gone; she was not one to stay behind.

33

She'd given her daughter to Tjipuka and said, 'Keep Maveipi safe. I will come back and we'll all be free.'

Fierce and brave Novengi. Even if Tjipuka were brave like Novengi, she wouldn't have been able to go.

'You're still nursing Saul. You need to stay here,' Ruhapo said. He kissed her. 'I will come back to you. I promise.'

No one knew how long the battle would take, or when they would return. *If* they would return. But Tjipuka waited with Maveipi and Saul. Maveipi was like her father, tall and quiet, responsible. Novengi's fighting spirit seemed to have missed her – she was more like Tjipuka in that way. She didn't try to change things; instead she watched and tried to understand. She waited to see what would happen. But she was not fearful like Tjipuka, just calm and patient. When her parents, mounted on horses, headed for battle, Maveipi neither cried nor screamed as the other children did. She held Saul against her and watched them ride off.

Once the dust had settled, and the sound of hooves had disappeared, she turned to Tjipuka. 'Will they return?'

Tjipuka put her arm around the girl she took as her daughter. 'Of course. They are doing this to make life better for all of us. You have very brave parents. You should be proud of them.'

Maveipi nodded and silently walked to the house, carrying Saul in her arms.

The day passed and they heard nothing. Night fell and the children went to sleep. Tjipuka waited at the cooking fire, busying herself with odd jobs. Mending a hem, a job she was particularly bad at. Anything to eat up the time between that point and Ruhapo's return.

When they came back, there would be celebration for their success. She forced herself to think only of that. When they arrived, there would be celebration. Only celebration.

She set her sewing down and decided to prepare for Ruhapo's return. She went into the hut, quiet so as not to wake the children. Maveipi lay on her side, her arm protectively around Saul. Tjipuka pulled a sheet over the two of them.

She went through the dresses in her wardrobe. She chose her favourite one, the one her father had bought her from the traders in town even though it was far too expensive. Now that she was grown, she sometimes felt bad that he had run up debts, debts the Germans often collected at unfair rates, so that she could have a dress made from the finest brocade. This one was burgundy. She'd had it trimmed with lace at the sleeves, around the neckline and along the bottom.

She distracted herself from her thoughts about what was happening at the battle by preparing for her husband's homecoming. He would come back. They would be successful. And she would be waiting for him as if going to a fancy party. When they returned the victors, there would be a celebration and she would be ready for it.

She sat down at the mirror and re-plaited her hair, thick, strong hair that grew to shoulder length. Sometimes she pulled it back into a bun like the missionaries. Tonight she plaited it in cornrows. She looked at herself in the mirror. Pregnancy had been good to her. She'd gained weight; she looked more substantial now, a woman, no longer a girl, her breasts full, her hips wide. Saul had just turned one. Soon she might have another baby. A girl this time, a girl like her dear Maveipi. She thought about Ruhapo's dreams for them. He was a good man, a man who loved her and wanted only the best for them. If he was sometimes reckless and excitable, it was only because he believed in himself. He believed in himself and had an unwavering optimism that assured him that, as long as he followed his heart, everything would work out.

Tjipuka applied kohl to her eyes. She'd learned of this from a Boer trader who had passed by from the south. He said the Indians who lived there in the south applied kohl to their eyes. She'd bought one of the short black pencils, but used it only on special occasions. She ran it along the rim of her eye. Her lashes were long and the kohl lined them in a way she liked.

She picked up things on her dressing table and set them back in place. She put on a beaded necklace, a pair of gold earrings, dangling ones. She took them off and replaced them with a different set, an orange necklace and different gold earrings. She added a bracelet. She busied her hands. She could not stop, stop and think. It was late and so many things might have happened. Thinking made her mind see Ruhapo lying on the street in Okahandja's white section. His beautiful eyes flat and dead. His mouth still. His hands at his sides. Or dragged to a tree, a rope tied around his neck, hanged until the air in his lungs was gone. She couldn't see any of that. She couldn't think any of those pictures were true. She only saw him walking through the door to her, walking, carrying the victory he had assured her of. She must think like Ruhapo, where success was the only option.

Saul cried and she went to him. She held him to her and rocked back and forth. He played with her earring, talking his baby talk, the language of the ancestors. She rocked him and sang softly about silky cows and new moons. Soon he was asleep and she laid him gently back next to Maveipi.

Then she heard noises outside.

Louder as they came nearer. Voices and horses. Ululations of celebration. In the mix of sounds, one was perfect. It was Ruhapo's voice. Jubilant. Victorious. Alive.

4
Okahandja, German South-West Africa
July 1904

'It's over. We're moving on.' Ruhapo began to pack their things. He pulled down a trunk from on top of the wardrobe.

'Over?' She bounced a crying Saul against her shoulder.

'We're taking the cattle to Ohamakari. There's good grazing there. We're too many now in Okahandja. All the Herero in one place are too many. Plus the Germans' cattle that we captured. It's too much, we need new pastures.'

'Will they follow? The Germans?'

'No, Samuel Maharero says his friend, Governor Leutwein, will negotiate now. We will go to Ohamakari and wait for him. The governor needs to consult the Kaiser, this takes time. We'll wait there. There's water and grazing. We'll wait for the governor to respond. The Germans have been taught a lesson. They can see now that an Omuherero is a man just like a German is a man. They have been taught who owns this land, that they were here at our mercy. They mistreated our hospitality. They understand that now. Now they'll negotiate, and we'll be left alone once and for all. Left to run our own affairs just as we always have.'

He took Saul from her and held him close. He danced around the hut, humming a song she could not place. 'My son will grow up free of all of this. He'll be a rich, powerful man, free of all of this sorrow and conflict.'

Tjipuka didn't like leaving their home, even if Ruhapo assured her they would return. It hadn't been as they had thought, as Ruhapo and Novengi had hoped: one battle and the Germans gave in. There had been months of fighting all over Hereroland. And now they were running to Ohamakari.

She watched Ruhapo and Saul dancing around their hut. Could she trust Ruhapo? Could she trust what he said? Could any of them trust Samuel Maharero? She told herself she had to, for all of their sakes. They'd come too far.

Tjipuka put her arms around her husband and her son. She swallowed her doubts. She was happy, she told herself. They were free again. They would go to Ohamakari and soon they would make a new life without any of this grief. Soon everything would be as it should be.

Ruhapo's father and mother helped them to pack up the homestead. They loaded everything into two wagons, and the cattle were herded ahead by the Berg Damara who worked for them. It was the end of July, winter, cool most of the day with clear, blue skies. Tjipuka sat at the front of one of the wagons holding Saul, with Ruhapo driving. The wagons and cattle spread out far ahead. The Herero were rich. They had endless cattle now. Though lives had been lost in the battles to win their freedom from the Germans, the people were happy. Samuel Maharero had assured them all the trouble was over. It would be only peace now.

Saul was happy too. He played with the small doll Tjipuka had made for him.

'Mama,' he repeated over and over. Not to her but to the doll. Tjipuka suspected he didn't know what the word meant. Perhaps he thought it was the doll's name. She hugged her son to her. Everything was going so well. Ruhapo was happy. Because of all his cattle, even though he was not from a royal family, he thought that when they got to Ohamakari he would be a headman. He would sit on the council with Samuel Maharero. The chief respected him. He was a fierce soldier and had acted with bravery in the battles that had subdued the Germans. Everyone had noticed, including the chief. Ruhapo was respected, and he enjoyed that.

The night before leaving, after making love, they lay talking. He had held her in his arms and spoken of the wonderful life they would have now. They would thrive in the rich grasslands of the north. Once the treaty was agreed, they would move back to Hereroland, the whole of it. The Germans could move to the cold, retreat to the desert along the coast. Or they could leave altogether. Ruhapo thought he and Tjipuka might move back to the south, to his family's land near Gobabis. He would have again what was taken from him, what was taken from his father. All would be set right. They had fought hard so that everything would be returned, so that justice for the people would prevail. And they had been victorious.

It was already a month later, and Tjipuka sat outside in the cold darkness high up on the plateau of Ohamakari. She liked to wake up long before others, she always had. She liked to hear the birds waking up, to watch the world reveal itself, to sit and watch the eastern sky change from black to grey and slowly to yellow and orange. She liked to sit near the cattle and hear their mooing, their contented grunts. Sometimes she would go inside the kraal and stand among them, rubbing her hand over their hides, letting the calves suck her fingers with their rough tongues and strong lips. She liked that alone time in the morning to think about things. To organise her thoughts.

They had been at Ohamakari for nearly a month. The pasture was good and the cattle were fat. She liked the place, but looked forward to the time after the peace negotiations when everything would be settled and they could go back home. She didn't like this in-between place; she liked security and certainty.

She sat quietly watching the sky for any lightening. It was black, still cold night. She heard a cock crow and realised she was not alone in waiting for the sun. She pulled the blanket tighter around her shoulders. Then she noticed that something was not right. The cattle were nervous – they were moving, but silent. She wondered if they smelled a leopard. There were leopards in the hills, though she'd never seen one. She stood up and walked further from their hut, towards the edge of the plateau on which they had set up the encampment. She pushed though the bush and then she saw what was unsettling the cattle.

Below her, in the first thin light of morning, she saw horses. Horses and soldiers. Many of them, the line stretching back around the curve in the road and disappearing. The horses pulled big guns behind them. More and more were coming.

And then she understood.

The Germans were not going to negotiate. They had not been waiting to hear from the Kaiser about how to make peace with the Herero. Samuel Maharero had got it wrong. The Germans were not going to retreat to the coast. The war was not over. The Germans had been getting organised. They had been getting organised to come back and punish the Herero. They needed time for the ships to arrive from Germany, ships loaded with weapons and soldiers. Now the Schutztruppe had arrived and they had come to fight.

She slipped back through the bush and rushed to Ruhapo. 'They're here!' she cried.

Still sleepy, he groaned and tried to take her into his arms, but she pulled back. 'The Germans! They're here! They're here to fight us!'

He woke up. 'They're here?'

'Yes, down below. There are many, the line is still coming. They have lots of weapons! They've brought big guns. Ruhapo, they've come to kill us!'

Ruhapo stood up and dressed quickly. He collected all his ammunition, his gun, his enga. 'You wait here. No matter what – you wait here. If they come, you hide in the bush with Saul. No matter what happens, I will come for you. Don't go. Wait. Are you listening? Do you hear me?'

She nodded her head through the thick fog of fear. He kissed her and disappeared into the night.

She strapped the sleeping Saul to her back. She collected her jewellery and the money she had. She packed her expensive dresses. Then she sat on the bed and waited.

The smoke was so thick Tjipuka could barely see. Saul cried on her back. She could wait no longer. The noise was all around her. The Germans would come for her, sitting there waiting. They would shoot her dead right on the bed her father had bought them. She sneaked out of the house and checked her father-in-law's hut; the beds were empty. They'd fled already. Outside, the kraal was open, the cattle gone. In all of the noise she had heard nothing.

She headed for the bush. Her eyes burned. Smoke of burning houses filled the cold morning air; she couldn't see clearly where she stepped. She tripped and fell, and when she turned her head, she saw a foot. She followed the ankle to the leg, to the body. The stomach was burst open, the insides spilled to the ground; ants already crawled on the intestines. It was her mother-in-law, Mama Ruhapo.

Tjipuka did not scream. She kept her head. She swallowed her fear. She stood and ran again. More careful now. She saw that the bush was littered with bodies. Tens, maybe hundreds. She did not look. She didn't know these people. They were not the people she knew. She couldn't know them and still keep running, so she must not know them. She ran, and stumbled, and ran again. Saul screamed on her back, but it didn't matter. No one could hear a single baby's voice above all the noise of killing.

She found a place, in a bush, hidden, and sat. She remembered being a girl, remembered her skill at stillness. She sat as the day heated up and then cooled down. Night fell and she sat in the same place. She did not go any further. Ruhapo would not find them if she went too far. It was cold. She was wise to bring two blankets. She wrapped them around herself and Saul, suckling at her breast. They waited. They waited the next day in the hot sun.

She hid and stayed silent and still as a stone when the three Germans passed. She covered Saul's mouth with her hand. But a woman, a distant cousin, married with five children, stood up out of the bush not far away. She'd been still too, so still Tjipuka hadn't seen her though she was quite near. She stood and walked to the soldiers.

'Please … please do not kill me. I'm surrendering,' she said in German. She walked towards them, her hands up.

They laughed at her. Tjipuka was a stone. She did not yell out a warning to this woman, a warning that no mercy would be found with these men. Tjipuka saw it in their faces, but she was a stone. A stone felt nothing. A stone could not help anyone.

The taller German, his blond hair speckled with blood, moved forward. He took the woman's hand gently. He spoke his language, but it was soft and soothing so as to calm the woman, not its usual clustering of harsh guttural sounds. He led her away from the bush, to a clearing. The other two German soldiers laughed. One had teeth that stuck out. The other was younger and nervous. He laughed, but it was out of fear, Tjipuka could hear that.

The tall German ran his hands down the front of the woman's dress. With sudden violence, he ripped the dress open and tore again at her petticoat underneath, revealing her bare breasts. She brought her hands up to cover herself, and the tall German slashed them with a knife – one, two – and red strips appeared and dripped down each hand as she pulled them away. They bled, but she made no sound. She put her arms at her sides and waited. The blood dripped down her hands and fell to the ground – the ground so greedy for Herero blood.

The tall German turned her around and bent her over. He lifted her dress and used his knife to tear away her pants. He pulled out his manhood, already stiff, and pushed it into her. She was silent. The bush was silent. He finished and looked at the young, nervous boy. He spoke and the buck-toothed one laughed. The two pushed the young, nervous boy forward. The boy was still smiling, his teeth dry from the effort.

The young boy unbuttoned his fly with shaking hands, but his member was flaccid. He could not do what they wanted him to. The tall German and the buck-toothed one laughed and pushed him to the side. He stumbled, but stayed standing. The buck-toothed one took his turn with the woman and then moved away. As he put his penis away and was buttoning his pants, the tall German pulled the woman up. He grabbed her breasts. He tweaked the nipples with his fingers and smiled at her kindly. Her face was blank. No one was there.

Then the tall German took out his knife, grabbed her by the back of the head, and sliced the knife across the soft skin of her neck. He jumped back to avoid getting soaked in her blood. She fell to the sand where the last of her life gurgled away.

The Germans laughed again and headed back towards the centre of the plateau. The young nervous one, still a child really, looked back once. He spotted Tjipuka crouching in the bush, trying her best to be a stone. Their eyes met; for a second he looked at her, and then he turned back and followed the other two soldiers, saying nothing.

Tjipuka watched the evening sky fade to grey and then black. Later the ice-cold stars twinkled in the black sky as if all was well and as it should be. The night-time sky she'd watched her entire life looked down at her unchanged. Such a betrayal, she thought. How could the stars not be changed by all this evil they had witnessed?

The night was long and cold. Hungry and thirsty, she was relieved when the sun came over the eastern edge and the first bird sang. Somewhere she heard the sound of a person moaning. Her mouth was dry; her muscles ached from sitting in the same position for so long. Saul sucked at her breast greedily.

She heard someone coming. She pulled Saul loose and covered his mouth with her hand. He seemed to know that silence was required, as if he already had a keen grasp of the rules of war. She waited. Then she saw they were men, two black men, Herero. Finally Ruhapo had come, just as he said he would. It was him, she was sure of it.

But then she realised the men were Kahaka and Waueza. Ruhapo was not among them. It was the sun or her state of mind that had tricked her. She wanted to cry out in frustration but she did not. She stood up and called to them, since they'd nearly passed her by. They rushed to her.

'You're alive,' Kahaka said. He spoke in a whisper. The Germans were still around. 'We came back to look for anyone, to find cattle.'

'Where is Ruhapo? Why is he not with you?'

Kahaka looked away. Waueza spoke. 'He's dead.'

Kahaka's head whipped around. 'No. You don't know that. It was only said by others, but you don't know that.' He helped Tjipuka to her feet. 'Come, Tjipuka, we need to go.'

'I can't. Ruhapo said he will come for me. That I must wait here. He's not dead. I know he's not dead. I must wait here. He'll come for me, he promised.' She pulled her arm from Kahaka's grasp.

'I saw him dead. I saw his body. He's dead,' Waueza said with finality. Kahaka looked at him, but said nothing.

Tjipuka did not let his words inside her. She steadied herself, and the words bounced away to fall on the dusty ground. But she allowed Kahaka to take her hand again. He led her away through the bush. Over bodies and bodies. Men and women and children. Slashed and bullet ridden. Over dead cattle. Over burned huts and piles of clothes and dishes. Iron pans. A blue necklace. A white teapot. A pillow, trimmed in lace. Everything strewn and left behind as the people fled.

She was led into the bush, into the desert, the only way out, she learned. The Germans had blocked all other escape routes. They would kill the Herero, or the desert would. Now she was only a stone. A hard, unyielding stone. A stone that no one could penetrate, no one could touch. No one could hurt.

5

Omaheke Desert, German South-West Africa
August 1904

Kahaka led Tjipuka and Saul into the Omaheke Desert. She was confused about where they were going, about what was happening. The sun was hot and Tjipuka's mouth was dry. Saul cried on her back, but she could do nothing.

They walked without speaking.

As the sun began to fall to the west, they rounded a slight hill and there were the people. Most sat on the bare ground, their arms at their sides, looking out into the dust. A few cattle grazed on the scattered tufts of grass in the distance. A baby cried. No one built any shelters, and, though night would soon come, no fires burned.

Waueza stopped and turned to her. 'Wait here.'

She stopped and stood. Kahaka removed Saul from her back. He carefully helped her sit and then handed the baby to her. Saul cried in her arms. She didn't notice.

'Nurse him,' Kahaka said. He watched as she mechanically removed her breast and stuck the nipple in the child's mouth. Her eyes scanned the crowd – where was Ruhapo? Why was she brought here if Ruhapo was not here? She needed to wait for him at Ohamakari; he would be looking for her there.

The people were lost. The chiefs were gone; they'd trekked quickly towards Bechuanaland, fleeing the Germans who wanted them dead. The people who were injured or too slow stayed behind. Others stayed to wait for the relatives they were sure would come eventually. They would come, and then together they would go back to Hereroland and start again. This was what they thought. They didn't know yet there was no going back.

A tall woman, her dress stained with blood down the front, walked through the crowd. 'Frederick!' she called. 'Frederick!' She checked behind bushes. She looked into the distance. 'Have you seen my son Frederick?' she asked Tjipuka.

Tjipuka shook her head. The woman continued into the desert. It was then that Tjipuka noticed she carried something in her hand. She looked closer. It was a small, bloody shoe.

Kahaka returned.

'Drink this,' he said, pushing a cup to her mouth. Tjipuka swallowed the salty water. 'Drink carefully, it's all we have. The Germans have blocked the waterholes this side. We'll not have water again until we go another fifty miles or more.'

Tjipuka looked down at Saul. Everything was so confusing. How were they expected to go on now with everything lost? With everyone gone? How was she expected to go on living without Ruhapo? She didn't know how that life worked.

Soon the people stood up. Kahaka warned that they needed to get further into the bush before they slept. The Germans were not far. The people listened to him; by default he had become their leader. They stood and collected their few belongings. Others rounded up the cattle and pushed them along.

Waueza helped Tjipuka to her feet and held Saul as she retied the blanket that held him in place on her back. 'Don't be afraid, I'll take care of you now, now that you're alone.'

Her hand reached out and slapped him hard across the face. She did not need his kind of help, ever.

'If you want to help me, go and find Ruhapo.'

Waueza held his face where her hand had landed. 'He's dead. I told you that. He is dead. Gone. You have no one. The day will come when you'll beg for me to help you, and I'll turn away and let you die just like your beloved Ruhapo.'

Waueza turned in the other direction, away from the people. He marched back to where they'd come from. Tjipuka said nothing. She followed Kahaka, who walked ahead with the others. Now she could see Novengi walking nearby. She hadn't wanted to ask where Novengi was for fear she was back on Ohamakari with all the others. She rushed to her, but then noticed – *where was Maveipi?* Tjipuka stopped her thoughts from going to where they might. Maveipi was fine, she told herself.

Tjipuka caught up with Novengi and took her hand. 'You're here. You survived it all. Are you all right?'

Novengi looked at her. 'I'm fine,' she said, as if Tjipuka were a stranger she'd met at the marketplace. As if everything was the same, not fallen apart and broken, unable ever to be fixed again.

Tjipuka stopped her and grabbed her by the shoulders, forcing Novengi to look at her. 'You're not fine, none of us are fine. Where is Maveipi?'

In a flat voice, squeezed clean of any feeling, Novengi said, 'She's dead. She's dead like all of them.'

Novengi continued walking with the others, but Tjipuka could not move. Maveipi was dead. She looked back from where they'd come. How could they go and leave Maveipi behind? Leave Ruhapo behind? She ran after Novengi and grabbed at her arm, pulling her.

'Stop. We need to go back. We need to find her, find Maveipi. We need to find Ruhapo.'

Novengi yanked her arm away viciously. 'They're dead. They're all dead. What can we do about that? Make them live again? Are you magic like that now?' She walked again.

Tjipuka couldn't believe that Maveipi was dead. Saul's big sister, gone like all of the others. The little girl with an entire life in front of her. The boys she would love, the children she would have – all dead, all disappeared. Over what? What had they done? What had they done to bring all of this upon them?

She wanted to know what had happened, where the girl's tiny body lay, but didn't ask. Novengi was not up to such questions. She was always the brave, strong one, but Tjipuka could see that she was missing now. She was a thin shell, barely holding up against the pressure. Her Novengi was gone and might never come back.

Tjipuka needed to take care of her now. For all the years that Novengi took care of her, it was now Tjipuka's turn. She carefully took Novengi's hand in hers and said nothing more.

There were no tears. It was too much for tears. In Novengi's eyes Tjipuka saw the death of Ruhapo. She felt his death. She knew now, he was dead like all the others. After everything, he was not special. They were not special after all. She would not be exempt. Not this time.

They were the only ones left, this handful of broken people. There might be a few more tattered groups trying to survive the desert trek, but that was all. The Germans had nearly accomplished what they set out to do, to kill all of the Herero. These few people were all that was left, and what was left in them could hardly be described as life. Everyone had lost someone, some had lost everyone. Their spirits were gone. Everything that made them people, human, was left on Ohamakari.

But they needed to live. They needed to live if only to win. To make sure the Germans did not succeed. She thought of Ruhapo. Somewhere back there his body lay among the others, rotting in the hot sun. She could do nothing about that, but she could live for him. She would live for Ruhapo. And she would live for Saul. For Maveipi. And for Novengi.

She held Novengi's hand tightly, saying nothing, and they walked deeper into the desert.

After two days they reached a waterhole. The people rushed to it. The little water they'd had was finished the first day. They ate only tubers

48

they dug from the hard, sun-dried ground. The cattle were giving no milk as they too were thirsty and starving.

'Wait,' Kahaka yelled to the people who ran for the water. Some had already drunk from the well. 'Wait, let the animals drink first.' The people protested. 'No, you must wait. We must make sure the water is safe.'

Tjipuka was not sure who had warned Kahaka, but within minutes they could see something was wrong. They couldn't stop more cattle from pushing to the water, driven by thirst. The people tried to chase them back, but they pushed forward wildly, and the people did not have the energy to fight them. The cattle drank their fill and moved off to search for bits of dried grass in the sand. The people looked at the water, but did not touch it. Then the cattle began to moan. Soon they were crying, filling the air with their painful calls. They fell to the ground, legs thrashing. Saliva poured from their mouths.

The people watched as the cattle died, one by one. The few people who had drunk the water before Kahaka stopped them began to hold their stomachs and moan too. They rolled on the ground, vomiting. Nothing helped. Within two hours all of the cattle, goats, and sheep were dead. Seven people – four women, one man and two children – lay dead as well. Now they were down to thirty-one people: seven women, nine men and fifteen children.

The fit men went to dig graves for the dead; the rest sat in the short shade of the stunted acacias and watched the surface of the glistening water as they licked their cracked, dried lips.

Ruhapo

6
Omaheke Desert, German South-West Africa
August 1904

It was at Ohamakari that the people scattered. When Ruhapo saw the endless line of horses and the big guns, he knew they stood no chance that cold morning, though they tried. Ruhapo grabbed his gun, leaving Tjipuka and Saul; he grabbed his gun and ran to meet the enemy. They fought, but it was futile. They were not ready – they thought the battle had been won and that they were the victors. They were not ready for what came to meet them.

Men were killed in the fight. Good men who fought like warriors. But this was not a battlefield – women and children were there, and the Germans showed no distinction. They killed everyone. Women shot through, the children on their backs killed with the same bullet that killed the mothers. Old people, sick and unable to run, burned in houses. Ruhapo stepped over a small boy, alone in the sand, dead, his hands cut off.

When there was a lull in the fighting, Samuel Maharero called the people together. He stood in his German uniform, a red feather in his hat, his defiant clothes in contrast to his defeated stance.

'It is lost,' he said. 'We must save ourselves. I am going to Bechuana-land, to the British. Each one of you can do as he chooses. The war is lost.'

Ruhapo wondered what leader left his people like that. It was as he'd always expected. Maharero was only Leutwein's puppet, nothing more. A coward in the end.

The Germans were everywhere. People fled in all directions, leaving everything behind. They had no time. Ruhapo needed to find Tjipuka and Saul – he needed to get them and go to the British. The people ran, but he knew Tjipuka would wait for him. Ruhapo couldn't get to her, though. The Germans were blocking him everywhere.

He went into the Omaheke Desert, the only place to hide from them. He would wait, he'd wait until the Germans left and then he'd go back and he'd find her. He knew she would find a way to wait for him. She was strong and she trusted him.

Ruhapo hid in a nearly dry well. He heard people pass, but waited. There were cries and the sound of bullets, and the long guns boomed without rest. Two days he waited, then a third, until finally it was quiet.

As night fell, he crept out of the well. He was weak from hunger but he had to find his wife. There were a few Germans left behind, guarding the area, but they were easy to get by. He crept back up to where they had set up camp. The smell greeted him before he saw the wreckage: the smell of rotting bodies. As he neared, he saw that they were everywhere. No one was intending to bury them: they were not the bodies of humans; the respect of burial was not required.

Jackals ran away as Ruhapo approached. One carried a child's hand. Vultures, too, heavy from feeding, unable to fly, huddled in groups under trees waiting for the morning updrafts to assist their bodies weighted now with human flesh.

Ruhapo tried not to look at anything. He tried not to think about what he might see. He sneaked to the side of where his father's hut had stood; all the huts were burned to ash. It meant nothing, he told himself. It didn't mean anything.

He stepped over bodies. He did not look. He told himself no one he loved was lying in the sand dead, being picked apart by jackals and vultures. He crept carefully through the bush. Occasionally a German soldier passed, but they could not see him. He was invisible. He was silent as a leopard.

Something caught his eye. It was familiar and he could not look away. The material was familiar. A dress made of thick blue cotton. He fell to his knees. He took the corner of the dress in his hand; he rubbed it on his cheek. He knew then. The animals had already taken most of her body. Dug it apart, fighting for her organs. But her face was there. His mother's face, contorted in pain. Pain was the last thing she felt before she died. She was meant to die an old woman, in her sleep. But here she lay, slashed apart by a German's knife, gutted as if she were an animal. He could not bury her but he could not leave her like this either. He grabbed anything he could find and pulled it on top of her. A thrown blanket, a wooden chest, a large branch. He piled everything on top of his mother's body. The animals would have no more of her. He could not show her the respect she deserved, but he would not let her be eaten as if she were not a human being.

Ruhapo went further and found his father, the old man's head cut clean from his body. His uncle lay nearby, shot twice in the chest, his uncle's wife next to him, lying serenely, her hands crossed on her chest, a tiny bullet hole through her forehead.

Everyone was dead. He found one after another. Inside him everything went quiet. It was as if the world had ended. All were dead. His world was slashed bare; only he walked among the ruins to see what the Germans had done. To be a witness. If he was alone, he alone would need to carry the burden of finding justice for the dead.

But Saul and Tjipuka were not there. Though he looked and looked through bodies torn to pieces, they were not among them. They must have escaped. He still held on to that small hope. They had to have escaped. He was sure of it.

He found a metal chest, the one his father had used to keep everything important. He pried it open and inside he found his father's rifle and ammunition. He couldn't believe they were still there. The Germans must have been too busy killing to look for it; besides, they had ample ammunition and guns. His father hadn't even had time to get his gun out to fight.

Ruhapo collected the gun and the ammunition and headed into the desert to find his wife and son.

7

Omaheke Desert, German South-West Africa
October 1904

Ruhapo heard the springbok before he saw it. He crouched in the thorn bush, ignoring the long, hard white thorns poking into his flesh. He hadn't eaten for two days and he would not let this meal pass him by. He stayed still and waited. There were three springbok. He was sure he'd be able to shoot one, though he was weak and his hands were shaking. He aimed the rifle and squeezed the trigger. As one fell and the other two bounced off into the desert, Ruhapo fell to his knees and cried. He knew this meat would keep him alive. Alive another day to continue the search for Tjipuka and Saul.

He made a fire. He didn't care if the smoke would be seen. He would deal with the Germans if they spotted it, if they found him; he'd done it before.

He had seen the barbed-wire barrier the Germans had erected to keep the people from going back to their land. They had only one way to go: east. Soldiers patrolled the fence and shot anyone who came near. Women, children, the old. The Germans didn't care if they were armed or if they were begging for mercy – they shot them down and left their bodies in the hot desert sun. Ruhapo saw the dead, nothing more than bones, having spent weeks wandering the desert with no food or water. One man held a white flag, still clutched in his hand, but there would be no surrendering. All Herero must die.

There were troops moving around the desert. He'd seen some on camels the day before. They guarded all waterholes, and those they couldn't guard, they poisoned. They were around, but Ruhapo didn't care. Tonight, he would build a fire and cook his meat. He needed the strength; he had far to go.

He'd been searching for over two months now, he realised. He'd found scattered groups of Herero, but Tjipuka was not among them. No one seemed to know where she was. People tried to convince him to give up the search and join them. They were all searching for people and it was better if they were together. They'd all lost wives and husbands, children and parents. They didn't know if the missing ones had died at Ohamakari or if they were safely in Bechuanaland with Samuel Maharero and the other chiefs. They didn't know if they'd died on the way from the heat or thirst. If lions had attacked and killed them. If they'd drunk the poisoned water. So many people were missing, so many questions about what had happened. What was one woman? What was so special about one woman among the thousands and thousands of dead?

Ruhapo didn't care what anyone said. He would find Tjipuka. If he had to search the whole of Africa, he would find her and Saul.

As Ruhapo turned the meat on the fire, he decided that he would go to Bechuanaland. He was sure Tjipuka must be there. If she was in the desert, he would have found her by now – he'd searched everywhere. She must have made it safely to the British. He would find her there.

He cut a piece of sizzling meat from the roasted springbok. Others thought he was mad, but he knew Tjipuka was alive. And his son, Saul. They had made plans. Plans to be happy, to have many children – bright, healthy, beautiful children. To take care of their cattle, to live a life that they chose. Their plans had been solid things, they couldn't just disappear into the air. If not for this, if not for all of this, everything would have been fine. He couldn't understand how the Germans could come all the way over the sea to take their land. To steal their cattle. To desecrate their dead. To abuse their women. And now to kill – to kill everyone. To destroy his future, the future he and Tjipuka had so carefully constructed. What would their god say to them when it was their time to meet? Would they have any reasons for what they had done?

Two weeks before, he'd been nearer the German fence, about fifteen miles into the desert. Someone he'd met had told him there was a group of Herero who had set up a semi-permanent camp. They had a few cattle and were waiting for them to gain strength before they headed north. Someone thought Tjipuka might be with them.

Ruhapo searched but never found the group. Maybe they had left already. But on the second night of his search he came upon a group of three German soldiers, probably out looking for Herero in the area. They sat at a campfire, eating their dinner. Ruhapo could see clearly that they had left their guns leaning against the tent, too far away for quick retrieval.

He lined up two bullets and put a third in his rifle. He shot, and the first German fell at the fire, his plate of food still in his hand. The second stood, alarmed, and took two steps before Ruhapo shot him in the chest. The third one almost had a chance. He was reaching for his rifle, but he was just that bit too slow.

Ruhapo went to where they lay. They were young, all three of them, but he tried not to think of that. Instead he reminded himself that if Tjipuka and Saul had been out here with the group he was looking for, these men would have killed them both. He forced his mind to remember his father and mother. To remember the child he saw with the hands cut off. The baby dead on his mother's back. Monsters – these were monsters, not humans.

He stripped them and pulled them to lie one next to the other. He smiled as he saw the sand around them darken with their blood. They would stay here, in this land where they did not belong. Their ancestors would never find their spirits; they would be lost in the next world forever.

He took off his own clothes and pulled on the uniform of the tallest of the three. He wished now he hadn't killed them. He wished he had only wounded them, so that they could be alive for the next part.

He sharpened his knife on a stone until it was like a razor. Then, one by one, he castrated the men. He threw their private parts out into the darkness of the desert, screaming into the night, shouting the wild, mad insults of the possessed. His hands dripped with blood; it ran down his elbows into the sleeves of the stolen uniform. He wiped his hands down the front. The desert echoed with the screams of his victory.

But then it was over and all was silent.

After a while, the blood on his hands dried and flaked off. He sat by the fire, looking at the three men. He stopped his mind from thinking that these were sons of women, brothers to men, lovers to those who waited for their return, who even thought of them at that moment as alive, somewhere far away, soon to return to them. To stop such thoughts, he shut off part of himself. He shut off a part that, at the time, he didn't know could never be brought to life again.

Now, as he seasoned his springbok with salt he'd taken from those soldiers, he thought about the three Germans lying there dead in the desert, as he had quite often over the days since, and he felt nothing. He cut pieces of the sizzling meat from the carcass with the same knife he had used to castrate them, and ate until his stomach was taut.

After such a big meal, he slept soundly. In the morning, he woke when the sun was already over the horizon. He packed the remaining meat and headed east. He wasn't sure how far he was from the border. He had backtracked in his search and he suspected he was nearer to the German fence than he had first thought.

He walked east all day. It was summer now and the sun had little mercy. The Omaheke was better than the Namib, though. Ruhapo had seen the Namib when he was a boy, when his father was leaving Gobabis. It was endless sand, with only the occasional low plant, a crazy mixed-up plant with two long leaves that split and broke in the wind. Otherwise it was hills of rock, and sand, flat or in high dunes.

The Omaheke was a different kind of desert. It had tufts of dry grass scattered in the hard ground. There were short thorn trees and bushes, so at least some shade could be found where springbok and duiker took cover from the hottest part of the day. He'd seen a male lion and two females pass once. He'd hidden in a patch of thorn bushes to let a herd of elephants be on their way. They were most likely in transit to better places. They wouldn't last long without water, but they knew the course of ancient rivers. There were hares and mice. Ruhapo had killed a puff adder that lay still on a warm rock and eaten it for breakfast one morning. You could survive if you had a gun, as he did. And if you had water or knew where to find it.

Night was falling, but still Ruhapo continued eastward. He didn't mind walking in the night, especially when the sky was as clear as it was that night and the moon full. The blue light gave the desert a kinder edge and the coolness was welcome.

He walked and thought of Tjipuka. After they married, people spoke about when he would take a second wife. He was a wealthy man and could support many wives. He'd laughed, but never said anything. He loved Tjipuka with his whole heart; there was no room for anyone else. He would never take another wife. From that first day, when he told her she would be his wife, he loved her completely. He didn't know if it was that way for everyone, but it was that way for him. Without her he knew who he would be, especially now after everything he had done, and this was why he had no option but to keep looking for her.

Riette

8

The Transvaal
July 1897

Riette was eleven when Koos died. He was such a competent boy that when their father first carried him into the house, Riette never considered that her brother might not recover. The horse, a mean-eyed stallion Koos had vowed to tame, had reared and come down on his leg. Setting the broken bone was easy enough for their mother. Having grown up on the isolated farms of the Transvaal, it was important for her to know such things; nurses and doctors were hard to come by. Riette was told to leave the room and from outside the bedroom door she heard her elder brother scream as the bone was put back in place and the splint applied.

But it hadn't been the biggest problem, that leg, broken, crooked at an odd angle – it had been only the beginning. After a few days of lying in bed, Koos developed a fever. Mother applied poultices made of marula bark and made a bitter tea for him to drink, but it didn't help. In the second week, he began to have spasms that left him unable to breathe properly, and by the end of the week he was dead.

They buried him on the hill behind their house, next to their grandmother and the three baby boys their mother had lost during childbirth. As the soil fell on top of her brother's coffin, it seemed to cover all of them in a bitter darkness. Her mother and father sank in on themselves; they spoke little and seemed only to be going through the motions of life, just waiting for the end and final relief.

Riette felt helpless watching Koos die. She knew that if they'd been in Cape Town or even in Kimberley, at a hospital with modern equipment and medicines, Koos would have survived.

She made a promise to herself then that she would become a nurse. She would become a nurse, and boys like Koos would live under her care, not die. On that sad, silent farm, Riette waited until she could break free. When her chance arrived, she took it.

Now, as she looked down at the letter in her hand, she felt Koos's presence. The letter, which she'd received two weeks before, was from the Colonial Medical Council. She had passed her nursing examinations, with distinction even. Soon she could go back to Kimberley Hospital, the hospital where she had trained. Sister Mary Alice liked Riette and had assured her of a nursing job once she passed her examinations.

Riette folded the letter and put it in the pocket of her apron. Although she'd known the results for two weeks and had written to inform Sister Mary Alice, she'd not yet told her parents. She would only tell them when everything was in place for her return, when they would not have the chance to ruin her plans.

They had agreed, reluctantly, to her nursing training. They never expected her to pass; they expected little from Riette. But she had, and she would finally be free of them, with their strict rules and old-fashioned ways, all covered with the loss of the only child they'd ever really valued.

As she bent down and collected the last of the brown chicken eggs from the wooden nesting boxes and headed to the house, Riette smiled, thinking about her escape. She just needed everything to be right and she would be gone.

Inside, her father was already sitting down to his coffee, and Riette realised she must have let time get away from her. Time was a problem for Riette. She liked to set her mind free to go where it liked, and time disappeared in the swirl of her daydreams. She'd been thinking of herself in the hospital, now a qualified nurse. She saw herself in her blue cape, easing people's suffering. She must have lingered in the chicken house, and now she was in trouble.

Her father had been up since dawn, out doing chores. He had a strict routine and he didn't like it disturbed. When he came in from the barns, he expected his breakfast to be set before him. He sat now with only his big enamel cup of sweet, milky coffee in front of him and a scowl on his face.

'You were dawdling again,' her mother said. She snatched two eggs from the basket Riette held and cracked them into the hot oil already on the stove. 'Sit. Your father needs to talk to you.'

Riette sat down. She looked at the stern, hard face of her father and wondered when last he had spoken to her directly. For him she was a disappointment. She was already almost twenty-five and unmarried. He needed help on the farm – he was aging, and, with no surviving sons, he struggled to keep things running alone. By now she might have given him some grandsons who could assist him, and a son-in-law. But instead he was stuck with a plain daughter whom few boys looked at. To compound things, she'd wasted his time and money training to be a nurse, a profession he found unsuitable for an Afrikaner girl from a good home.

As she sat waiting for her father to say what he needed to, she wondered if this was the right time to tell her parents about the exams. Sister Mary Alice was sending a train ticket; perhaps it had already arrived at the post office in Rustenburg. She would rather have waited until she had the ticket in hand, but maybe it was the right time now. Maybe this was her opportunity.

Her father cleared his throat to make space for the unfamiliar passage of words. 'I've found you a husband,' he said, looking down at the plate of eggs and bread his wife had set before him. 'You'll be married next Friday.'

Riette sat back in her chair. Had the words actually hit her? It felt as if they had. Nowhere in her imagination had she thought her father was going to say that. She struggled to understand. How did he think she could be married now? They had gone through all of this when she left for her training. She was too old for marriage, the very reason they'd allowed her to leave for nursing training in the first place. Why were they back to this again?

She took the examination results from her pocket, unfolded the paper and placed it on the table. 'I've passed my Colonial Medical Council examinations. I'll be leaving soon for Kimberley. I have a job waiting for me.'

Her father put his fork down and placed both forearms on the table. 'There will be no Kimberley. No nursing job. You'll be marrying Henk Venter next Friday.'

Henk Venter owned the farm bordering theirs. He was almost her father's age. His wife had died the year before, leaving him with two daughters to raise on his own. Riette didn't know what her father was thinking. She couldn't marry Henk Venter. She was going to be a nurse at the hospital in Kimberley. It seemed so straightforward to her; why was it not the same for him?

'But they're waiting for me in Kimberley. It was agreed.'

'You will not disobey me. You will marry Henk Venter. We've agreed to join the farms and work them together. He has two nearly grown daughters who can help. It's the best thing for everyone.'

Riette looked at her mother, standing behind her father; she looked away from Riette. Everything was decided. They were a united front, her parents, and she had no chance of winning against them. She stood up. She'd had enough. This was her life, not theirs. She was not going to be the wife of an old man like Henk Venter. She was not going to become like her mother, nothing but a tool for her father. A compliant tool with not a shred of life left in her.

'I will not marry Henk Venter. I'll be leaving for Kimberley tomorrow. You'll have to tell your friend Henk to find a wife somewhere else.'

She grabbed her exam results and put them back in her pocket. She stood and moved towards the door, but her father was on his feet, blocking her escape. He hit her once in the face and everything went black.

When she woke in her room, it was dark. She lay, trying to remember what had happened. Her cheek was sore and her eye swollen. She tried to get up but found her leg was chained to the bed, and then she remembered. She remembered everything.

She spent the week like that. Her mother was her only visitor, bringing her food and water, taking away her chamber pot. She applied salve to Riette's face. She spoke little, only reminding her that she would be marrying Henk on Friday and that it made no sense to fight it.

'He's a good man. The best a girl like you can expect.'

The best a girl like her could expect. By the end of the week she began to believe the words were true.

Friday morning arrived and Riette knew she would not fight. She was nothing to them. Her dreams were nothing compared to theirs.

Her mother helped her put on her navy dress usually reserved for Sunday church. Riette followed her parents to the wagon and climbed in at the back next to her already packed trunk. She sat at the back as they made their way to the Dutch Reformed Church two hours' drive away.

Henk Venter waited for them at the door, his two girls beside him. He'd not bothered with a suit, but he'd put on a new pair of overalls. He nodded at Riette when she walked up to him, but said nothing.

There was no one else to witness the marriage. It was not a wedding of celebration, just a bit of housekeeping to tie up the loose ends. The minister kept things short; in thirty minutes they were back outside. Henk lifted Riette's trunk from her father's wagon into his. He climbed up onto the seat and his girls positioned themselves next to him. Her father helped Riette into the back of the wagon next to her trunk again.

Henk and her father spoke for a few minutes about their plans for the following week. Then Henk flicked the reins and the horses headed out.

Riette watched her parents standing at their wagon. She did not wave. She did not cry. She just watched them disappear in the dust.

9

The Transvaal
December 1899

'You're not my mother, so don't think you can tell me what to do,' Martie said.

Martie was Henk's eldest daughter, thirteen when Riette had moved into their house. The death of her mother had hardened her, as Riette expected it had hardened Henk. Martie had been forced to be an adult before she was ready, and she resented that. Now here was Riette, giving her the opportunity to go back, to let go of some of the burden, but she wouldn't. It was her house now and Riette needed to know her place.

She was right, Riette thought. She was not her mother and had no interest in being one. She had no interest in controlling anyone. She'd leave her to do what she wanted. Wasn't that what she'd always desired as a girl? To be left to do what she wanted? To explore the bush alone, or with Modise and Wamodimo, the children of the farm workers her parents employed. Or with Koos before he died. They'd explore the Magaliesberg and shoot birds with their catapults, birds they'd cook on the small fires they made in the bush. They'd swim in the ice-cold streams in hidden spots in the mountains.

She had been left alone until her mother decided it was time she learned how to be a wife, at about twelve. Then there had been all sorts of rules for how a wife must behave. But Riette had no interest in imposing rules on these girls, Henk's daughters. They could do what they wanted, and she wished that they would.

Martie was tall for her age, with long, smooth blonde hair and bright-blue eyes. Men in the area were already eyeing her as wife material, and Riette suspected Martie had her preference. She'd spotted her after church speaking to a lanky boy from the other side of the valley, and she'd seen her sneak away in the night, Riette guessed for secret meetings with the same boy. Martie could do what she liked – Riette didn't mind, and she'd never think of telling Henk.

Riette wished they were closer, though, close enough for her to warn the girl. Warn her to flee, find a husband who would take her far from this place. To somewhere where the strict rules of Afrikaner society would not touch her. To the Cape or to Europe. Anywhere but here. Riette knew that whatever she said to Martie would be taken as grounds for a fight. If she told her to leave this place, she thought Martie would do everything in her power to stay, so Riette kept her words to herself.

Riette accepted that there would be no connection between them, so she kept to herself too. Her days were filled with cooking and cleaning. She had her chores on the farm. She kept the big vegetable garden and cleaned the chicken run.

It was different with Annemie, though. She was eleven when Riette had moved in. At first she'd sided with her sister, but she hadn't been able to hold out forever. One scorching hot day, Riette had left her chores and headed for the dam behind the farm. Martie had gone to town with her father, and Annemie sat on a blanket in the shade of the gum trees at the front of the house.

'Do you want to come?' Riette asked.

'Where?'

'For a swim … in the dam.'

'But Pa says we mustn't swim in the dam.'

'Your father's not here.'

Annemie hesitated, then followed. The dam was circled by a grove of trees. Riette stripped off her clothes and dived in with a loud shout when the cold water met her hot skin.

Annemie sat on the shore watching her. 'Is it cold?'

'Yes, it's wonderful.' Riette dived under and swam further out.

'Is it deep?'

'Not too deep. You can come, I'll hold you. Don't be afraid.'

The girl hesitated, but then Riette could see that a decision was made and it was more than a decision to disobey her father. It was a decision to defy her sister, one in support of herself and her own opinions. Annemie liked Riette and she couldn't hold on to animosity that she didn't truly feel.

She took off her pinafore and her dress, slip and pants. She stepped carefully to the water. She often acted timidly, but Riette could see that she was not timid in her heart. She was the opposite of her sister, who acted as though she were brave and strong but inside was scared of most things. Annemie had an adventurous heart, like Riette.

Riette walked to the shore and took Annemie's hand. They walked slowly into the water and, with each step, Annemie looked up at Riette and Riette nodded. 'We'll be fine.'

After that day, they did many things together when Martie was not around. Annemie still had to keep up the appearance of being against Riette for her sister's sake, but when Martie was gone – and she was gone a lot, as she liked to visit neighbours and was the one who went to town to sell with Henk – Riette and Annemie were best friends.

When they were alone, they left their chores undone. Riette would take Annemie into the bush to search for traditional medicines. They would dig up tubers and peel bark and collect seeds. Sometimes they would ride the mare together out to the village where the blacks lived, to visit a traditional doctor Riette knew who helped her identify what she'd collected and who taught her how the plants could be used.

Sometimes they fished or swam in the dam. If Henk and Martie were gone overnight, they would sleep out under the stars, something Riette loved to do. She'd found a book about constellations in the storeroom behind the house, and she and Annemie tried their best to identify the stars they saw in the wide night sky. The book was called *In the Heavens*. They both liked poring through its pages, trying to memorise bits to impress the other one when they were alone at night.

'There's the Milky Way.' Annemie pointed out the wide expanse of scattered red and white for Riette. She was much better at finding things in the night sky than Riette was.

'Yes, you're right. It's quite beautiful tonight.'

They lay quietly for a while and then Annemie turned over onto her stomach and looked at Riette. 'Do you think one day I could study the stars? I mean really – go to school and learn about them, become an astronomer?'

'Certainly. Why not?'

'My father won't allow it, I think.'

'We'll make a plan. When you want to go, let me know, and we'll make a plan,' Riette said. She took Annemie's hand in hers. 'We should all follow our dreams, even if they lead to the stars.'

They both laughed.

'I'm sorry I need to be mean to you when Martie is here,' Annemie said.

'Don't even think about it, I know how it is. You and I know the truth.'

'Yes, we know the truth. It's sort of nicer to be secret friends.'

Riette smiled. 'Yes, it is.'

Living with Henk was like living with an odd sort of stranger. He rarely said anything to her except what was absolutely necessary: where he was going, when he would return, what she should do while he was not there. The oddest parts were the nights. Riette wondered how two people could be so unknown to each other, and yet so intimate.

Her mother had never told her anything about the night-time relations of a husband and wife, but she knew a bit from watching animals on the farm. She'd learned a few things at nursing school too. She expected that with humans there would be more to it, though, and she guessed that with other humans there probably was, but for her and Henk, there wasn't – it was a strictly physical thing, like the need to eat or drink or defecate. Emotions didn't play a role. Nothing soft and sensual, nothing beautiful.

He never spoke except for that first night. Before blowing out the lamp he said, 'It will probably hurt this time. You'll just get through it. It will not hurt after this, it will get better.'

He'd been right; it had hurt the first time. He'd forced himself into her and she was sure he'd torn her apart. But he'd been wrong about the second part – it never got much better. He'd blow out the lamp, push up her nightgown, and pull her thighs apart. He'd push himself inside her as if she were a hole dug in the ground. There were no kind words, there was no kissing, no touching. He'd finish and move off her, falling asleep within minutes. Riette did not blame him. She suspected that with his first wife it had been different, that they had loved each other. She thought she was likely as much of a disappointment to Henk as Henk was to her.

Afterwards, she'd get up and wipe as much of his seed away as she could. Though she knew it wouldn't keep her from becoming pregnant, she didn't want any of him inside her and tried to remove as much as possible. She knew somehow that her eggs would never be accepting of Henk's sperm. She never feared getting pregnant. The last thing she needed was another reason to keep her from running. A baby would tie her down and she still had plans. Riette was waiting for her chance to escape.

Though the two farms were within walking distance, she never visited her parents. She saw her father occasionally when he came to speak to Henk. There were often men visiting Henk and, increasingly, discussions of war. Since gold had been discovered on the Witwatersrand, more and more foreigners were entering the Transvaal. There were more foreigners than Afrikaners now, and they were agitating for rights. They wanted to vote, but President Kruger knew that that would mark

75

the end of the independent Afrikaner republics. The British wanted the gold and they would get it, no matter if it meant war. The men were already speaking of heading off to join the commando units. They had not suffered through the Great Trek just to have foreigners take their land from them yet again. There was anger brewing; there was reckless war talk in the air.

At breakfast one morning, Henk said, 'I'm leaving today for Pietersburg. I'll not be back until the work is finished.' Riette knew what he meant. He meant the work of pushing the British back to their place.

Riette said nothing. Martie jumped to her feet and said, 'So you're leaving us with her?'

'I'll not have any trouble,' Henk said. 'We all need to make sacrifices. This will not be the first, there will be many, and I expect you and your sister to be brave and strong. This war is for our freedom. Everyone must be ready to fight it.'

Later that day, a wagon already full of men and boys from the area stopped to collect Henk. Riette saw her father among them but made no show of recognising him. Riette and the girls watched Henk leave. Martie stood tall and still and Annemie cried silently next to her. Riette watched the wagon pull away and inside she rejoiced. The time had come – the time had finally come for her to make her escape.

She'd been saving money secretly since she arrived at the farm. Bits of money from the sale of eggs and the chickens she kept, from money Henk gave her for personal items. She had enough to get a lift on a wagon to Pretoria and take the train from there to Kimberley. She knew Sister Mary Alice would take her in immediately. Nurses were always needed, more so with a war starting. With Henk gone, it would be easy to go. There was no one to stop her.

She carefully planned the night she would leave. She'd packed food and a small bag of clothes. She would take one of the mules, and ride to Rustenburg. She'd leave the mule there; Martie could collect it if she wanted. She wrote a note explaining everything. She would go and finally be free to live her own life, the one she had chosen.

When the night came, it was perfect, a cool night with a full moon. It would be an easy ride.

Riette looked in on the girls, who were both sleeping. Annemie lay curled on her side, her blankets kicked off. Riette pulled the blankets back over her. She kept a wedding photo of her parents next to her bed. Riette picked it up and looked at Henk standing behind his young, dark-haired wife, Cora. She wore a quizzical look on her face, as if she wondered how the camera worked or why she was there, married to Henk. Or maybe she wondered why her life would be cut so short, dead at twenty-nine, barely a life lived.

Riette liked the look of Cora – she saw a lot of her in Annemie. She'd never really known Cora, though she'd been their neighbour. They had seen each other at church, but that was about all. Riette's family had done no socialising after Koos died. Riette had heard that Cora liked to sing and dance. She could see that in her eyes – there was a sparkle there that even the dour Henk had not put out. Though married and burdened with two children at such a young age, she'd seemed happy. Riette wished she could be content with the life she was given. She wished she could be more like Cora, but she knew she was not built for it. She was different. This life, this small life defined for a girl before she left her nappies, was a life that would kill Riette.

She looked down at Annemie sleeping. Where Martie was her father all over, with blonde hair and crisp blue eyes and a hard, rigid character, Riette guessed Annemie's soft, kind heart came from Cora. She carefully put the photo back and ran her hand gently over Annemie's cheek. She'd miss her and she suspected Annemie would be the only one who would miss Riette.

Annemie turned and groaned. Not fully awake, she said, 'Ma?'

Riette watched Annemie for some time. She thought of their nights together under the stars, and then she remembered the promise that she had made, the promise to help her follow her dreams. Annemie had believed Riette, believed that she was telling the truth. At the time Riette was sure she was too. But now? What did that all mean now?

Riette sneaked out of the room, picked up her bag by the door, carried it back to her bedroom and unpacked. Perhaps she'd known all along that she couldn't go. War was coming, and leaving the girls, leaving Annemie, alone to face it was a step too far for her.

She'd wait for the war to end, and then she'd be on her way, she promised herself. She'd be on her way as soon as the war was over. Maybe she'd leave with Annemie then, take her to her school to learn about the stars. That's what they would do. After the war, they'd go off and live their lives – exactly the lives that they wanted to live.

10

The Transvaal
January 1901

It was difficult to run the farm alone, only the three of them, especially with the shortage of supplies. British soldiers, the Khakis, had destroyed the railway lines, so provisions couldn't get through. It was just over a year since Henk had left. They'd had news that his commando had been captured. Captured men were sent off overseas, and they'd heard that both Henk and Riette's father had been taken to Ceylon.

When Martie got the letter telling her that her father had been sent so far away, she said to Annemie, 'Don't worry. He'll come home soon.'

In a way, Riette envied the girl's way of seeing things. There was a just and right way and, in Martie's world, that way always won. Her father was fighting on the side of good, so he would survive and come home. It made life much easier if you believed that, Riette thought – believed there were rules that were always observed.

Riette and Annemie kept the big garden going and the chickens that fed them. Martie, with the farm workers, managed the orchard and the cattle. She drove the wagon into town to sell oranges and meat and pick up the few supplies that were available. Together they managed.

Riette hoped that the Khakis would leave their little valley alone until the end of the war. Then Henk would return and she would escape.

One morning, Martie woke early and, with the help of Isaiah, one of the farm workers, loaded the wagon with smoked meat and bags of oranges. They hitched up the mules and, after breakfast, left for the day. As soon as Annemie and Riette were sure the wagon was over the hill and out of sight, they looked at each other.

'A picnic by the dam?' Annemie said.

'Perfect,' Riette replied.

They packed koeksisters Riette had made that morning, some biltong and oranges and a bottle of tea. Riette grabbed their fishing poles and a blanket, and Annemie collected her sketchbook. Drawing was her new interest and she was becoming quite good at it. She was particularly good at portraits, and her sketchbook was full of portraits of Martie and Riette and her friends among the workers' children, Refilwe and Keitumetse.

The clouds of the morning burned off in the hot January sun, and by noon they were swimming in the water while the two fish they'd caught cooked on the tiny fire they'd made. Annemie was an adept swimmer now, swimming deep into the middle of the dam with strong, confident strokes. Riette swam out to her and floated on her back, letting the hot sun fall on her bare breasts and stomach.

She thought she heard something and looked to the far shore, where she was surprised to see her mother, her hair pulled from its usual tidy bun, her apron still on. She saw them in the water, and waved and shouted for them to come in. Something had happened, it was clear – something serious. Her always tidy, never excitable mother would not behave like this.

'Something's wrong, Annemie,' Riette said. 'Hurry!'

When Riette was out of the water, she looked back at the other side of the dam where her father's farm was and saw smoke rising. By the time Riette and Annemie had pulled their dresses back on, Riette's mother had made her way to their side of the dam.

'It's the Khakis! They've burned everything!'

80

What Riette had feared was happening: the war had come to them. Annemie gasped and Riette put her arm around her. 'We'll be fine,' Riette said, wishing she could believe it.

Riette's mother carried a blanket and a photo of Koos and nothing else. 'I managed to leave before they saw me. They burned the house. Even the animals. They've burned everything and they'll be coming for yours. We must get what we can!'

At the house, Riette and Annemie packed what they thought they might need in bags that were easy to carry. Riette knew that Martie, like Henk, hid money. They thought they were hiding it from Riette, but she knew the place. She went out to the barn and moved the big milk tank to the side. Under it, at the back, was a metal box. She opened it to find gold British sovereigns. Tearing open the hem of her dress, she pushed the coins in. Then, with the needle and thread she'd brought, she quickly sewed stitches between each coin to keep them from hitting against each other. She'd only just finished her work when Annemie rushed in.

'They're here! Oh god, Riette, they're here and they have Martie! We can't run – they have Martie!'

Riette's mother came into the barn. 'We must slip out the back. Now! We must leave now or they'll find us!'

She pulled at Riette and Annemie, but Riette broke free. 'We can't,' Riette said. 'They have Martie. We can't leave her.'

Her mother looked at Riette and said nothing more. She grabbed one of the bags they'd brought from the house and ran out the back of the barn into the veld. She would join the laager deep in the mountains where people were hiding from the soldiers.

Riette took Annemie's hand. She was crying and Riette pulled her close. She could hear the soldiers outside; they needed to go. 'We'll be fine,' she told her. 'We're going to be fine.'

Outside they found a contingent of ten British soldiers. They had Martie and Isaiah standing to the side, where one soldier kept his gun on them. The leader of the group spotted Riette and Annemie. He spoke to them in Afrikaans. 'Join the others!'

Annemie ran to Martie and they held each other. Riette stood to the side. It was then that she noticed the open wagon. Inside sat Tannie Lena and her three children, Johan, Emily and Marika, from the farm on the other side of the valley. They were dirty and smudged with ash. Tannie Lena held the children tightly and they all sat weeping together.

They'd heard that Lord Kitchener was losing his patience with the Boer commando units fighting a guerrilla war against the British. They burned forts and blocked supplies. Kitchener had issued a scorched-earth policy. All women and children should be collected in camps, and all houses and other property burned to the ground so that the commandos – their support systems dismantled, their loved ones imprisoned – would come out of hiding and surrender.

Riette had heard of this, but thought they were safe here in their protected valley. It was all so far away; the war had little to do with them. They were not feeding commandos; they were not assisting anyone. Riette had no feelings one way or the other when it came to the war. In a way, she'd been her happiest since the war started and Henk and her father had gone off. She told no one how she felt. She knew that emotions were high and anyone who spoke against the war and the independence of the Afrikaners was considered a hensopper, a traitor.

They watched as the soldiers poured paraffin on the house and barns, even on the orange groves, and lit the fires. Thick, dark smoke filled the air, and they covered their mouths with their pinafores, but still it filled their lungs and made them cough. When the soldiers were sure everything was burning, they pushed the women towards the open wagon.

'Don't touch me, you dog!' Martie said to one soldier who tried to help her into the wagon. She spat in his face and he slapped her so hard that she fell to the dirt. Annemie tried to help her up, but Martie shook her off. 'Leave me!'

The soldiers allowed them to take the bags they'd packed with blankets, extra clothes and food. Before they were taken to their destination, the soldiers stopped at two more farms. The women, farm workers and children were collected, and they all watched as houses were set alight with everything the families owned inside. Cattle were killed with bayonets. Horses burned. Nothing would be left to rebuild their lives after the war.

As the sun set, the open wagon headed for Pietersburg, the air thick with the smoke of destroyed lives.

11

The Transvaal
July 1901

The camp in Pietersburg housed four thousand people, primarily women and children, with a few men too old to fight. They were housed in white canvas tents with no floors save the dirt of the bare ground. Riette, Martie and Annemie shared a tent with a family of four: a mother, her two sons and her baby daughter. It was crowded and dirty and smelled of sweat. They were given cots to sleep on, but no bedding. The camp was infested with lice, so they immediately cut their hair off. The farm workers were taken to a different camp for the blacks. Riette suspected it was far worse there.

Because Henk was a commando, they were put in the lowest group for weekly rations. They were issued cards to collect their meagre supplies: some mealie meal (full of bugs), a small amount of coffee, an eighth of a tin of condensed milk, a bit of meat (when available) and sugar.

Their tent mates had arrived a month before. Tannie Aggie said they'd come from the north. Her sons, Riaan and Danie, were quiet boys who spent most of the day outside. Tannie Aggie was a little older than Riette and helped her and the girls to learn quickly how camp life operated.

Tannie Aggie laid baby Anke down on the cot and waved a towel back and forth over her to create some wind in the stagnant and scorching tent. Anke was very thin. The condensed milk that came with the rations was not enough for a baby of her age and now she had developed a fever. Tannie Aggie wiped a wet cloth over the baby's tiny body to try to cool her, but the child was still and quiet, her sunken eyes watching Riette.

'They think bringing us here will break the commandos,' Tannie Aggie said. 'But it won't. It will make them even more passionate about the fight. I hope my Willem kills a hundred of these Tommies. Thousands.' Her eyes glared with hatred.

Riette didn't understand that sort of passion amid all the suffering. Was any of this worth it? She needed to be away from this woman and her crazy thoughts. This woman with her dying baby – for, despite what Riette said, the comforting words she offered Tannie Aggie, she knew Anke would not last much longer. She'd seen malnourished babies at the hospital in Kimberley. Once they got past a certain point, there was no return. Anke was past that point.

She stood up. 'I want to see if they brought water.' Riette picked up the empty bucket and left the tent. She didn't know where Martie and Annemie had gone. Martie insisted on Annemie joining her to move among the tents to find the women they knew from their area. She felt that they could work together, that it was better than staying alone. Riette didn't think it made much difference.

There was hardly a breeze outside; it was nearly as hot as the tent, but at least the air smelled better. They'd been at the camp for a week and in that time she'd seen five children and one elderly woman die. Besides the lack of food, the hygiene was poor and disease was rife in the camp. Measles, typhoid and dysentery killed many. There was a marquee set up as a hospital, but few people took their loved ones there. It was manned by a British doctor and British nurses, and the people believed they killed the patients instead of helping them. Riette doubted it was true; it was just that patients were taken there too late.

Riette stood near the hospital and looked inside. The floor was bare earth, just like their own tents, which didn't lend itself to hygienic conditions. There were about twenty cots, each with a patient.

As she looked inside, one of the British soldiers passed. 'Do you have someone in there?' he asked in faltering Afrikaans.

Riette spoke to him in English. She'd learned English from the British sisters at the hospital in Kimberley. 'I'm a trained nurse. I thought perhaps I could help.'

She took out the letter with her exam scores. It was old and a bit tattered now, but she kept it with her at all times – it was her most valuable possession. The soldier took the paper, read it and handed it back to her.

'A nurse who knows both English and Afrikaans. I think you could be very useful.'

He said he was a trained medic, his name was John Reilly, from Ireland. He seemed young to Riette, maybe twenty-two or twenty-three. He had bright-red hair and kind eyes. He spoke in a sing-song way that Riette liked, words in the middle of sentences going up like a question and then sinking down again.

She followed him inside the tent, where the suffering of the patients became clear to her.

'Sergeant Miller,' John Reilly said to a man who seemed to be in charge. 'This woman is a trained nurse, speaks English too. She wants to help.'

Sergeant Miller looked Riette up and down. He hesitated as if he wanted to refuse. 'A nurse, you say?'

'Yes, sir.'

'You won't get any favours by working here, no additional rations.'

'That's fine,' Riette said.

'You'll take care of her then, Reilly. Any problem, I'll be looking to you.'

'Yes, sir.'

Riette never thought for a moment that working at the hospital might be a bad thing. She would be helping the people stay alive. But some in the camp, including Martie, saw it otherwise.

'What were you thinking?' Martie said a few days later. 'You're help-ing them.'

'No, I'm not,' Riette said. 'I'm helping us.'

'They're calling you a hensopper. You should quit.'

Riette was surprised when Annemie spoke up. 'She's helping to keep people alive. I don't think that's being a traitor. How could it be?'

Martie looked at her sister, her face red with fury. She stood and left the tent.

Annemie went back to her sketchbook, where she was trying to draw her father from the photo that had sat next to her bed on the farm and she now kept in her pocket.

'You shouldn't have done that,' Riette said.

'Why? That's what I think. I'm tired of Martie. She's trying to get the women to stand up against the soldiers, do you know that?'

'No, I didn't. How could they? They have no weapons.'

'They're making them. Making spears and knives. I think they'll get killed. All of them. I told her she was being reckless and she called me a coward. This camp is too much for her. She's going mad. She can't stand things that make no sense. This camp makes no sense to her.'

Riette said nothing else. She knew it was no use speaking to Martie, but, if the women were planning some sort of a revolt, she was afraid. Annemie was right, the soldiers had guns. No handmade spears and knives would stand up to that.

'You stay out of it. Do you promise?'

Annemie nodded. 'Yes, Martie already knows I won't be involved.'

The next day Riette showed up at the hospital after breakfast. John Reilly was already there. 'We've had a bad night. Two children with typhoid died. We've had four new patients and not enough beds. I've got children sharing.'

Riette got to work straight away. There was much to do and the day slipped away. She was kept busy bathing patients, feeding the weak-est. She administered the few medicines they had. Her first chance to sit down came as the sun was nearly below the horizon. She sat on the ground at the back of the hospital and watched the red sun through the barbed wire. She'd wrapped a ball of pap in a handkerchief and put it in her pocket before she'd left in the morning. Now she unwrapped it and ate slowly, watching the sun go down.

'Is that your dinner?'

Riette looked up and saw the smiling face of John Reilly. He had a plate stacked high with bread and meat with gravy. She'd grown used to the constant feeling of hunger, but smelling John Reilly's food was too much. She feared she'd burst into tears.

He sat down next to her on the ground. 'Would you like to share mine?'

He handed her the plate and she tried her best not to eat it all down in a flash. She wondered if she might be able to sneak one of the big slices of bread for Annemie and Martie, but decided not to take a chance, not today anyway.

'It's a funny place this,' John Reilly said. He looked out, past the fence, at the bush. 'Nothing like my home.'

He made no move to share the food, and Riette realised he'd brought it for her all along. 'What's your home like?' she said.

'Ireland? Green from top to toe. I miss the rain and the green. The smell of home. That's what I really miss, the smell of home.'

'How long have you been out here?'

'Two years next month. Seems so much longer. Seems ages.'

'You're young. You've not had many years yet. One year feels long when you're young.'

John Reilly laughed. He had a lovely laugh, an honest kind, Riette thought. 'You talk like you're an old lady. I'd guess we're about the same age.'

'You'd guess wrong. I'm twenty-nine, and I guess you're not more than twenty-two.'

'Twenty-three, I'll have you know.'

'Well, twenty-three then. Just a baby, really.'

Riette was speaking honestly – she felt miles older than him, why, she couldn't say. Maybe it was the war, the marriage, the responsibility of two children. She didn't know, but she knew she'd lived longer in her twenty-nine years than most.

'So what about you, Riette? What about this place?' John Reilly seemed interested in what she had to say. She wondered when last that had been the case. Perhaps with Annemie, but no one else had ever been interested in her thoughts. Not her parents, not Henk. She smiled up at him. It was nice to have someone listen.

'Well, there is something,' John Reilly said. 'I think that's the first smile I've seen on ya. You should share it more – you've got a lovely one.'

Riette felt suddenly shy. 'Not much to smile about here, I think.'

John Reilly seemed to have forgotten the situation. Forgotten that Riette was the enemy, a prisoner. 'Sorry. It's bad ... all of this, horrible. Sorry, really, it was stupid of me to say that.'

'It's all right.'

'No, it's not. I wish all of this could end and we could all go back to our lives. What would you do, Riette Venter? If all of this was finished?'

'First, I'd get my girls somewhere. Well ... they're not mine really. I'd get them back to their father. And then I'd get a job as a nurse in Kimberley. I have a job waiting for me; it's only I got delayed, lost a bit along the way.'

'You're a good nurse. Any hospital would be lucky to have you.'

Riette looked down at the empty plate. 'Sorry, I ate everything.'

'It's all right. I'll feed you here, despite what Miller says. You give your rations to your girls. It will help them. Food is the problem here. There'd be a lot less sickness if there was a bit more food.'

Riette wasn't sure what to think about John Reilly. He was the enemy, one of the nation that had caused all of this. Then, too, he was a young man missing home, confused about the point of it all. Willing to go against orders and give her food. She liked him, though she knew she shouldn't.

They heard noise from the hospital tent, so Riette and John Reilly went back inside. Tannie Aggie and her elder son, Riaan, were standing there. Tannie Aggie held baby Anke in her arms.

'Help her! Please help her!'

Riette knew, even from a distance, that Anke was past help. She stepped forward and took the dead child in her arms, and led the mother to the back, to another tent that acted as a mortuary.

12

The Transvaal
August 1901

The work in the hospital was difficult, but Riette slowly began to realise that she was happy there, happy because she was being useful, if only to make people comfortable before they died. But also she was happy to be with John Reilly. She knew she should feel guilty caring so much for a British soldier, but she didn't. To her he was not a soldier, he was a man. A kind-hearted, lonely man, who missed his home. The first man who looked past her plain face and saw who she was underneath and truly liked that person.

One night when it was time for them to go home, John Reilly turned to Riette and said, 'Could we walk a bit?'

Riette wondered where they might go. They couldn't walk through the narrow lanes between the tents. Already she was suspect; that would give the women even more reason to call her a traitor. And they couldn't walk among the soldiers' tents, as she wouldn't be allowed there.

'My mate is on duty at the side gate, the supply gate. He'll let us walk out in the veld.'

Riette's heart jumped. To be free of the wires, free to roam through the bush? Happiness flooded her and she could not speak; she only nodded her head.

John had been right. His mate let them pass without notice. They rushed away from the camp to a nearby koppie. They climbed to the far side and sat down on the sun-warmed rocks and watched the last rays of the day fall below the horizon, leaving the sky painted red and pink, which faded to grey and then finally to black. Riette lay back on the smooth rocks and sighed. What joy to be there, away from the camp.

She saw the first sliver of the waxing moon appear above her. Its horns faced down, a bad sign. She didn't want to think it, but her mind went there anyway. The Tswana believed that a waxing moon with the horns facing downwards meant that the moon was dropping disease on the people. Disease and bad luck. She didn't want those thoughts in her head now. She tried to think of other things.

John turned to lie on his stomach and looked down at her. 'You're beautiful,' he said.

Riette laughed. 'You know that's not true. You don't need to lie to me. If you want to kiss me, just do it. Between us, let's be honest.'

John leaned closer and gently placed his lips on hers. She smiled and he kissed her again. She always knew that all of those nights with Henk were not making love; she was sure there had to be more to it than that. On that koppie, she found the answer. With a single kiss, John showed her it could all be different.

John's kiss opened something in her. She felt reckless and free, as if the door to her true self was revealed after being hidden for so long. She wanted John to touch her – she kissed him back, letting her mouth open and allowing his tongue inside. Everything stopped except for the feelings. She pushed him onto his back and climbed on top of him. As each kiss became more passionate, she could feel him harden under her. John unbuttoned her dress and reached for her breasts, and she groaned at his touch. She slipped her underclothes off and pushed him inside her. Then, as he rolled her onto her back and slowly moved against her, she wished it would never end. She pushed up to meet him, her body

92

responding to his every move. The excitement built in her flesh as she'd never felt before. All of those times with Henk had been something else, not this. Tonight she was a virgin again; what she felt was absolutely new.

They fell apart reluctantly when it was over. It was properly night then and Riette looked at the Milky Way strewn across the sky. They were nothing, just two inconsequential people in the long history of the universe, nothing at all of significance about them, about that night. But that night they were everything. Riette knew that her life had changed. Things had shifted in her that could never be shifted back.

They lay on the rocks and Riette taught John about the night sky of southern Africa while he traced swirl patterns along her neck and chest. It grew cold and they finally, reluctantly, made their way back to the camp.

As they neared the camp, they could and see something was happening. The gate was unmanned and they could hear shots near the supply house where rations were distributed. John turned to her.

'Go to the hospital. You'll be safe there. I'll go and see what's happening.'

Riette did as she was told. She made herself busy, checking patients. After some time John returned.

'There's been a revolt of some sort, at the rations queue. The women were armed with knives, and they attacked the soldiers there. People have been shot. They'll be bringing them soon, we must get ready. It's not good, Riette, not good at all.'

John was not made for war, not like other men. What he'd seen had upset him terribly. He went to the storeroom to fetch stretchers and ran out to the soldiers waiting for him.

Riette looked out of the front of the tent. In the dark it was hard to see, but she thought she saw Annemie and Tannie Aggie carrying someone towards the hospital. Riette ran out to them, stumbling on a rock. She fell and got up again. She told herself that it was not what she thought, it was something else. But then she was next to them and she could no longer lie to herself.

Annemie screamed, 'It's Martie! She's been shot! Oh, god, Riette, save her!'

Riette grabbed Martie's legs and helped them get her to a bed. Her dress was soaked with blood, but she was still alive. Riette tore the dress apart and saw the two wounds where the bullets had entered, two dark holes in her chest. Her breathing was shallow and gurgling.

Riette pushed Annemie away and turned to Tannie Aggie. 'Take her out of here, please.'

Others were arriving – women shot and soldiers stabbed. She saw at least five women taken directly to the morgue tent. Riette tried to stop Martie's bleeding, but she knew there was no hope for her. She held the girl's hand, for she was still a girl even though she'd taken on all the responsibilities of a grown woman. She was only seventeen, far too young to die.

'Riette,' Martie whispered through the pain. 'Take care of Annemie.'

'I will, Martie, I will, I promise.'

Riette could hear Martie's lungs filling with liquid, each breath more difficult than the one before. She held her hand, feeling ineffectual because there was nothing more that could be done. In a few minutes, Martie was gone. Riette held her hand for a while longer. It was still warm, still holding on to the last bits of life. How unfair this all was, how unfair that a young girl like Martie, with so much passion and life ahead, had to die – for nothing, really. Despite all the animosity between her and Martie, Riette had still loved her. They were very different, but Riette would miss her.

There was no time to mourn, though; the hospital was filling up. She called two passing soldiers with a stretcher. 'Take this one to the morgue, we need the bed.' Businesslike words hid her breaking heart.

Then she made her way out of the tent and found Tannie Aggie holding Annemie in her arms. Riette went to them.

'Is she all right?' Annemie asked, her dear face wet with tears.

'No, she's not. She's dead, Annemie, I'm sorry. You must be strong for her now, though.' Riette tried to keep her voice steady.

Annemie fell to the ground, weeping into her hands. Riette sat next to her for a time but needed to get back to the hospital.

'Tannie Aggie, please take her back to the tent. I'll come when I'm finished here.'

Riette wished she could take Annemie's pain and carry it for her. Her kind heart might break from the loss of her sister. Riette thought of how lost she had been when Koos died. But Riette would keep her promise; she would take care of Annemie. They would survive this war, this horrible, bloody war, and find their lives on the other side.

13

The Transvaal
August 1901

Riette never lied to herself. She knew she was in love with John. Who could have imagined, in a camp filled with such suffering, that she would find love? But she had. She was not foolish enough to think it would last after the war. John had told her about his young wife back home in Ireland waiting for him.

Riette didn't mind. She knew that when all of this was over she didn't want to be bound to a husband. She was almost positive about that – even a husband like John. She would make her own life, on her own terms, finally. One thing John had showed her, though, was that happiness could be part of her life. She'd never thought that before him; she'd thought she was a woman not meant for such things, a woman not made to be loved.

Winter arrived, and the cold was harsh on the women and children in the camp. Most had brought little except the clothes they were wearing when the soldiers arrived. Riette and Annemie were lucky; they had the blankets they'd brought in their bags. They shared some with Tannie Aggie and her boys, since they had only one blanket between them. Still, it was difficult. Riette wondered how much longer the war would go on. According to John, the British had taken over most of the Boer republics. It was now just for the last of the commandos to surrender, but they seemed unwilling to do so. They wanted to fight until nothing was left.

Riette sometimes wondered about the fate of her mother. Was she also in a camp somewhere? Or was she out in the mountains assisting the commandos?

And her father? And Henk? How were they faring so far from home? They'd heard rumours that many of the men taken to Ceylon had died there. So many had died – were they among them?

When they had the chance, she and John managed to slip away from the camp. Riette knew that if she ran away when they were out of the camp, John would do nothing to stop her. They never discussed it, though. When they were outside the wires of the camp, they talked of everything but her escape. Outside the camp they were just a woman and a man in love.

'Tell me about your brother,' John said one day. He lay behind her, holding her body to his, leaning against a big rock.

'Koos? He was always so clear about things, so confident that nothing could stop him. He was brave, I suppose, so unlike me. I used to watch him and wonder where that came from, his bravery. Our parents were not brave; they followed where others stepped. But Koos, Koos was going to make his own way. I wonder sometimes what he would think of this war. Would he have charged into battle with the others, or would he have tried to speak peace? I hope he would have tried to find peace; I try to think that's what he would have done. That would have been the braver way to go.' Riette turned to John. 'He was a bit like you, really. I remember that the old tomcat we had killed a mouse near the chicken run once. Koos found the nest of babies the dead mouse had left behind, all pink and blind. I found him out there crying. He was so tough and brave on the outside, but inside he was gentle and soft. Like you. And, like you, the things that got through that tough outside affected him forever. Like Annemie too. I'm scared for her, John.'

'Did the tonic I gave you help?'

'She's out of bed now, but she's not better. The loss of her sister has been too much, I think. Her heart is broken, that's not something that can be fixed with tonic.'

'Give her time. She'll come right, I'm sure of it.'

Days passed and Riette could see that Annemie was trying her best. 'When we leave here we'll find a school for me to learn about stars, won't we?' she asked as they sat outside the tent next to the small fire they'd made. She leaned in to warm her hands in its inadequate warmth, the cold wind at her back.

'Yes, of course. Maybe an art school where you can study the stars. You're very good at drawing – you have a gift, I think,' Riette said.

Annemie considered this. 'Yes, perhaps.' She became quiet. 'What do you think Martie would have wanted for her life?'

'I don't know,' Riette said. 'I think she liked the farming life.'

'She did, you're right. Did you know she was in love with a boy?'

'Not really. I suspected, but I knew nothing for sure.'

'Yes, his name was Cornelius. He left to fight with our father. He was in the wagon that day. Martie cried for a long time after watching him leave.'

Riette was surprised to hear this. She struggled to imagine Martie crying over anything. 'He'll be sad to hear Martie died.'

'No, he's dead already. He got shot in the first battle. Martie changed then, when she heard. She had so much hatred for the British after that. I'm sure that was part of what led her to start the revolt. Anyway, maybe they're happy now, together in heaven.'

'Yes, I think they are.' Riette stood up. 'Let's go inside. You're not yet well. The cold night air is not good for your lungs.'

Riette first realised some new infection had come to the camp when she saw children dying in the hospital. Three or four a week were coming in with a bloody cough. A few recovered, but most died. Annemie had a

98

straggling cough from the week after Martie died. Riette hadn't realised how bad it was until she found Annemie washing out a handkerchief stained with blood.

'What is that?' Riette asked when she found her behind the tent.

Annemie closed the handkerchief in her hand. 'What?'

Riette reached down and took the cloth from her. 'It's blood! Are you bleeding when you cough?'

'I didn't want you to worry.' Annemie looked close to tears.

'For how long?' Riette could not prevent her fear from rising to the surface, where it appeared as anger. Losing Martie was difficult, but losing Annemie would be the end of her. She realised now that she loved her as much as she'd ever loved anyone.

'I don't know.' Annemie began to cry. 'A while. I'm sorry I hid it from you – please don't be angry.'

Riette grabbed her up in her arms. 'I'm not angry, never angry with you. I'm scared, though. This is serious. I want you in the hospital. You need rest. With rest and care you can recover. I know it.'

Annemie agreed to go to the hospital, where Riette and John kept watch over her. They steamed her lungs. John managed to get some of the tonic for consumption, which was rare and difficult to find. Riette kept it aside, only to be used by Annemie. Other children died, but she would not let that trouble her. She needed to keep Annemie safe, needed to heal her. But, despite the tonic, Annemie was not improving.

Riette would have easily stayed at Annemie's bedside through the night, but John insisted she go and rest.

'I'll stay with her, I promise. You're no good if you don't rest. You'll get consumption yourself if you don't watch out.'

Riette went reluctantly back to the tent, where she fell into a dreamless sleep. She woke up suddenly after many hours, in a panic, guilty that she'd been so indulgent. She splashed water on her face and rushed back to the hospital.

She found John sitting on an upturned tin outside the hospital tent, holding his head in his hands. At first she thought he was sleeping, then he looked up. He looked up and she saw it in his face.

'No!' Riette said, running into the hospital. She stopped when she saw Annemie's empty bed. 'Where is she? Where did you take her?'

John, usually careful not to show his feelings for Riette in public, took her in his arms. She struggled to break free, but he wouldn't let her go.

'She died this morning, Riette.'

For the first time since everything had happened, Riette cried. When, at last, John let her go, she went to the morgue and knelt next to the young girl. She laid her head on Annemie's tiny body, already cold and stiff. She had failed her, Riette thought. She had failed Martie too.

Day bled into night, but Riette could not leave her Annemie. Tannie Aggie came. 'Riette,' she said, 'we need to bury her. You need to come away now.'

Riette heard nothing. She screamed and fought the women who came to take Annemie. Finally John stepped in. He spoke softly to her. Riette collapsed into his arms and he led her away. The women watched but stayed silent. As the women of the camp buried Annemie, John took Riette to their special place behind the koppie. He held her in his arms and rocked her; he smoothed her hair and told her everything would be better with time.

The sun rose and found them still in place. Riette's tears were finished. She had thought nothing could hurt her more than the loss of her brother, but now she knew otherwise. Loving was a dangerous, hurtful business. Her special, kind, talented Annemie was gone, and Riette wasn't sure she could go on. Nothing seemed to have any light left in it.

'I think you should leave this place. There's no one to keep you here now. I can help you get away,' John said.

Riette wondered why he'd said that. *He* kept her here in this place. As long as he was here, she would stay. He was all she had left. It was then that she realised she hadn't been honest with herself after all. She needed John, and she hoped he would stay with her. That was all she hoped for now.

When Riette got back to the camp, she could sense that something had changed. She walked to her tent and eyes followed her. As she neared the entrance, a woman from across the way, one she didn't know, came running at Riette and said, 'Hensopper! Dirty whore!'

Riette ducked into the empty tent and sat down on the cot she had shared with Annemie. She picked up Annemie's sketchbook, which lay next to the cot, and paged through images of herself and Martie, of Tannie Aggie and her boys. Drawings of Cora and Henk. When Riette got to the end of the book, she was sad to discover there was no drawing of Annemie herself. Riette had no photograph of her either. She wondered how long Annemie's face would remain in her mind. Would time pass to a point where Annemie was only a feeling of loss and nothing more? She could not bear to think that.

Tannie Aggie came into the tent as if someone was chasing her. She rushed to Riette and knelt in front of her. 'Riette, listen, you need to find a place to be safe. The women ... the women are angry. They know about you and the Tommy.'

'What do you mean?' Riette had told no one about her friendship with John. It was bad enough that she worked in the hospital; she knew anything more would be too much.

'They know about you and John Reilly, that you are ... friends. They saw you at the hospital, how he was with you. I heard a woman say she'll put blue vitriol in your sugar. They want to kill you, Riette.'

Riette waited until morning to leave the tent. She woke early and crept to the hospital at the back of the rows of tents. John was already there.

'I need to leave,' she whispered. 'I need to leave today.'

'I'll organise it,' John said. He must have known something because he asked no questions. 'Go and get your things and come back. Be careful.'

Riette didn't want anyone to see her carrying a bag. She still had the gold sovereigns in the hem of her dress. All she wanted from the tent was Annemie's sketchbook, the star book they so loved, and Koos's photo. She stuck them in under her dress and went back to the hospital. John met her at the door.

'You'll go tonight. I've organised everything.'

The day passed slowly. Riette feared the women would find her and drag her from the hospital, but they didn't. Once it was dark enough and the camp had gone to bed, she and John slipped out of the gate. He led her to the back of the koppie. She was surprised to see a wagon there. A black man sat on the seat waiting for them.

'Dumela, Rre Molefi,' John said to the man.

'Ntate,' the man replied.

'You can trust Mr Molefi. He's a friend of mine. He's going to take you to Mafeking. He'll take you to my friends, the Woods. They're British. They know about you. Wait there for me. When the war is over, I will come for you.'

'But your wife … you must go home to her.'

'I love you, don't you know that? How could I leave you?' John helped her into the wagon. 'Wait for me, I'll come to you. I promise.'

Rre Molefi flicked the reins and the horses set off. Riette looked back only once, and then looked ahead at what lay before her.

14

Mafeking
April 1902

'Give me four yards of the blue cotton. I need to get three dresses from it for my girls.'

Riette pulled out the bolt of fabric and measured out four yards on the ruler nailed to the long table. She cut the fabric and folded it into a square. 'It will be more than enough for your girls, Mrs Corning,' she said. She took the money from the woman and handed back the change.

'Good day, Mrs Corning,' Riette called after her as she left.

It was a quiet day in the shop. Woods General Dealer was at the centre of Mafeking and was usually busy, but not today. Mr and Mrs Woods had gone off to the meeting. There was talk that the end of the war had finally come. The Woods were happy because they were devout Quakers and had never believed in the war in the first place. A town meeting had been called to discuss the new developments.

Riette was not interested, Mrs Woods – Abigail – had said they could close the shop for the day, but Riette saw no reason. She'd much rather stay behind and wait on the few customers who arrived than listen to more talk about war. She was tired of war.

Since she'd been in Mafeking, she'd received only one letter from John Reilly. She'd responded, but hadn't heard back again. That was more than seven months ago. She didn't know what that meant. Maybe he never received her reply. Maybe he'd already gone home to Ireland. Maybe he was dead. She didn't know, so she waited. In some sort of purgatory, she waited for what she didn't know, fed only by her hopes of what might be.

The bell above the door jingled and Riette looked up. It was Mrs du Plooy. Most of the Afrikaner women had been released from the camps around Mafeking. Before the war, Mrs du Plooy and her husband had been rich business people in the area. They'd bought and sold cattle. Her husband was still missing, maybe dead or still in a camp overseas. She waited for him in their big, empty house near the centre of town. Their eldest son had followed his father off to fight and the youngest one had died of dysentery in the camps. It had been a hard war for her.

Mrs du Plooy's face fell when she saw Riette. 'I thought you'd be gone to the meeting, happy to hear your friends have won and will now take what is not theirs.'

Riette ignored her words; she'd learned how to smile through almost anything now. 'What can I get you today?'

'A pound of sugar. And make sure it's a pound. Last time you cheated me by quite a bit.' Riette scooped sugar into the weighing pan. 'They closed your camp there in Pietersburg, did you hear?'

'No, I hadn't heard.'

'Last month already. Cleared out the lot of them. The women went home to their burned farms, the Khakis back to their lives in England. Not a care in the world for all they did here, the evil bastards.'

Mrs du Plooy snatched the bag of sugar from Riette and threw the money on the counter even though Riette held out her hand to take it.

'No problem, though, for women like you, the whores of the Tommies. You did yourself fine. Set up here with those British swine, saved yourself from the worst. In the end, the women and children were dying ten or twelve a day I heard. But not you, no. You opened your thighs just to make an easy life for yourself. But don't worry, God will punish you, be sure of that. God will see that you go to hell with the lot of them.'

She turned and left. Riette knew how the Afrikaners in the area felt about her, so the accusations were nothing new. There seemed to be a bush telegraph that alerted everyone about her, or perhaps she wore a scarlet letter only they could see. Mrs du Plooy would not have had the courage to speak that way to her if Abigail and Mr Woods had been around. She'd had an opportunity today, that was all. She was angry and she'd taken her chance.

Riette went outside to the tap. As she held the enamel mug under the water, she was surprised to see her hands shaking. The woman's words were harsh and she wasn't sure they were not true. John Reilly had made things easier for all of them – for Riette and Annemie and Martie. He'd helped her escape and found this place for her at the Woods'.

Then she remembered what else Mrs du Plooy had said: the camp was emptied, the soldiers gone home.

It must have been recently or the Woods would have told her. They were friends of John Reilly. They'd helped him when he had first arrived. Abigail especially had a soft spot for John Reilly. She said he reminded her of the young brother she had left behind in England when she followed her husband to Africa. Abigail would tell her if she knew anything about John Reilly, Riette was sure of that.

Maybe he was on his way to her even as she thought of it. Coming to her so she could restart her life instead of being stuck in the purgatory she'd been living in since she arrived in Mafeking. She did as she had been told and waited for him; he had promised her he would come for her. And now she could marry again. She'd got word that Henk was dead, so she was a widow – free to marry whomever she liked.

Maybe they could live in Kimberley and she could work at the hospital. They might have a child. Knowing that he was free of the bonds of the army set her imagination going. She saw the two of them together, happy, with their children. She knew a life with John would be a good one. She'd lived variations of it in her mind almost every day since she'd left the camp.

Abigail and Mr Woods came back from the meeting when dinner was nearly ready. They rushed in, hot and dusty, and went to bathe and dress for the evening meal. They were a bit older than Riette, Abigail already forty, and they'd taken her in as if she were their daughter. They gave her a room in their small house, and she repaid them for their kindness by working in the shop, cooking, and cleaning the house. They were kind people and she suspected they cared about her, and she cared about them as well.

'It's over, really,' Mr Woods said when he finally sat down at the table. 'Next month the treaty will be signed and this horrid war will be a thing of the past.'

'We're grateful to God for that,' Abigail said.

'Yes,' Riette agreed. They ate in silence for a while before Riette got up her courage. 'Mrs du Plooy was in the shop.'

'She's an awful woman,' Abigail said.

'She's suffered a lot. Have some compassion, Abigail,' said Mr Woods.

'Yes, well ...' Riette hesitated. Maybe it was easier to wait. To be hopeful for a while longer. 'She said the camp in Pietersburg closed.' Abigail looked at her husband, then down at her plate. 'Did you know this?'

Abigail stayed quiet.

'Yes, we knew,' Mr Woods said, breaking through the silence. 'Riette, John Reilly went home to Ireland last month.'

'Oh? Last month already?' Riette kept her voice steady. 'Well, isn't that nice. That's very nice for him, I know he missed home so much.'

Abigail looked up and Riette could see the pain on her face. 'We knew it would be hard for you to hear. We were waiting, I don't know for what. I hoped a time would come that would be the right time to tell you. I'm so sorry, Riette.'

Riette covered Abigail's hand with hers. 'There's no need to be sorry. John Reilly has a wife waiting for him in Ireland. I myself told him he needed to return to her, that she'd sacrificed a lot to have him come here and fight. I told him to return to his wife. And I'm glad he did. Really, I'm glad.'

Riette spent the next month waiting for peace to be officially declared and for her heart to stop bleeding. Everything was in flux and she needed things to calm down, but she knew she was finished with this country. There was nothing here for her except sadness. She didn't want to live with the shadow of who she was and what she'd done forever darkening her life. She wanted to leave all the loss behind. The loss of Koos and Annemie; the loss of Martie. The loss of John.

She wanted to go to a place where no one knew her, where who she'd been would mean nothing. She wanted to go to a place so foreign she could be somebody else, a place so remote she'd finally be free. Riette still had her gold sovereigns; she would wait for the right moment to use them and finally be free.

And soon she found her chance.

Stanley Williams was a merchant who often bought from the Woods' shop. He stocked up a covered wagon and headed north to sell to the people there. North was Bechuanaland, a sparsely populated wasteland. Riette wasn't sure if he made a profit, but she assumed he did, since he went there regularly.

The next time Stanley Williams returned, Riette negotiated a deal with him. She asked him how far he went before turning around and coming home to Mafeking.

'Up deep in the bush,' he told her. 'At the edge of the Okavango River. A wild place. But there's a village there. I often do a good business in that place, with the blacks and all. Got some bit a wealth up there, selling ivory and cattle. Them, they call it Tsau.'

Then Tsau it would be. Even the sound of it on her tongue suggested a place where every single thing would be different, the exact kind of place she needed to start a new life.

German South-West Africa
October 1904

He was a tall man. He stood straight and proud. He knew he was correct. He was always certain of himself and didn't understand those who were not. To him the uncertain were cowards, nothing more. His bushy moustache covered his top lip, trimmed straight as a ruler. The Germans were the chosen people, he knew this as law, and he was a warrior on their behalf. He had a mission. The stars had shown him that the mission was true and correct, and he would follow his path until success.

The soldiers and settlers gathered in front of him. He would read the words, words inspired by the Kaiser, but written by him. His troops would clean the land, make it free and safe for the good German women and children, for the expansion of the German nation, for the chosen people.

Lieutenant General von Trotha began to read to the gathering:

'I, the great general of the German soldiers, send this letter to the Hereros. The Hereros are German subjects no longer. They have killed, stolen, cut off the ears and other parts of the body of wounded soldiers, and now are too cowardly to want to fight any longer. I announce to the people that whoever hands me one of the chiefs shall receive 1,000 marks, and 5,000 marks for Samuel Maharero. The Herero nation must now leave the country. If it refuses, I shall compel it to do so with the "long tube" [cannon]. Any Herero found inside the German frontier, with or without a gun or cattle, will be executed. I shall spare neither women nor children. I shall give the order to drive them away and fire on them. Such are my words to the Herero people.'

Tjipuka

15

Omaheke Desert, German South-West Africa
December 1904

'Everything will be fine,' Tjipuka told Saul. He was crying – there was never enough food. She gave him everything she could, but her milk was barely there so he needed to eat. Despite all her efforts, he was melting away in her hands. At least he was still crying. She'd learned that once he stopped crying, he'd be dead soon after. A lesson learned by watching the other children slowly – silently – disappear.

They'd been walking for weeks, but now they'd set up camp and stayed put for a few days; the people needed rest. They found some groundwater. The men had dug with sticks deep into the hard soil. Kahaka believed that the way the land tilted meant water lay beneath, and he'd been right. The water was salty, but they drank it; at least they knew it was not poisoned. Since the poisoning, they'd come across a few cattle in the desert, abandoned by others, which they'd collected. The cattle were in a bad state, but the hope was that, waiting here where they could get water, they might soon begin to produce milk again.

Five children had died so far. Though Tjipuka didn't want to think it, she felt sometimes that it was a blessing. Children shouldn't have to suffer like this. Saul was still healthier than most. She was happy for this, but she knew it wouldn't last long, not without milk and food.

Waueza was gone. When he'd walked alone into the desert, he'd left forever. It was better. He'd challenged Kahaka for leadership and it had caused tension the small group did not need. Kahaka cared for the group, not just himself, so he was a good leader. He'd found water and everyone was thankful for that. They welcomed the rest too.

Novengi sat down next to Tjipuka in the cool shade. It was midday and the sun beat down, causing the land to appear watery in its heat. Most people were sleeping in the shelters they'd made with sticks and branches. Kahaka believed the Germans were far enough away for them to camp for a while – for how long, no one knew.

'Wa uhara,' Novengi said, sitting down and reaching out for Saul.

Tjipuka handed the child to her. Novengi often spoke of Maveipi as if she were out playing and would soon return with a funny story or a shiny stone she'd found. Tjipuka left her to those thoughts. They comforted her. What did it matter? What was the truth? Were Ruhapo and Maveipi not gone somewhere to be met again when they all joined the ancestors? Would they not have new stories to tell? Would they not give them presents of shiny stones when they all came together again?

'Saul is such a good baby,' Novengi said, kissing him on both cheeks. 'We'll be fine now. Kahaka says he will come back with some meat. Maybe a springbok or a hare. We'll be fine just now. All of it is over.'

Tjipuka doubted he would come with meat. There was no ammunition left. Maybe he could kill something with his enga, but she doubted it. Maybe. It was best to be hopeful, though.

'Are you well today, Novengi? Is your stomach ache better?' The salty water was troubling her.

'Yes, it's better.'

Tjipuka looked at her friend. She was so thin, her face just skin sculpted over bones. Even when there was food, she could eat only tiny bits.

'Kahaka is our saviour. If it were not for him we'd all be dead. You made a good choice with that husband,' Tjipuka said. 'Who could have thought that skinny boy with knees that knocked on each other would grow to be such a wise, powerful man?'

Novengi smiled. 'Yes. He was very skinny, this is true. Skinny and naughty. Do you remember how he used to shoot stones at me with his catapult? He thought it was the way you showed a girl you loved her. He nearly knocked my eye out that time. Do you remember?'

They laughed. Such a simple thing, but now so rare. Tjipuka rubbed Novengi's back and they both watched Saul fall asleep in her arms.

That evening they were lucky. Kahaka and the other men had caught a big lizard, a monitor as long as a leg. Though it was not food they would have considered eating before, they were thankful for the meat now. They sat in a circle, each taking a bit along with a cooked tuber. Even the tubers they'd been living on were becoming scarce; they had to look further and further for them. But for that night they had food and water, they had a place to rest, and that was enough.

The small group spoke very little so it was easy to hear sounds from quite a distance. The desert air was clear and unhindered. Suddenly Kahaka dived to the fire and pushed dirt over it to put it out.

'Someone's coming,' he hissed.

He motioned for everyone to hide behind the shelters and wait. The men moved forward, the few with weapons at the front, the others behind. If it was required, they would fight with bare hands.

It was a person on a horse. As the horse neared, they could see that the rider was not a German – he was black, Herero they suspected. Kahaka walked to him. The man dismounted. They spoke for some minutes and then the man got on his horse and headed back to where he came from. Kahaka returned to the group.

'He says the Germans want to negotiate. He's an Omuherero. His group has gone into the German camp, about fifteen miles south of here, and he says they are telling the truth. They want to talk and they'll give us land to live on. This is what he says. He seems to be truthful. I don't know him, but I know some of his people. They are from Otjeru. He's not a traitor – at least I don't think so. What should we do?'

115

The people discussed what they should do. In the end, it was agreed they would leave in the morning and go to hear what the Germans were saying.

At sunrise they packed up their few belongings, filled the bags with water, and headed south. They left the cattle behind; they would come back for them if everything was as the man on the horse had said.

As the sun set in the west, they saw the camp in the distance.

Kahaka turned to the group. 'I'll take three men with me. Everyone else wait here. We'll find out what the Germans want. When it's safe, we'll come back for you. Don't come to the camp unless one of us comes for you. Only one of us, no one else.'

Novengi stood and went to her husband. They spoke in quiet whispers. Kahaka placed his hand on her shoulder. Then he turned with the others and headed for the Germans.

Night fell, but the group left behind did not make a fire. They waited. It was cold but Novengi had brought her blankets and pulled them around herself, Tjipuka and Saul. They spoke little. Tjipuka wondered why Kahaka had not returned. If the Germans were being honest, he should have returned straight away. She was scared something was wrong, but said nothing.

When the moon rose, they saw two Germans riding towards them. They didn't have guns. One dismounted and came closer. He spoke Otjiherero. He told them that all was well and that Kahaka had sent him to come and collect everyone. The Germans had made peace with the Herero. They would all be safe now.

The people collected their belongings and walked behind the riders, who moved at a slow pace so as to not overexert the tired, weak people. Tjipuka put Saul on her back and he quickly fell asleep.

Novengi took her hand. 'We will soon be fine again. We will find Maveipi and then everything will be fine again.'

'Yes, Novengi,' Tjipuka said. 'Let's go now.'

The camp had many tents, with fires burning all around, and many German soldiers, at least fifty. Tjipuka became nervous. Why were there so many of them if they were here to make peace? Why were there so many weapons around? Something was not right. They did not look like people wanting to make peace.

Then the fire flared and she saw them. On a long branch some distance to the east of the camp. The man who had come for them, the Herero man on the horse who had said everything was all right, that the Germans wanted to make peace, hung from a strand of wire attached to a long, thick branch, his arms at his sides, his head tilted at an odd angle. Next to him were the three men from their group and then Kahaka. The strong, wise Kahaka hung from a wire, his trousers soiled, his eyes open and bulging out.

Tjipuka stopped and the group continued ahead. She held Novengi's hand and waited for the others to pass. She needed to be careful, they needed to get away unnoticed or they would have no chance. She whispered into Novengi's ear, 'It's a trick. We need to run. Hold my hand. Do not let go. Whatever happens – do not let go.'

They turned back and Tjipuka ran as fast as she could, pulling and sometimes dragging Novengi behind her. She ran into the darkness. She could hear the shooting behind her. She could hear the screams. They ran and ran, back into the desert. They ran and ran until the moon told Tjipuka they could stop. Then she pulled Novengi into a circle of bushes and held her tightly, rocking her in her arms until the sun rose.

16

Omaheke Desert, German South-West Africa
December 1904

Novengi, Saul and Tjipuka walked and walked. Tjipuka's shoes were becoming thin on the soles and she could feel the sharp stones underfoot. Thorns poked through and pricked at her feet. Sometimes she stopped to remove them. Sometimes she did not.

Novengi was lost to her completely. She mumbled words. Sometimes she asked where Kahaka was or Maveipi. Tjipuka told her what had happened, that Kahaka was dead, killed by the Germans. But she told her only once. To tell her again would be too cruel.

They stopped during the hottest part of the day. They were heading east – Tjipuka knew now there was no hope of them returning to Hereroland. The Germans would lie to them, only to catch them and kill them. They needed to get to Bechuanaland. It was their only hope.

They'd eaten very little. Two days earlier they'd found three dead cattle. She suspected they were Herero cattle left behind by the fleeing people. There was still a bit of meat on the carcasses – one looked to have died maybe a day before. Tjipuka made a small fire and cooked the meat though it was already covered with flies. She wiped away the small worms it was full of. She cooked it hard and fed bits to Saul and Novengi. She ate what was left when they were finished, and was happy when it did not make any of them them sick.

Since then they'd had nothing. Water was a constant search. She learned that if you woke very early, the leaves of the plants, though they didn't look wet, had a thin layer of moisture. She taught Novengi how to move around and lick the moisture before the sun stole it away. It was nothing to quench their constant thirst, but it allowed them to live another day.

Earlier they'd stumbled upon a small band of Bushmen, who gave them three spiky green fruits they roasted in the fire. Tjipuka had seen these fruits before, but they didn't look edible. The Bushmen had many of them and explained that they must be roasted first. They also showed them a sort of melon, round and green, that grew on vines along the ground. It was fleshy and full of juice.

Tjipuka had seen the melons but feared eating them. Kahaka had warned them not to eat anything they were not familiar with. The Bushmen had shown them the melon, given them three of the spiky fruits, and gone on their way, heading north.

Tjipuka and Novengi sat in the stingy shade of an acacia tree while Saul slept on a blanket. Tjipuka cut bits of melon and handed them to Novengi. They would only eat half, saving the other half for later.

Novengi rubbed the melon on her dry lips before putting it in her mouth.

'Will we die here?' she asked.

'No.'

Tjipuka was firm on this. She would not allow the Germans to win. They had killed Ruhapo; they had killed Maveipi and Kahaka. They had killed everyone else, but they would not kill them. She would leave this desert alive, she and Saul and Novengi.

'I wish we would. In a way I wish we would,' Novengi said, looking out at the shimmering desert.

Tjipuka felt the rage flash in her and she slapped Novengi hard across the face. Stunned, Novengi held her cheek and looked at Tjipuka with a hurt expression.

'Never. Never say that,' Tjipuka shouted. 'Never.'

She dropped the melon onto the blanket and stood. She walked into the sun. She needed to get away before she did worse to Novengi. The rage had not disappeared with the slap. She could stand a lot, but she could not stand such betrayal. Not after all they'd been through.

They often passed piles of things in the desert. Discarded blankets or a photo, a small stack of jewellery. Priorities changed. Something you'd needed desperately before suddenly weighed too much to continue carrying. Tjipuka knew that where they were going they would have nothing. Anything they came with would help them to make a new life. She kept the blankets. She learned to wind them into tight balls and tie them to one another. She wore them like a hat; it helped against the hot sun. Novengi wore similarly odd headgear. Tjipuka's pockets jangled with the jewellery she'd found. She never took glass beads or strings of fake pearls. She searched the clasps carefully for bits of gold. She'd snap off the gold bits and leave the rest.

As they trekked further into the desert, she stopped keeping track of days. The day of the death of Kahaka and the others seemed a long time ago now. Maybe a week, a month, maybe longer. She didn't know any more. Days were only bits of time to get through, better measured by miles walked over the hard ground.

'What is that?' Novengi said one morning. She pointed into the distance at a camp of some sort.

'We need to be careful. It could be Germans.'

They moved closer, slipping among the thorn bushes and bigger stones to hide, but then waited in a patch of bush to the side. It was a camp, but where were the people? There was a hut, a round one made of branches, a temporary structure. A fire pit. They moved closer. It looked empty. Tjipuka told Novengi to wait with Saul, and she crept closer still. There was no one. She looked in the hut, then quickly moved away from it.

Novengi came out of the bush where she'd hidden, carrying Saul.

'What is it?' she asked, seeing Tjipuka's face.

'A woman. Dead. And a child, dead too. They must have left her behind. Maybe she was too weak. Don't go in there.'

'Did the Germans kill her?'

'No, the desert did.'

Tjipuka suspected the woman's group had left her. Maybe she was sick, too slow to keep up. There was an empty calabash. The water had run out, and then it had been just a waiting game for her and her child.

Tjipuka and Novengi looked around for anything they could use, anything that might be helpful later. There was nothing. There was a crudely dug well nearby. It looked as if it had once had water; perhaps this was why the group had stayed, but it was dry now. Tjipuka was desperate. Saul had stopped crying and she knew this was a bad sign. She called Novengi.

'Find a stick to dig. I think there's water here.'

She put Saul on a blanket in the shade. The women dug all day in the scorching sun. Tjipuka was sure she could smell water. It was just a bit further, if only they could keep digging. Eventually, Novengi collapsed and Tjipuka pulled her into the shade with Saul. She continued working. She must find water now. The hard digging in the hot sun had made everything worse. It was no longer a choice. They needed water or all of them would die here with the unknown woman and her child.

Night fell and still she dug. She heard the deep belly roar of a lion in the distance. She wondered what they ate and drank in the desert. She and Novengi had heard their roars often. She hoped that didn't mean they were being tracked by them. She tried not to think of that.

She sat back on her haunches to rest. The air was cool now, which she welcomed. She covered Saul and Novengi with blankets. They slept without moving. They slept like the dead.

She went back to her work. She kept a strict rein on her mind. There were too many places it could go that would bring her pain. As she worked, she allowed her thoughts to go to Ruhapo. She was happy he'd died in the battle at Ohamakari. That he didn't have to see the abuse the Germans had brought upon the Herero since then, all of the suffering and pain. They were a proud people. Now the Germans treated them like animals. The women were used as the soldiers liked. The men were made to beg for their lives but then hanged from trees to die a slow death, for the wire used did not break their necks – the men suffocated instead. The Germans did not want to waste the scarce rope they had on a Herero. A wire worked well enough. It was cruel and inhumane, but it got the job done – eventually. Tjipuka knew that the ancestors and Omukuru could not allow such things. The Germans would be punished many times over for what they had done to the Herero. It had to be. Either that or there really was no god. Either that or the world was a place of evil.

As morning neared, Tjipuka felt moisture at the bottom of the pit. At first she thought she might be imagining it because she wanted it so badly. She dug deeper and waited. Soon tiny trickles of water dripped into the hole. She wanted to cry. She sat back on her haunches and watched the trickle and thought that it might be one of the most beautiful things she'd ever witnessed. She got the calabashes and slowly collected the water. She drank carefully, not too much. She'd learned her lesson. After so much time without proper water, if she drank too much it would result in terrible cramps. She drank a little at a time. She rubbed the water on her dry lips. Let it soak into her heavy tongue.

She waited until she had two calabashes full before she woke Saul and Novengi.

'Novengi. Novengi!'

'Kahaka? Are you there?' She did not open her eyes; she only reached out for him.

'I have water. Sit up.'

Novengi opened her eyes, but could not sit. Tjipuka held Novengi's head in her hand and put the calabash to her lips and let her sip. Then she picked Saul up. He did not open his eyes either; he groaned at her touch. His little body was painful. She slowly dropped water into his mouth. He opened his mouth to receive it, but did little else. She was scared but told herself he would be fine now, they would all be fine now. It was not too late, the water had not arrived too late.

'In my dreams everything was right,' Novengi said. Tjipuka didn't reply. 'I wonder, when we get that side, if things will ever be right again.'

'I don't know.'

Tjipuka did not dream, nor did she hope. She had only one thing to focus on – that they live. She could think no further than that.

The water kept flowing into the hole they'd dug. They decided to stay put for the moment. They needed to gain some strength, to rest. Each day they moved away from the camp to search for food. They ate anything. Mostly insects and small lizards Novengi had skill at catching. They found tubers they knew were edible. They ate the melons the Bushmen had taught them about. They found more of the spiky, bitter fruits and roasted them for themselves. Slowly they gained strength. On the second day, Saul cried. On the fifth day, when he sucked at Tjipuka's breast, the milk arrived. She was cautiously hopeful.

17

Omaheke Desert, German South-West Africa
January 1905

'We need to get moving again,' Tjipuka said after a week had passed. 'We may be near to the border. We don't know. It might be just a few days' walk to safety.'

'No,' Novengi said. 'We should wait a bit longer. We're fine here.'

It was better there than walking, but they needed to move on. Tjipuka could see she would have to force Novengi eventually, but she would give her a few more days. They were all three gaining strength. Though the food was minimal, they were becoming more and more adept at finding what they needed in the desert. Tjipuka had fashioned a type of bow and arrow using the blade of a small knife she'd found in the hut with the dead woman. The day before she'd used it to wound a duiker. She stood over its writhing body, the knife stuck firmly in its back leg. Her childhood love for the bush and its animals fell away. She did not hesitate to bring a rock down on its head, crushing it. Killing was easy if it was a matter of you living only if it died.

It was early morning of the ninth day they'd been at the waterhole. The water poured so freely they'd even bathed in it and washed their clothes. Tjipuka was bathing Saul. He was still thin. She tried not to notice the way his skin stretched over his tiny ribs and instead focused on the way he was livelier and no longer in pain. He was solidly alive, not wavering in the in-between as he had been.

He was a handsome child. He had Ruhapo's round eyes and Tjipuka's strong nose with a slight hook at the end. He had long arms and legs. She knew he would grow very tall like his father. When he was old enough, Tjipuka would tell him everything she knew about Ruhapo. How he had fought hard to get back what the Germans had taken from them. How he was an exceptional cattleman. How he knew exactly which bull to mate with which cow to produce calves that were strong and healthy. He knew the right food to make them shiny and beautiful. He knew where to find sweet water that made sure they got no diseases. She would tell Saul about how his father led men. How he spoke with thought and wisdom, and how people respected him for that. He was proud, but not recklessly so. He believed in himself and his abilities, and this was where his pride emanated from. It was an honest, earned pride. And he was a kind and loving man. She would tell Saul how he had come to her mother's house, against all custom, when Saul was only a day old. He needed to see his son. He didn't care if it was wrong. He crept in and warned Tjipuka to keep quiet. He kissed her for the gift she'd given him. Then he picked up his son in his large, strong hands. He held Saul in the patch of light coming in from the window. His eyes searched all over the baby, looking for anything out of place. Then he held him to his chest. He held his son and rocked him in his arms.

She would explain to Saul what a good husband Ruhapo had been. How he knew his role was to keep his wife happy and protected. He made sure to think before doing things, to consider not only his position and how it might affect him, but also his wife's. She would teach Saul so that he too would grow to be a man like his father had been.

She took Saul out of the water and wrapped him in a blanket. She wondered what was taking Novengi so long. She'd gone off to look for something to eat for breakfast before the sun became too hot. Tjipuka squinted into the distance but saw nothing. Novengi must have had to go further than she'd expected. They'd been camped here too long; food was becoming scarce. They needed to move on. It was good Novengi was struggling to find food – perhaps that would show her that Tjipuka's view was the correct one, that they had to get moving again.

She hummed a song to Saul as she rocked him to sleep. This stop-over had saved them, she knew that. Saul had been nearly dead. The ancestors had stepped in and saved him. He was special, she knew; they would keep him safe.

He fell asleep and she laid him on a blanket in the shade. Just as she was about to stand, she heard something behind her and turned. There was Novengi, escorted by two men, Herero men, with guns.

'What is it?' Tjipuka asked indignantly. She'd gone through enough and had no compassion for rogues lost in the desert wanting to take advantage of them.

Novengi struggled against the hands that held her, but could not break free. 'They're from the mission station. They've been sent to collect us. To take us into the mission. They say to help us, but I don't trust them.'

The bigger man, the one with the harder face, shook Novengi. 'Are you calling us liars?'

'Liars and collaborators!' Novengi spat at the man and he slapped her. She fell to the ground.

'We'll not go with you,' Tjipuka said firmly. She stepped forward and helped Novengi to her feet. They stood together in front of the sleeping Saul. 'We know about these Germans. Our group was killed for trusting them.'

The kinder-faced man spoke. 'It's not like that. There's plenty of food and water there at the mission. The war is over now. The missionaries have been asked by the German government to help collect the people and resettle them. The Germans are tired of war. You know the missionaries, they have never been part of the killing, not like the settlers and the soldiers. The missionaries are good people. They want to help.'

'The Germans never tire of war,' Tjipuka said. 'We have seen the Germans' way of making peace – we want none of it. We're going to the British. We don't have far now.'

The hard-faced man laughed. 'You don't know that. You could be a footstep away or hundreds of miles.'

'It doesn't matter. I'd rather die looking for the border than surrender to the Germans.'

The hard-faced man took a step towards where Saul lay. Tjipuka stepped between him and her child.

'He's thin,' the man said, looking down at Saul. 'I don't know of a mother who chooses her child's death over a chance to save him.'

'Don't speak about my child.' Tjipuka spoke in an even, flat voice that did not show anger, but did not allow for dissent.

The hard-faced man laughed. He was near enough for Tjipuka to smell the alcohol on his breath – the pay from the missionaries, likely the only pay. He looked Tjipuka over and smiled.

He moved closer to her. Slowly. He reached out his hand and ran it gently over her cheek, down her neck, to her breast. Tjipuka stood still. He grabbed her breast in his hand and smiled at her. With one quick determined move, she brought her knee up hard into his groin and he fell to the ground. He moaned there while she looked down at him.

Tjipuka picked up Saul and strapped him to her back. She knew that running would not be the answer – the men had guns. They would probably shoot them. She could see that these two had lost all affinity for their own people. For them it was about collecting what was needed for the Germans and getting their pay. Allegiance to their people played no role in the equation.

Force would not work, she knew. She and Novengi needed to talk their way free, to try to remind the men of who they were before everything, and Tjipuka suspected the kinder-faced man might be the key to their freedom. He watched his partner on the ground, but made no effort to help him. This made Tjipuka believe he wished the man harm, or at least would not be unhappy if harm came to him.

'Why don't you escape with us?' Tjipuka said in a low voice only the kind-faced man could hear, not his partner. 'Life is good over the border. We will all have land and the British are not greedy like the Germans. They will leave us alone. Come with us. Staying only means you are a slave to the Germans forever.'

The man looked at Tjipuka. He seemed to be considering her offer, but then he pointed his gun at her. 'Collect what you need. We need to get going.'

The hard-faced man was on his feet. He said nothing to any of them, but started walking back towards the west. The other man hurried them by shooting two shots at their feet. The dust filled Tjipuka's mouth and she realised they had no choice. They packed their things, carried all the water they could, and headed back to the Germans.

18

Omaheke Desert, German South-West Africa
January 1905

When they arrived, Tjipuka thought the two men had not lied after all. There were five rows of houses set up for the Herero. Tjipuka estimated there were about fifty Herero there already, mostly women and children and old people. They were around fires, cooking, and children were playing. When last had she seen children playing? They were inside a fence, but still they looked as if they were being treated properly.

They were met by a tall German man. He wore a stern black suit, the jacket and shirt buttoned high despite the heat.

'Welcome!' he said. His smile was cold, on a face not used to smiling. 'I am Franz Schneider. I am the minister here. We must first get you some food and water.'

He called to a Herero man behind him. 'Joseph, please take these women to the dining hall. After they're finished, show them to their living quarters.'

Joseph came forward. He was a handsome young man, dressed smartly in a suit. He spoke German fluently though he was Herero. His face was soft and he moved carefully, cognisant of the people around him, people who had suffered. Somehow, amid all of the cruelty, this young man had managed to maintain his humane heart.

As they followed him, Tjipuka looked back and saw Franz Schneider giving money to the two men who had brought them in from the desert. She turned to Joseph. 'Is it safe here?' she asked in Otjiherero.

'It's fine. This is the collection camp. The war is over. From here you will be taken to your new homes. All of the Herero will have new homes where they can live happily with no bother from the Germans. All of the badness is over now.' Joseph smiled.

He was young, younger than Novengi and Tjipuka. He struggled a bit in Otjiherero. Tjipuka guessed he was one of the children the missionaries liked to take as their own. They took them into their homes to make them into small black Germans, often leaving the real parents out in the servants' rooms. The Herero did not take up Christianity easily, and the Germans thought that if they could raise a few of the Herero people within the Church, then those selected few might do better at converting the rest. Over time, these children, boys almost exclusively, lost their connections to their own people. They no longer knew where they belonged. She wasn't sure if this young man, Joseph, could be trusted to be on their side or the side of the Germans. She suspected, from how he behaved, that he was not sure either.

Joseph took them to a place where tables were scattered in an outdoor eating area. 'Sit here,' he said. 'I'll bring food and water.'

Tjipuka and Novengi sat down. Tjipuka took Saul off her back. He looked at her with tired eyes. They had travelled for three days to arrive at the collection station. The men had pushed them to move quickly. They had rations but they gave Novengi and Tjipuka the smallest amount possible. They were both exhausted, but at least Tjipuka's milk was still flowing.

She stuck her nipple into Saul's mouth and he suckled. As long as she had milk, she would let him suckle until they were finally settled.

'I don't trust this place,' Novengi said.

'Why? It seems all right.' Tjipuka looked around. There were no soldiers. No guns. 'I think that the minister and Joseph are telling the truth. Why would Joseph lie to us?'

'Because he doesn't know the truth.'

The days spent at the waterhole had helped Novengi. She seemed better, stronger, more herself – nearly her Novengi again. They did not speak about Kahaka and Maveipi, though. They just went forward with the life they were now in, as if the past had dropped away.

Tjipuka considered what Novengi had said. Perhaps, but they could stay here for a few days. Get stronger. Then, if it was a bad place, they could easily escape. There was nothing but a thin fence to keep them in; it would be easy to leave.

The food arrived – meat and bread and cabbage. There was a tall pitcher of clear water. They ate slowly but steadily. Tjipuka could not believe how wonderful everything tasted after such a long time.

When they were finished, Joseph reappeared. 'Shall I take you to your beds?'

They walked back towards the hostels set up for the Herero. At the fence, a watchman appeared. He was Herero. He had a gun slung over his shoulder, the first gun they'd seen at the camp aside from the ones carried by the men who brought them in. Novengi looked at Tjipuka knowingly. The watchman unhooked keys that unlocked the gate of the tall fence and they went inside. He locked the gate behind them.

As they walked, the people already there stopped and looked at them, but said nothing. They seemed healthy enough, at least not starving. Tjipuka thought that was a good sign. They did not greet Novengi and Tjipuka, though. They looked, but they were not interested. They only looked. There was something missing in each of them. Tjipuka knew it was also missing in her and Novengi. They were no longer complete humans. They were something else. Something less than that. They were alive. Their systems ran. Their hearts beat. Their blood moved through their veins. But something shifts in a person when the only hope they have is to live and nothing more. Just to live another hour, a day if they're lucky. The world becomes a tiny, insulated box, untouchable by anything outside it. That world is so small they cannot see beyond it, cannot risk a look beyond it any more. They are not dead, but they are not alive either.

Tjipuka looked away and walked on.

Joseph led them to a small house at the end. Inside were four beds, two of which were empty. 'Here, take these two. I'll bring blankets.'

Two women sat on the other beds. They greeted Tjipuka and Novengi. 'Where have you come from?' the smaller one said.

'The desert,' Tjipuka said.

'No, before that.'

'Okahandja.'

The taller one sat quietly listening. She was older than all of them. Her face was lined and her hands hard-worked. Her dress was torn but clean; in some places it was very thin. She sat straight on her bed though she looked exhausted. Tjipuka wondered why she didn't lie down and sleep.

The smaller woman was called Lucinda, the older one Mara. 'Mara doesn't talk,' Lucinda told them.

She explained that they'd both been in a group that fled the battle at Ohamakari. They were heading north, trying to get to Ovamboland. A man who was their leader knew a chief there. He was sure they would be given refuge, that they would be able to start a new life there. But something went wrong. They got lost in the desert and then they were ambushed by a band of German soldiers. Most of their group were killed. Only seven remained, among them Lucinda and her seventeen-year-old son, Tjirwe, and Mara.

'And Mara, has anyone survived for her?' Novengi asked.

Lucinda shook her head in a way to say this was not something that could be discussed.

'How long have you been here?' Tjipuka asked.

'Three days.'

'And the others?'

'Most a few days. Some a week or more. They say they come to collect people after two weeks.'

'And where do they go? The people?' Novengi asked.

'No one knows. But they say there's land set aside for us, for the Herero. They don't say where exactly but it's there, they say.'

'Do you trust them?' Tjipuka asked. 'Are they telling the truth about this land?'

'I don't know. You've met the man Joseph?'

'Yes,' Novengi said.

'I know him. From when he was a child. His mother worked for the Rhenish missionaries in Otjimbingwe. Those missionaries were good people. They were not rough like the settlers. They took care of Joseph's mother. They took Joseph to school, even to a college in the Cape. He's a minister now too. He even preaches to the white people. He has told me that it's all fine. I think I believe him. He tells the truth. He's a good man.'

'The truth as he knows it.' Novengi believed none of it; Tjipuka could hear it in her voice.

'You never know, Novengi. Maybe these are good missionaries like the ones Lucinda knows in Otjimbingwe. Like the ones who ran our school.'

Tjipuka wanted to believe that it was all over now. She was so tired; she just wanted to stop and rest. She needed to find a calm place to raise her son. She hoped this was where they would be going, a place where there was food and water and they could live a peaceful, quiet life. She wanted nothing more than that now. Let the Germans do anything they wanted, she only wanted to be left alone.

Novengi looked at Mara, who was rocking slightly on her bed, then turned back to the others. 'But maybe they haven't told Joseph. The Germans never trust a black person, this I'm sure of. No matter what they say.'

'I don't know,' Lucinda said. 'I know Joseph, I trust him. I don't trust Franz Schneider, though. I've seen him angry. He beat an old man with a sjambok. The man nearly died. He beat him because he could not lift a bag of flour. The old man had just arrived; he was so tired and sick. My son says we must wait and see. If they come for us we will see, we will see how it is. If we don't like it, we're going back to the desert. We'll find our way to somewhere safe.'

'This is what I think,' Novengi said. 'This place is not difficult to escape from. Only the watchman has a gun and he's Herero. He'll not shoot a woman. We can stay and eat their food, sleep in their beds. But if things look wrong, we must go.'

Tjipuka agreed. Somewhere along the way their roles had shifted again. Novengi was suddenly the strong one. That was fine with Tjipuka. She was tired of fighting. She wanted to sit in quietness. Her mind was so weary. She wanted to have no fear. This place was good enough. She could live here for now. And for now was all she could think about. She let Novengi take over their future.

19

Omaheke Desert, German South-West Africa
February 1905

The four women stuck together. Lucinda's son, Tjirwe, was too old to stay with them, but they sat together when they went for food. He was a moody child, full of anger. Only seventeen, but he seemed much older. He should have been with his friends, learning about cattle, learning how to hunt. He should have been playing with girls, preparing to marry. But instead he was sullen and quick to take offence. He had seen too much, Tjipuka thought. She was thankful Saul was just a baby. She hoped this all would be forgotten, that he might be able to recover and be a normal child one day. But she knew there was little hope for Tjirwe. He'd carry the scars like all of them, perhaps deeper since he was so young and unable to understand it all fully.

'Look at him,' Tjirwe hissed, staring at Joseph. 'If I were him, I'd slash Schneider's throat while he slept, his wife's too.'

'Tjirwe, don't say that. They'll hear you. Schneider hates you already. He keeps his eyes on you,' Lucinda whispered.

They'd had a confrontation a few days before. Tjirwe would not carry wood into the mission house. Schneider had got out the sjambok and, as he'd raised it to bring it down on Tjirwe's head, Tjirwe had grabbed it. Schneider had frozen. No one challenged his authority. But Tjirwe's move had shown everyone how vulnerable the minister was. In a flash he'd been made impotent. He had let go of the handle and walked into the mission house. Immediately, the guard with the gun had come to Tjirwe, his gun raised and aimed at the boy. 'Give it to me!'

Tjirwe had dropped the sjambok on the ground, forcing the guard to pick it up for himself, and walked away. He'd made two enemies, enemies who would get their own back, everyone feared.

'Do you think I care what they hear?' Tjirwe said, louder.

'You should. Your words could put us all in danger, including your mother. It's stupid to anger people when you're not forced to,' Novengi said.

This quieted him. Despite everything, he loved his mother ferociously. And she in turn loved him. There had been a father and two sisters, all dead now. They, all three, were killed at Ohamakari. They had only each other now, and Tjirwe would do nothing that would harm his mother. He got up without speaking and headed to his sleeping quarters.

'He can't help himself. He hates them; he can only see that rage. He saw both of his sisters killed, it broke something in him.' Lucinda turned and looked out through the fence, into the desert. When she turned back, the sadness was hidden again where she kept it locked tight. They had to learn to find a place for the sadness and rage, or it would eat them up, as it was eating Tjirwe. 'He'll come right later, when we've settled at the new place. It will take some time, but he'll come right, my boy, I know that. He's a good boy.'

Tjipuka and Novengi said nothing. Who knew? Maybe they would all come right one day. They'd been at the camp for a week and already Saul was much better. Tjipuka gave him as much food as he would eat, even if it meant she went without. Joseph sometimes brought extra food to Tjipuka for the small boy. He'd taken a liking to him. Saul's body was filling out again – she could no longer feel the edges of his bones under his loose skin. He played a bit and slept less. A couple more weeks and he'd be back to normal. He would be two years old the next month. He could walk but preferred not to. He was content just to lie or sit. She tried to ignore this, tried not to think it was anything important. She was sure it was just the situation and he would walk once they were resettled. Saul would be fixed just like Tjirwe would be fixed. They'd all be fixed.

Mara suddenly stood and walked towards their sleeping quarters, leaving a slice of bread on her plate. Lucinda was always looking out for Mara; she had no sense any more. She had to be reminded to drink water, to wash herself. Like a child.

Lucinda grabbed her arm. 'You're not finished eating.'

Mara pulled her arm loose and continued walking. Lucinda picked up Mara's plate and pushed it towards Tjipuka. 'Best you eat this. You give everything to the baby, you need your energy too.'

Tjipuka took the bread. 'Thank you.'

They'd become a team: Tjipuka, Novengi, Lucinda, Mara, Saul and Tjirwe. Tjipuka hoped that when they were resettled they'd be together. She liked Lucinda. She hoped one day Tjirwe would open his damaged heart to let Saul in. He could act as his big brother. Mara would play the role of grandmother to the boys. They would create a family in the vacuum where others had been.

Tjipuka was surprised that her mind was allowing such thoughts. When Ruhapo died, she was sure that all hope had left with him. But slowly, as she recovered physically, her dreams came back, even if they were only fragments of what they'd been before. Small, contained dreams – but at least they were dreams.

'What happened to her?' Novengi asked, indicating the retreating back of Mara.

Lucinda's face changed. 'She had a difficult time.'

'We all have,' Novengi said, jaded.

'Not like her. Mara was a fighter. At Ohamakari she had a gun. She killed and wounded German soldiers. She was wild at the battle. She had an enga too. She slashed at them as they came near to her. She fought beside her two sons and husband. Her husband was injured, shot in

137

the arm. She and her sons carried him with our group into the desert.

'He survived for a while. But the wound became infected. The arm darkened and one night he died. She was sad, but still, she was fine. She was still herself then. Strong and resilient. She's the daughter of a chief, a very proud woman. There were times that she led the group; people respected her – she knew many things. She knew a lot about the desert. She was fearless. Her knowledge saved us, I think. I've never known a woman like her.'

Lucinda placed her hand on Novengi's arm for emphasis. 'You must believe me; she was not like this. You must try to see her as she was. That's the way I see her even now. This is temporary. She was a strong, proud Herero woman. She was not broken like this.'

Novengi nodded and placed her hand on top of Lucinda's.

'But then the Germans who found us, they were vicious. Horrible … so cruel. It was as if they were scared of us, but by then we had no ammunition. We were weak – they had nothing to be afraid of. All the same, they lashed out like a lion caught in a trap. Mara stood up to them. That's where she did the wrong thing. That's where it went wrong.

'In front of everyone, before they began the shooting, they raped her. One by one. But before that, when they'd only just begun, her sons tried to fight them off. The elder one was shot in the forehead, dead before he hit the ground. But the younger one, a sweet boy, not even fourteen, they made him suffer. They shot his feet so he could not move. Then they took turns on his mother. No one in our group raised a voice to help her. They saw what they would get if they did. I covered Tjirwe's eyes, but he knew what was happening. Everyone knew. When they were done with her, they shot the boy in the eyes. She fell to him, Mara, she fell to her son and never spoke again. Everything died then.'

Tjipuka wished Lucinda hadn't told them. She didn't need more such pictures in her mind. She had enough already.

'I just feel I must watch out for her now,' Lucinda said. 'She has no one but me. She did so much for our group. She was a good woman – *is* a good woman. She's a good woman.'

'We'll help you,' Novengi said. 'I'm sorry. I shouldn't have asked.'

Tjipuka kept quiet. She wondered if kindness was making sure Mara ate and drank water. Was keeping her alive kindness? Keeping her alive for what? To remember such cruelty? What was kindness anyway? Was it not actions to help alleviate pain? To make the journey through this cruel life better? Helping Mara to live was not kindness. Tjipuka knew kindness and it did not look like that.

20

Omaheke Desert, German South-West Africa
February 1905

They'd been at the mission station for three weeks, apparently an unusual situation. The longest anyone had stayed before was two weeks, according to Joseph. Every day they were sure the wagons would come for them, but they didn't. People spoke more and more about the place where they were going, what they hoped it would be like. They were impatient to arrive at their new home, to begin their lives again. The deprivation of the desert was receding into the past; they were impatient to move on to their future.

Tjipuka liked to wake early, before the sun, the way she always had before. She liked to sit at the edge of the camp, look out at the desert and wait for the sun to slowly lighten the sky, then rise over the edge of the world, casting gold on everything. For a few minutes, before it got too high, everything looked lovely, special and transformed.

One morning, some days after they'd arrived, Joseph found her there. 'So you're an early riser too,' he said when he came upon her unexpectedly that first time.

Tjipuka nodded. He sat near her and they watched the sky together.

He was quiet by nature, like her. There was a calmness about him so that one didn't feel a need to fill the silence with words. Because of this Tjipuka didn't mind his intrusion.

She didn't know how to think of Joseph. He was one of them, really. He was free to come and go, but he didn't. He chose to stay with the Germans of his own free will. He was not a captive, but he was not completely free. He was one of them, but not quite. He existed in an in-between place.

The sun rose that first day and Joseph drifted off without a word.

Other days Tjipuka found him already there. When she found him alone, when he looked out into the last dregs of inky night, she thought she saw the truth of this man. He sat not only looking out at the desert, but searching the horizon. She realised then that he waited for someone. There was someone he missed, someone gone whom he hoped might return one day. Maybe that was why he stayed there; he hoped the person might arrive and find him still at his post.

'Wa penduka,' Tjipuka said, walking up to him one morning.

'Mba penduka. Ove wapenduka vi Mama Tjipuka?' She smiled at him.

It was cool but not cold. The days were still so hot that the morning coolness was a blessing. They sat together in silence.

'It was bad the battles, is it true?' Joseph asked, as if they'd been in the middle of such a conversation.

'Yes, Ohamakari was bad. We didn't expect that. We thought if the Germans came they would come to talk. The battles before were a success; we'd subdued the Germans. The war was over, it was time to talk, that's what we thought – but we were wrong. They came to kill us. They nearly did, they nearly succeeded in killing all of us.'

'In a way I feel a traitor that I was not there. The mission sent me to study in the Cape Colony. They've been good to me. I don't know sometimes what to think. I see and hear everything, horrible stories about how the German soldiers behaved. But I know, too, the kindness individual Germans have shown me and my mother. Maybe those soldiers were the Germans from overseas, not the settlers or the missionaries already here. I wish none of it had happened. I feel so torn. I wish we could all go back to before it all happened.'

Tjipuka did not mention that it was not just the German soldiers, it was also the settlers. Some settlers were worse than the soldiers. 'Yes, I think we all wish that.'

Tjipuka could hear the pain in his voice. He was old enough, a man now – he could go off. He was no longer tied to the Germans. She couldn't help but blame him in a way. He was complicit, at least partly, by being so close to them.

'What do you hear about this place we're going?' Tjipuka asked.

'They don't speak about such things when I'm there.'

'Is it somewhere in Hereroland?'

'I don't think so. I think it's far away. Organising wagons is always an issue. They need to bring them for supplies for the journey. Sometimes the people must walk if the wagons are not enough. Some walk and then later I think some get on the train, that's all I know.'

'Not in Hereroland? But then what will we do? We need to be near our ancestors. If they take us far, where we have no history, how will they find us? How will we find each other again?'

Joseph shook his head. 'I don't know.'

'I think you do.'

'I don't know,' he insisted. He continued looking out at the bush. A single bird sang an undulating song in the distance. Tjipuka could see he was trying to make up his mind. 'But … but I don't think the place is good. I think the settlers need the good land now. They are coming every day and the new settlers need land, lots of it. Everyone must go to the new place, though. No Herero will be allowed to be where the settlers are.'

'What right do they have to our land? They have their own country – why can't they go home to it and leave us alone?'

'I don't know. They believe this is their land. For some of it treaties were signed. To the Germans, treaties are important. Their law says if the treaty was signed the land is theirs.'

'Treaties? You want to talk of treaties signed by chiefs pushed into corners, with no options on any side?' Tjipuka was losing her temper. Joseph was one of them – how could he talk like that if he was not one of the Germans? 'What about their side of the treaties? Samuel Maharero signed the treaty to give them land on the condition that the Germans protected us from the Nama raiders. The invasions became worse after the treaty was signed. The Nama left many Herero impoverished, without a single head of cattle. And the Germans were nowhere! They never kept their side of the treaty that you say they believe in so faithfully, but they still want to take the land. If they want their laws, they must follow their laws. There are no treaties. They're invalid. The land belongs to us!'

Joseph watched her, but Tjipuka could not understand what his face was telling her. He was upset, but whether he was angry or sad she could not say. 'I know the treaties were not fair,' he said. 'I know what the Germans have done is wrong. Do you think I don't know that?'

'But how can you accept it? How can you help these people to do this?'

'Do I help them?' he asked, mostly to himself, as if questioning his own motives. Joseph stood and looked out over the land, now covered in a weak grey light. 'Do I really help them? What choice do I have?'

'You could go. You could go south, you know the place, the Cape Colony. I think things are better there. You have your education; you could make a new, better life for yourself away from the Germans. When you stay here, when you help them, you are guilty too. Can't you see that?'

Joseph shook his head sadly. He spoke only after some minutes. 'Things are no better there … in the Cape Colony. To be black is wrong wherever you go. You're not wanted. You're less, no one can see beyond your black skin. I can't hide my colour, and my colour is all they see. I'm nothing but my colour. I'm educated; I was top of my class. I could be a lawyer, a teacher, a priest, even a doctor – if I were white. I could be anything my heart wanted. But now I must wait for the generosity of whites. I must sit with a begging bowl and wait for their crumbs. They'll decide what I will be. They'll set my destiny. Not me.'

He did not look at her. He stayed looking out at the desert, the shadows of scrub bushes, patches of grass, stones.

'I'm not sure what this place is. I'm not sure where the people go, my people, your people, but I need to be here. I'm not helping them, the Germans. Everyone thinks I'm helping them, but I'm not. I'm trying to help you, you and Saul – and all the other people. I try to make things easier. I'm trying to help. To do anything I can to make things … this untenable burden … less. I don't know if it matters. But it's all I can do.'

Tjipuka felt ashamed. She didn't know his life, just as he didn't know hers. Maybe he was right. She'd noticed herself that when Joseph was around Schneider was reluctant to bring out the sjambok, to speak harshly to the people. It was as if he didn't want Joseph to see him that way. Joseph helped with so many small kindnesses. She'd overlooked all of that.

They sat quietly and let the air between them settle and the emotions smooth away. The sky glowed orange, preparing for the sun's arrival.

'Who do you wait for here?' Tjipuka asked, her voice kind now.

Joseph turned and looked at her. He didn't hide the pain in his eyes. He spoke with effort. 'There was a girl, at the mission school … before I went to study in the south. We promised we would be together. I don't know where she is. I suppose she's dead. I don't ask people. I don't want to know if she is. I just want her to walk through the gate. To appear on that horizon, making her way to me. I wait for her. I'll always wait for her, I promised her that.'

They both kept quiet. When the sun was completely up, he walked away without saying anything else.

In the collection camp, a lot of the time was spent waiting. They cleaned their sleeping quarters. They washed with the little water they were given. Then they waited. They sat together in small groups. When Joseph had free time, he would sometimes come and read to them from his books. Sometimes bits of the Bible, but better still, from his adventure books he'd brought from the Cape. Tjipuka loved the story of Robinson Crusoe, stranded on an island with his friend Friday. She loved how they found ways to survive and become friends against all the odds. It was a relief to listen to Joseph read in his smooth, deep voice, a relief to be somewhere else for a little while.

One morning, Tjipuka, Novengi, Lucinda, Mara and Tjirwe sat with Saul between them. It was nearly midday. They were trying to encourage Saul to walk. He would stand only, then sit back down. Tjirwe pulled him to his feet again and stepped back; a glimpse of the kind young man Tjirwe had been before everything shone through when he was with Saul.

'Come now. Come to me. Walk like a man, Saul,' he said, attempting to shame Saul into walking.

Saul looked at him thoughtfully through Ruhapo's eyes. Tjipuka could almost remember the whole of Ruhapo's face by looking at those eyes. Saul scowled at Tjirwe then sat down.

'That method will not work with this one,' Novengi said. 'He will not be bullied. He's a decisive man. He'll decide when the time is right to walk.'

Novengi scooped Saul up in her arms. She kissed his cheeks. They all clung to Saul. He was like the sun they revolved around.

Tjipuka smiled at her son. He played with the fringe of Novengi's shawl and mumbled 'Mama', for both she and Novengi were mama to him.

Joseph came up to their group. He greeted everyone, then asked Tjipuka if they might talk in private. They walked towards the outdoor kitchen. Wood smoke filled the air. Pot lids clanged. Tjipuka could hear the cooks talking inside.

Joseph spoke in a low whisper. 'I've heard something. This place, the place where they're taking you, I think it's not good. It's not good at all. You need to leave before they arrive with the wagons. You need to escape. You mustn't go to this place.'

'Why? What did you hear?' Tjipuka was so tired of running. She needed solid proof before she ran back into the desert.

'I heard them last night. Frau Schneider was complaining. She got a letter from a friend at the coast. There's a camp there, full of Herero. That's the place where you are going. The people are sent there only to die – not to make a new life, but to die. They die, even ten a day, maybe more. Frau Schneider asked her husband if this was where the people from the collection station are taken. He would not speak. But he was angry. I could see it. He got up and left. I pretended I wasn't paying attention. I continued reading my book. I knew then. I knew that's the place. It's at the sea. There's no food and it's bitter cold. And there's a terrible sickness there. Everyone's dying. You can't go there, you can't take Saul there.'

Tjipuka couldn't think. She'd become used to the idea that it was all over, that the trouble had passed. Now suddenly it was back again in a new form. Now suddenly they had to run back into the desert, back to the uncertainty.

'Do you know when they're coming for us?'

'No, but it's soon. The camp is too full. I heard Schneider telling one of the cooks that everyone would be leaving within this week. You need to leave now. He won't come after you now. He doesn't have enough people. When the others arrive, it will be different. They come with regiments of soldiers who escort the people to the place. Then they'll have the manpower to track you – but now I think you can get away.'

Tjipuka thought about this. 'All right, we'll go tonight. I'll talk to the others. We'll leave tonight.'

'I'll help you. Let me sort things out. We'll speak later.'

She took his hands. She'd come to care about this man quite a bit and she knew he felt the same. 'Thank you, Joseph, thank you.'

Joseph got the keys to the gate, Tjipuka didn't ask how. Lucinda, Tjirwe, Novengi, Mara, Tjipuka and Saul had prepared for the journey. When the group got to the gate that night there was no watchman. Joseph had performed magic yet again. He'd packed food and water for them. They carried blankets on their heads.

Once out of the gate, Joseph whispered, 'Your only hope is east. You must go to Bechuanaland. Do not rest for two days, keep walking. Walk east without stopping. That will be far enough so that they won't come after you. I'll pray for your safe passage.'

Tjipuka took his hands in hers. 'Come with us, Joseph. What do you have here? Come with us.'

Joseph looked at her for a moment longer, as if he were considering the option, but then he shook his head. 'I can't. You know I can't. I need to go back.'

He turned and walked back through the gate, locking it behind him. Once inside, he watched as the small group disappeared silently into the night.

21

Omaheke Desert, German South-West Africa
February 1905

They did as Joseph had advised them. They did not stop for two days. They walked without sleeping. They ate walking, drank walking. They needed to get far enough away from the collection station so that Schneider could not send someone to find them.

On the third day, when the sun had risen to its hottest point, they stopped. Tjirwe and Lucinda built a shelter with blankets and branches, and they all climbed under it and slept the solid black sleep of exhaustion. Tjipuka woke just at dawn of the next day. Saul slept between Novengi and Tjirwe, his tiny hand resting on Tjirwe's cheek.

Tjipuka climbed out of the shelter into the cool morning air. The sun was not up yet, the sky only beginning to lighten. She sat down and looked through their provisions. Their water would be gone that day. They would need to find some soon. She took a small bit of dried meat and ate it. Joseph was wise with the food he'd packed for them – light, but with staying power. Food that would keep them going for a long time. Dried meat, nuts, rusks. He must have taken from Schneider's own pantry. Tjipuka hoped the theft would not be noticed. Joseph had risked a lot for them. She already missed him and his calmness, his quiet way, even his sadness.

She'd dreamed about Ruhapo at the tail end of her long sleep. The dream was about a time shortly after they got married, when they were both so very young, and so happy.

They'd slipped off to the bush that day.

'There is a place I want to show you,' Ruhapo said, his eyes twinkling in the naughty way he had.

They walked, holding hands. Every few steps he would stop to kiss her. He always struggled not to touch her. They climbed a hill, mostly rocks and thorn bushes. In parts it was quite steep. Ruhapo would go ahead and reach back to pull Tjipuka up over a large stone or a steep section of the path. He would push back thorn branches to let her pass easily. They climbed first up the hill, and then down the other side into a valley of sorts.

'It's not far now.'

Tjipuka had travelled through most of the bush around Okahandja when she was a girl. She'd never been content sitting at home, sewing or helping her mother milk or make butter, like her sister. Her mother would scold her, but her father always insisted she be left alone. 'She will be a grown wife soon enough, let her be a girl now,' he said.

Tjipuka knew the bush around Okahandja, so was surprised that she didn't know this place Ruhapo was taking her to.

'It's secret. I made it just for you,' he said, his eyes shining.

'You made it?' she asked.

'Yes, Wife, do you doubt your husband's powers?'

She smiled. 'No, never.'

They pushed through the bush where it grew thicker. The trees were getting taller and taller, and the air smelled moist and organic, the smell of growing things. Then the trees opened and Tjipuka gasped. Before her was a field of yellow and white flowers. They led to a small pool fed by water that fell from the high cliffs that framed it.

'It's beautiful. How did you ever find it?' she asked.

'I told you. I didn't find it, I made it for you,' Ruhapo said.

He took her hand and led her through the knee-high flowers. Butterflies and bees flew up as they passed, disturbed from their feeding. Purple and blue butterflies, yellow-and-black-striped ones.

The pool was clear and she could see that the bottom was rock. Ruhapo turned to her and began unbuttoning her dress.

'Do you expect me to get naked and swim here, Mr Ruhapo?' she teased. 'You know I'm a married woman now, not the bush girl you used to know. I have standards to maintain.'

'I packed the standards up nicely. They're safe and sound back in the village. You can take them out and put them back on when you return. The bush girl is free of all that here.'

Tjipuka stepped out of her dress once it had fallen to the ground. She pushed off the straps of her petticoat and let it fall to where the dress lay. She stepped out of her pants. Now naked in the warm sun, she said, 'And you, Ruhapo, are you not joining me?'

In seconds, he was free of clothes. He ran up the side of the cliff, about halfway, and jumped into the pool. The water splashed high and Ruhapo roared with pleasure. Tjipuka laughed at him from the edge, then leaped into the icy cold herself.

They played until their skin was wrinkled. Then Ruhapo pulled her to him, holding her tightly. She wrapped her legs around his waist, he entered her, and they moved gently in the water together. He left his seed in her, the seed she was certain made Saul. It was a perfect day like that. Everything the best it would ever be. Everything magical and drenched in warm love. She was sure that from that perfect magical day Saul had been created.

Her dream had been so clear. She'd heard the water falling, smelled the flowers as she walked through them, heard the bees buzzing, felt the smooth rocks under her feet. She'd felt Ruhapo's hands on her body. She'd been there. It had been so real. Waking up seemed the falsehood. How could a man as alive as Ruhapo be dead? It must be a lie, it could be nothing else.

It took some minutes for her to accept the truth again.

She looked out over the endless desert before her. Sometimes she forgot Ruhapo was dead. She couldn't remember that he lay on the ground at Ohamakari. He was dead, she told herself. He was dead. She needed to remember that, but it was hard when he still seemed so alive to her in her mind.

She'd never cried for him. The grief and sadness were too much, tears could not come. But the dream had weakened her. The tears broke through, first slowly, then in a flood. As the sun rose, already showing its merciless heat for the day, Tjipuka, all alone in the desert, everyone still asleep, finally cried for her dead husband.

22

Omaheke Desert, German South-West Africa
March 1905

They saw the doves flying up into the clear desert sky and knew there was a waterhole in the distance.

'There, look,' Novengi said, pointing at the brown doves, a cloud of them circling. 'At last, water.'

They were still quite far away. Lucinda took Mara's arm to hurry her. They'd run out of water the night before and all of them were desperate for a drink. Just seeing the doves had lightened their mood.

Tjirwe took Saul from Tjipuka. 'Come, little man, let's run.'

He put Saul on his shoulders and trotted off ahead of the group, making horse noises, rearing his head and whinnying every few steps. Novengi came up next to Tjipuka.

'Saul has helped that boy,' she said. 'He's found the place for love again in his heart, thanks to your son.'

'Yes, I think it's good for both of them.'

The waterhole seemed to be man-made. There were tracks leading out from it into the desert, perhaps made by Herero herd boys. It was not uncommon for them to trek cattle into Bechuanaland if the rains had not been good in Hereroland and they needed to search for better pastures. On the tracks that they followed in search of the good grazing, they would dig waterholes that they remembered on their way back. Tjipuka decided this must be one of them. The birds were drinking and not dying, so the Germans must not have found this one yet.

Tjirwe and Saul arrived at the waterhole first. Tjirwe took Saul off his shoulders and set him on the ground along with the pack he carried. He pulled out a calabash and went to the hole, which was surrounded by thorn branches to protect it. He dragged one of them away and stepped forward to enter the enclosure. Tjipuka saw him suddenly stop. He took a step back and then another, and that was when they saw them.

Three men emerged from the waterhole, all of them armed. Tjirwe scooped Saul up and stumbled backwards, pushing the others back with his free arm.

The tallest man said, 'Stop.'

Tjipuka looked at Lucinda and Novengi. They were still far enough away; they might be able to run without being shot. Novengi knew what the look meant and shook her head.

'No. We're together.'

They continued to the waterhole. The three men were all Herero. The two shorter, older ones spoke little. The taller one seemed to be the leader.

'Six thousand marks,' he said to the other two. 'I knew if we stayed here a few days we'd make our money.'

'I doubt the baby will fetch a thousand,' one of the small ones said.

'Why not? They said a thousand marks per person – is that one not a person? I'll be damned if I'll let them cheat me.'

'You know the Germans – they'll cheat you every side if they can,' the smaller one with a battered leather hat said.

The women arrived and stood next to Tjirwe and Saul.

'Nice of you to join us,' the big one said.

Novengi looked at Tjipuka, her eyes indicating something was wrong.

Tjipuka shook her head slightly to indicate she didn't understand. Novengi had noticed something. Tjipuka looked around but couldn't figure out what she meant.

'Get the ropes. I want their hands tied. I don't want to lose one on the way,' the taller one ordered.

One of the smaller ones began tying their hands while the other one went behind a sand dune and collected three horses. The big one kept his gun levelled at the group.

Tjipuka looked at Novengi, trying to figure out what she was attempting to communicate. She kept indicating the big one with her eyes. Tjipuka looked at him. He was a battered-looking man with a hard, pockmarked face. He moved with his shoulders hunched, like so many too-tall men. Looking again, something about him seemed familiar, but she was sure she didn't know him.

'What're you looking at?' he asked her and moved closer. He looked her over, up and down, and then he suddenly laughed. 'Could that be you?'

He moved around Tjipuka, looking at her carefully. 'You're not the fresh young woman you used to be, that's for sure. Not so full of herself either.' He ran his finger along the side of her face. When she pulled away from him, he slapped her.

With that slap she knew. He looked older, and something had happened to his face. She suspected he had survived smallpox, from the look of the scars. But she knew this man – it was Waueza. She wished she had a knife to slash his throat, she hated him so much. But she needed to think of the others. If she did things correctly, they might be able to get free. Her knowledge of Waueza might help them escape.

'Waueza? I didn't know it was you at first.' She smiled. Her hands were not yet tied so she held one out to shake his. He took it, but didn't let go. 'We thought you died,' Tjipuka said. 'We thought you gave up and walked back to the Germans to die. I'm so glad to see you're still alive.'

He relaxed a bit. He looked at the others. 'Is this Kahaka's wife then?' he asked, indicating Novengi.

Novengi shrank a little at hearing her husband's name spoken.

'Yes, yes it is. We've survived. The others in the group didn't,' Tjipuka said.

Waueza looked at them. He seemed at a loss how to behave. Before he'd recognised them, they were just prey to be hunted, to be turned over for a reward. Now they were people he knew. Tjipuka was aware he had no kindness in his heart, but she hoped he was at least human enough to see them as people now.

'Where did you go when you left us?' she asked.

'I headed east. But then I got caught. Things worked out all right, though. I made a deal with the Germans.'

Tjipuka swallowed her anger, so bitter in her throat. She would not let it get the best of her, not now. She needed to keep her head. 'That was better. The men in our group were not as lucky. Perhaps they weren't clever enough to know how to make such deals.'

She looked at Novengi. She didn't want to hurt her, but she needed to do this.

'Of course,' Waueza said. 'I know the Germans, I know how their minds work.' He tugged at Tjipuka's hand and pulled her away from the group. 'You're too thin, this is true, but you're still beautiful. Didn't I tell you one day you would need my help?'

Tjipuka stood very still. Waueza ran his hand over her backside. He reached his hand between her thighs from behind and pulled her to him. Tjipuka did not fight. She would not fight. They would be free, she reminded herself, if she did not fight. None of this mattered, she told herself.

As he pushed against her, she could feel him hard on her stomach. He ripped at her dress.

Tjipuka whispered, 'Not here. Not in front of them. Not in front of the children, please.'

Waueza slapped her again. 'You'll not tell me anything. You're not Ruhapo's wife today. He's dead. I'll have you as I want you this time.'

He breathed hard, his eyes bulging, his lips curling back from his teeth. Tjipuka stayed very still. She would not fight him. He could do whatever he wanted if it meant that they would be let free. She kept telling herself that. Survival was the only thing. They must live; everything else was secondary to that goal. Everything.

She tried to separate herself into two: the physical body and her soul. Her soul moved away so it could not be harmed by anything Waueza did to her. She did not look at the others. She made her mind blank, made her body someone else's, not hers. They became two separate things, not related to each other, not affected by each other.

Waueza ran his rough, dirty hands over her now bare breasts. He pulled his penis out. She was not there. She could feel nothing. This would not harm her.

Someone gasped and then there was a hard thud. Tjipuka was not aware of what had happened at first. She felt something wet on her face. She wiped it with her hand. It was blood. She opened her eyes and Mara was there.

Tjipuka stood, her dress torn wide, her bare breasts dotted with drops of red. Mara rose and fell to the ground over the prostrate body of Waueza. She rose and fell and rose and fell. Only then did Tjipuka see the large rock Mara held in both of her hands, still tied together. She brought the rock down on Waueza's head, over and over, until his face was only blood and flesh. And still she continued. She continued until a shot rang out. She held the rock over her head and stopped for an instant. A flower of red bloomed on her chest and she fell backwards into the sand.

Tjipuka heard screams. Lucinda fell to her friend. Tjirwe went to his mother. Novengi, holding Saul, wrapped her shawl around Tjipuka's bare breasts and pulled her away from Waueza's body.

One of the men, the one with a flattened nose, moved forward.

'Let's get going,' he said.

He used his gun to push the group away from the two bodies. They had a long walk and the sun was getting no cooler. He let them collect water, the reason they had come there in the first place, and then they headed back west, leaving Mara and Waueza where they'd fallen, to be taken care of by the desert, like all of the others. Tjipuka realised it was getting easier to leave the dead behind, and she tried not to notice.

23

Omaheke Desert, German South-West Africa
March 1905

They soon realised that they were heading back to the mission station from which they'd escaped. The two men kept them walking both day and night, with only short breaks. They kept repeating that the shipment would soon leave and they mustn't miss it.

Tjipuka watched Lucinda look back only once at her friend Mara. She didn't cry. She just looked once and started walking. The encounter with Waueza seemed to have sparked something in Novengi. Tjipuka suspected it was the reminder of Kahaka's death. She walked without speaking. Though the men bullied her, pushing her with their guns, telling her to hurry, she never spoke back.

As they neared the station, Tjipuka could see something was going on. There were horses and soldiers all around. Wagons were being loaded, people moving back and forth carrying their few belongings. Franz Schneider must have seen the group as they arrived, because when they got to the gate he was waiting for them.

'So you've found the lost sheep,' he said to the two men. He did not mention that there had been three women and they were now only two, or that one of the men was gone. Schneider moved towards Tjipuka.

'You thought you could use my people against me. Is that what you thought?'

His sneering face was close to hers. He was not the man who had welcomed them when they arrived the first time. He leaned into Tjipuka; she could feel his warm, moist breath on her face.

'I must show you what your selfishness has accomplished.'

He grabbed Tjipuka's arm roughly and pulled her inside the gate. As the others followed, the people stopped working and looked at them. They all looked in the direction Franz Schneider pointed.

'Look. Look at what you've done.'

On the largest acacia tree – the one under which people sat during the hottest part of the day, under which Joseph used to read to them about the man stranded on the deserted island with his friend Friday – a man was hanging. His hands hung at his sides in resignation to his fate. Then a slight breeze turned him around so that his face was directly towards them.

Tjipuka hadn't needed to see the face. She'd only needed to see his kind, soft hands. The ones that turned the pages of books about adventures and told stories about people with dreams. The face of the man who waited for the woman he loved. The kind hands that had sacrificed everything for them. It was Joseph. They had killed Joseph.

Joseph was a good man. Brilliant and kind and better than almost anyone she'd ever met.

Tjipuka turned to Schneider.

'You call yourself a Christian,' she hissed. 'You're nothing! God will punish you for what you've done. You're nothing!' Her voice rose in a wild scream and she repeated, 'God will punish you!'

She ran to Joseph. She would not leave him hanging like a trophy for Franz Schneider to show off. She lifted his heavy body and tried to unwind the wire from his neck, but she'd hardly started and they were on her. The two men who had brought them in carried her kicking and screaming, biting, to Franz Schneider. He stood with a slight smile on his face.

'Hold her still on the ground!'

He brought down his leather sjambok on her back. She did not scream. She lay still. She would take anything. Though she blamed Franz Schneider for Joseph's death, she also blamed herself. Joseph would never have risked disobeying Schneider if it was not for her. She welcomed this punishment. She counted each time the sjambok bit into the skin of her back with a loud, hard thwack. At seventeen, everything went mercifully black.

Tjirwe carried Saul, and Lucinda and Novengi carried Tjipuka. They'd covered her slashed back with a blanket to absorb the pus that was leaking from the wounds. She was in and out of consciousness, but the soldiers had no mercy. She would walk with everyone else, or be left at the road-side for the wild animals to deal with, they didn't care one way or the other. So the others carried her. Everyone from the camp owed Joseph for one kindness or another. Because of this, they all owed Tjipuka for standing up to Franz Schneider when they hadn't. When Novengi or Lucinda became too weak to continue, others stepped in and took over.

There were about fifty in the group, almost all women and children, only a handful of old men. Some still believed that they were being taken to a new place where the Herero would be allowed to live in peace, to patch together a new kind of life. Some hoped they'd find their lost people there. They would have cattle again. They would be able to light the sacred fire. They would find their ancestors again and God would be able to help them. There were a few who were still hopeful.

On the second day, Tjipuka began recovering. An old man in the group found a plant in the bush that he said would help. He boiled it with some of the little water he had, and dabbed the tea onto Tjipuka's wounds. He had her drink some of the liquid too. She slept that night. In the morning, she was lucid and able to walk, with help. He did the same the next night when they stopped. By the third day of the treatment, the wounds had stopped leaking and were scabbing over and she could walk on her own.

Tjipuka and her small group knew where they were going. They were walking to the coast. They had not left the bushveld yet; they still had the deadly Namib to get through. And then they would arrive at the sea, a place she'd never seen before.

Joseph had said they put all the people together in some sort of camp. A camp where they would die. He'd been right, too, about the soldiers. Once the soldiers arrived at the mission station, there was no chance to escape. There were at least twenty-five soldiers, all well armed. Escape would mean death by a bullet in the back.

They would wait and see, Tjipuka thought. Perhaps the camp would not be as bad as Joseph had heard it was. For now, they needed to survive the walk through the Namib. After that they would decide what to do.

Ruhapo

24

Bechuanaland
January 1905

Ruhapo headed for the makeshift border into Bechuanaland. He'd been crossing the desert for months. He was sure Tjipuka was not there – he'd searched all corners of the Omaheke. She must have crossed over. He would find her in Bechuanaland. He believed it so much that he saw her in his mind, sitting with Saul, waiting. She was there, he was sure of it.

The border was little more than a wire fence. He could have jumped over it easily, but there was a cement building where the British colonial government kept an office. They tried to keep track of the many Herero fleeing into Bechuanaland.

At the border, he found small groups of Herero waiting with the border police. They were attempting to sort out their passing into Bechuanaland. They were weak and thin, barely alive in many cases. They had nothing, only what they wore on their bodies, and even those clothes were old and torn. They had no cattle. No small livestock. Nothing. Ruhapo moved among them, asking if they'd seen his wife or son. Those who could speak told him they hadn't. Others just looked at him with sunken eyes and silent mouths. But, at last, one thin young boy came forward.

'She was with us,' he said. 'I know her. She had a child named Saul.'

'Yes! Yes, that's her! Where is she now?' Ruhapo asked, grabbing the boy by his shoulders. 'Where are my wife and son?'

The boy seemed reluctant to say. Ruhapo shook him; he could feel the bones of the boy's arms poking into his hands. 'Where did she go? Tell me! Where is she?'

The boy began to cry, either from fear of Ruhapo or from being forced to remember. Still he spoke. 'The Germans said they wanted to make peace. We were with Kahaka. He went first. They sent a man, one of us, to tell us it was safe. Kahaka didn't trust them. He told us to stay, to wait only for him. But we didn't. We should have listened to him, but we didn't. When the Germans came in the night, we went with them. We thought it was for peace. One spoke kindly in Otjiherero. We thought he was one of the kind Germans. But they shot everyone.'

He began to cry harder, tears rolling down his face. 'They shot my mother in the head as she ran away. They pushed a bayonet through my grandfather and he fell to the ground. They hanged Kahaka.'

The boy cried, his body shaking with grief, his arms dangling useless at his side, but Ruhapo pushed him. He needed the boy to tell every-thing, to tell the truth.

'But Tjipuka, she ran away. She ran away from that,' Ruhapo said. 'Tell me. Where is she?'

The boy was fearful of Ruhapo's wild face, but he spoke anyway. 'No. Everyone died. I was near the front. Instead of running back where the soldiers were going, I ran forward. I managed to escape through the tents, unseen. I waited. I could see from where I was. No one lived. Later, after the Germans stopped shooting, two younger soldiers passed through and killed any wounded people with their bayonets. I saw it all from where I hid. None of them survived.'

Ruhapo dropped the boy to the ground and turned away. He walked away from the others, away from the border police who called to him. He went back towards the desert. When he could see the border no

166

more, he sat on a stone in the sun. He didn't care about the heat. He wished it would burn him up – dry him to nothing, to dust that blew away in the wind.

His hope was gone now. He only wanted to know where Tjipuka's body was, where baby Saul lay. He would go there. He would find them and bury them as humans should be buried. And then he would lie next to them and wait for death to come. The Germans had been successful after all. No matter how hard he had fought them, they had finally taken his life. They've taken it all now, he thought. Let them win – let them win and take everything; he didn't care.

As the air cooled and darkness fell, Ruhapo began to wonder if it was fair to blame the Germans at all. The Herero had made the decision to rise up against them. At the time, he'd been sure that it was the right thing to do. At the time, he was positive that death was better than allowing the Germans to steal everything, to humiliate them. His pride had compelled him to be among the ones who convinced Samuel Maharero to rise up against Leutwein. Maharero wouldn't have done it if he hadn't been pushed; Leutwein was his friend. He tried to tell the people that they should wait, that they should give him time to negotiate, but the people, Ruhapo included, were too angry. They would not listen. They convinced him war was the only answer and they had risen up. And it had all led to this. What he'd done had led to this, to Tjipuka and Saul gone forever. Was he not to be blamed as well for all of the bodies that were scattered throughout the Omaheke? His parents, his uncle, his friend Kahaka? Was he not the reason Tjipuka and Saul lay dead somewhere out there? What was pride? Land? Cattle? When compared to the life of his wife and son? It was all nothing.

Darkness fell and he sat. He could hear the distant song of an eagle owl. From somewhere it called him back into the desert. He needed to find Tjipuka and Saul, the song said. He needed to follow them to where they'd gone. He stood. The night was dark; even the stars were gone behind the clouds, the cowardly cold-hearted stars.

He walked for some distance back into the desert and then a hand stopped him.

'Where are you going?'

At first Ruhapo didn't recognise him. His face, which had always been full, was drained. He wore only a tattered shirt and trousers. But, after some moments, Ruhapo remembered him; they'd gone to school together.

'Tjizumo?'

The one who always rushed for food, the dandy boy who'd gone to the mines in the Transvaal and come back with pockets of money, showing off to the women, with his stomach full and round, the stomach he rubbed like a rich man.

'What are you doing?' Tjizumo said. 'We're here now. We must cross over and find Samuel Maharero. I'm sure he has made it safe for us with the British and the Tawana. We must cross over now. The British police are waiting for us.'

'No, I need to go and fetch Tjipuka and Saul. I need to go and be with my wife and son,' Ruhapo said. 'There's nothing for me over there.'

Tjizumo held his arm tightly. 'No, you'll go with us now.'

'I can't. I need to go to them.' Ruhapo struggled to get free.

'They're dead. Can't you understand that? They're all dead. Everyone's dead. The jackals and the hyenas have eaten them. They are not there, not even their bones. They're gone. They're all gone. You'll find nothing there.' Tjizumo shouted at Ruhapo, but he wasn't really speaking to him – he was talking to himself, to the universe, perhaps. When he was finished, he was breathing hard. It had been too much for his wasted body. He bent over and leaned on his knees, trying, without success, to catch his breath.

Ruhapo looked at his friend. He knew there was nothing for him over the border, but he also knew that Tjizumo would die soon. He would die unless he could make it to food and water and a place to rest. Ruhapo would not be responsible for another death; there were enough already that he would be held to account for. So he put Tjizumo's arm around his shoulder and helped him walk back to the border.

The border police took Ruhapo's gun. That had been the only thing that had ensured his survival all his days searching in the desert. Now, without it, he felt vulnerable.

There were about twenty Herero in the group that crossed over the border with him, headed for a place called Tsau, at the edge of the Okavango swamps. They had been told that Samuel Maharero and the others were there. Along the way, some gave up. They found jobs with the Batawana, the people of the area, who had farms and were willing to take people on as workers. Some took the jobs so that they could get food and water. There were a few farms run by Boers; some stayed to work for them. They were too weak to make the trek to Tsau.

When, after a week of walking, they arrived in the village of Tsau, they went to the kgotla. There they found the Batawana chief, Kgosi Sekgoma Letsholathebe. He said that they could stay, but he did not want any trouble. The Mbanderu, the Herero-speaking people who had crossed the border when Samuel Maharero was made the paramount chief of the Herero, did not want these new Herero here. They would not allow Kgosi Sekgoma Letsholathebe to recognise Samuel Maharero as their paramount chief. Kgosi Sekgoma Letsholathebe needed to keep the Mbanderu happy. He was the chief because of the many foreigners he had invited to settle in his country. Without them, he would lose his position. If they needed Samuel Maharero to be ostracised, then it would be so.

Ruhapo's group discussed what to do. It was obvious to him that pledging allegiance to Samuel Maharero would make life difficult for them in Tsau. It was not hard for Ruhapo to turn his back on Maharero. He still blamed him for taking his father's land and cattle in Gobabis. He'd been a weak, ineffectual leader at home, where the Germans had supported him and where he was rich; how would he help them in this new land where he had no power at all? Where he had no German friends to give him what he needed?

Ruhapo had heard that a distant relative of his – Katjimune – lived in Tsau. He hoped he would get help there. But when he asked Tjizumo to accompany him, Tjizumo declined, saying he was going to Samuel Maharero.

They parted, and Ruhapo went in search of his relative. He'd been directed to a farm outside the village. After walking among towering camel thorn trees through the white sand of the area, he found a Herero woman fetching water. She gave him directions.

The farm was not far. Katjimune's place had the big kraal of sacred cattle first. There was a holy fire in the yard. He was holding on to their traditions. Their traditions and most of their culture had got lost in the scattering. Seeing these, the kraal and the holy fire, made Ruhapo feel safe. It made him feel as if everything could be fixed and restored as it should be. Maybe even the broken things inside him.

He introduced himself to one of the wives, a tall, strong woman who called herself by the Setswana name MmaLesedi. She offered Ruhapo a chair while she fetched Katjimune.

When he arrived, Ruhapo was happy to see that the old man was strong and healthy. Bechuanaland had been good to him. He sat down opposite Ruhapo.

'Wa uhara, son of Ruhapo,' Katjimune said. 'So you have made it here.'

'Yes, it's wonderful to see you in such good health. We've had trouble. I'm sure you know about this.'

'Yes, this I know. Many people have arrived. All nearly dead thanks to that man of no worth.' Ruhapo nodded his head. 'So you have come to me, not him.'

Ruhapo needed to speak carefully; he could see emotions were still high. Battles fought in Hereroland had been carried to this place. 'When I have the option to make a choice, I always try to choose the wise man,' he replied.

Katjimune nodded, satisfied with that answer. 'I have many people here already. They've been pouring over the border since May of last year. Because I knew and respected your father, I can give you some cattle, a few only. I can help you to find a job, too. I know a good man, a Motawana; he's fair and he'll not cheat you. This isn't the case for all Batawana – some are taking advantage of our people and their problems. But this man is good. He's called Mogalakwe.'

'Thank you, I'm grateful.'

'Are you alone? Have you no wife?'

Ruhapo tried to speak without emotion. In a flat voice that would become the only one he had, he said, 'They have been lost in the desert.'

Katjimune nodded his head. He had heard too many stories of sadness. For now, sadness was all there was from the people who arrived.

Tjipuka

25
Lüderitz, German South-West Africa
April 1905

They walked for nearly a month. The Namib was not as bad as Tjipuka had predicted because the soldiers knew waterholes at regular
distances, though food was still scarce. They ate wild potatoes and
occasionally the leftovers of animals the soldiers killed. The group had
shrunk along the way. Now they were only twenty-five. The old man
who had saved Tjipuka fell one day and couldn't get up. They picked
him up and carried him, but he begged them to leave him. He wanted
nothing else from this life. They followed his wish. Tjipuka left him
all of the water and food she had.

On that day, the air changed. There were clouds in the distance. As
they walked, the smell of fish became stronger. Every few miles the
temperature dropped. The air was wet and heavy and cold.

'We're nearing the sea,' Lucinda said.

'I don't trust this cloud we're walking in,' Tjirwe said. 'It smells of
sickness.'

It was true; the air was like a cloud – as if the clouds had fallen to the
ground. And the air was so cold. Tjipuka wrapped a blanket around

herself and Saul, already strapped in a blanket on her back. She agreed with Tjirwe, the air seemed laden with something. It was difficult to pull into your lungs, and, once there, it sat like something solid.

She heard the sea before she saw it. A loud crashing of water, over and over. Tjipuka had never seen anything so massive, so destructive. Some of the people screamed and wanted to run back. The soldiers whipped at them with long straps and they went forward reluctantly. The water was like a monster fighting the land, fighting them.

The town of Lüderitz, next to the sea, was quite large, with brick buildings and many horses and ox wagons in the lanes between them. There seemed to be only men living there, though, rough-looking white men, mostly. Tjipuka wondered where they kept the women.

The soldiers pushed them through the town. The people of the town looked at them; some turned away, either disinterested or disgusted. There were only a few black people, some in leg irons. They wore hardly any clothes, though it was very cold. But they didn't shiver. Their faces were blank. They did not smile or frown. They just looked.

The group walked out onto a strip of land jutting into the raging sea. Tjipuka feared the water would come and grab them. The strip of land was fenced off with barbed wire. Tjipuka saw many small, badly constructed shelters far out on this piece of land. The wind was blowing hard here, straight over the ocean and out to the desert. Nothing stopped it on its way. Tjipuka wrapped the blanket tighter around her, but it was impossible to escape the biting wind.

The first part of the peninsula that pushed out into the ocean was a camp for the German soldiers. The group walked through this camp and continued. Where the soldiers' camp ended, they walked across a causeway with water on each side and came to another gate, manned by guards with guns. The soldiers who had brought them across the desert spoke to the two guards. The guards came forward and looked at the small group, then one of them indicated that the group must wait to the side. They sat in the sand banked at the edge of the road, huddled close to keep warm.

One of the guards fetched a book and a metal box from inside the small house where the guards had been sheltering from the wind. He approached the first woman sitting near the house. He spoke Otjiherero to her, but a choppy, mixed-up version that was not easy to understand. He wanted her name and age, which he wrote in his book. Then he took a small tag from the metal box and pinned it to her dress. He warned her that she must always wear that metal tag or she would be shot. He smiled when he said this.

He went through the group like that, one after the other, until all of them were given metal tags. Novengi's number was 8867, Tjipuka's 8868.

When he was finished giving everyone in the group their metal tag, he opened the gate and told them to go inside. Once they were all inside, he locked the gate. The soldiers who had brought them disappeared on their horses. The guards went back into their guardhouse to get out of the biting wet wind. Tjipuka saw that they had a small fireplace in the house. They sat near it and warmed themselves, the people outside already forgotten.

The group stood, not knowing what to do next. Tjipuka turned to look at her new home. It was only rock – rocks jumbled into the sea, not land. On both sides was the wild ocean. It crashed and sprayed onto the jagged rocks, angry and bitter. The people there, who she now saw were both Herero and Nama, had built their shelters out of anything they could find. Pieces of driftwood. Blankets. Even the rocks them-selves. The bits of space between the rocks were limited. Tjipuka won-dered where they would sit, how they would lie down.

The people already there sat looking out at the sea. Many were in clothes that were barely worthy of the definition, they were so worn and tattered – the remnants of clothes, really. Their bodies, only bones, were exposed to the elements. Babies didn't cry. Even though the people numbered many more than a hundred, Tjipuka estimated, the only sound was the loud, relentless ocean and its angry wind.

'But there's nothing here,' a woman in their group said. 'This can't be the land they set aside for us. We can't live in a place like this.' Tears streamed down her face as she spoke, as she realised the truth. She had still had hope that they were being taken to their new home, the place of peace. Only now did she realise that there would be no new homes, no new cattle. This place was where they had been heading, and they had arrived.

26

Lüderitz, German South-West Africa
June 1905

They decided that to conserve materials and heat they would build one house for all of them. Luckily they still had a lot of blankets and they built using the blankets and branches they found. The space was small for four grown people and Saul, but that helped to keep them warm. The cold, wet air pushed into their weakened bodies. Each night a heavy fog came in from the sea and settled on the camp. Tjipuka had never felt cold like this before. Even in the day, when the sun was beating down on them, the cold did not leave her body.

They ate very little. They were given uncooked rice, but they had no wood to cook with. Any wood that arrived on the waves was quickly grabbed to make shelters. Lucinda soaked the rice in seawater in an enamel bowl she had and set the bowl in the sun. By sunset the rice was softer and easier to eat.

At the edge of the water, they searched for things they might eat. Tjirwe pulled hard brown shells from the stones and said they must eat the slimy bit of meat inside. These were difficult to find since everyone looked for them, but Tjirwe did not fear the sea like most, and climbed into the rough water to find the ones others couldn't reach.

After two days, soldiers divided them into work groups. Lucinda, Novengi and Tjipuka were grouped together. Their group carried things from the ships docked at the shore to the waiting ox wagons. Tjirwe was taken away with a group of men; there were few men on the island, most of them old. The men were to build a railway line. The work was just beginning. There was talk that they all, women and men, even children, would work on the railway line eventually. Tjirwe said the work was difficult and the guards particularly harsh.

Each day was the same. They were up at dawn. They were marched into the town, men in leg irons. The men then veered off to the south and the women continued into town. The loads they carried from the ships were often very heavy. Lucinda, Novengi and Tjipuka always tried to work together. They were still strong compared to the others and were able to avoid beatings for dropping crates or for stopping work. If a woman failed to lift something, or fell from exhaustion, the soldiers beat her with long leather sjamboks. They beat her until she rose and worked again or had to be carried away. Often a woman carried away was never seen again.

They were constantly hungry, always exhausted and permanently cold. Each morning before leaving for the dockyards, the dead needed to be collected. On a good day there would be one or two, but most days they were five or six. The people held quick ceremonies, where the appointed priests read from small prayer books or Rhenish Bibles. The missionaries had tried so hard to convert the Herero; in the end the camp succeeded where they had failed. After the ceremony, the bodies were carted off to the desert to be buried in unmarked graves. Every day at the camp started with death.

The people in the camp were not only Herero, though the bulk of them were. There were also a lot of Nama people, the followers of Jan Jonker Afrikaner, who had risen up against the Germans after the Herero. But many Herero kept their distance from the Nama people, seeing them as their former enemies. At Ohamakari, Jan Jonker Afrikaner's people had fought with the Germans against the Herero. They'd been the enemy of the Herero people before the Germans and, in many ways, they remained so afterwards.

One evening, Lucinda, Novengi and Tjipuka sat in front of their tiny shelter looking out at the sea, which was calm for once. They were exhausted from carrying heavy crates from the ships all day. It was already dark and Tjirwe had not yet returned.

'The men are late today,' Lucinda said.

Novengi laid her hand on Lucinda's shoulder. 'He'll come.'

Tjipuka held Saul. He was quiet, too quiet. Her milk was gone again, and the food they had was too little and hardly nutritious. He was too thin. And tonight he was hot with fever. Tjipuka kept quiet, though; she knew Lucinda had enough to worry about with Tjirwe not back yet.

When they heard a noise, they all looked up. Two Nama men had arrived, carrying Tjirwe. He was awake, but barely. Lucinda rushed to them. 'What happened?'

'He was beaten. He went after one of the soldiers. He was beaten bad.'

They set him down on the blanket Novengi had laid out. 'Keep him on the stomach,' one of the men said. He pulled a handful of leaves from his pocket. 'Mix this with seawater and rub it on his back.'

They made to leave and Tjipuka thanked them. When she turned back, she saw that Lucinda had removed Tjirwe's shirt. His back was raw. The sjambok had dug his flesh out in deep gashes. Novengi fetched seawater and mixed the herbs in it, careful not to waste any, then gently applied the medicine while Tjipuka held Lucinda, who cried over what they had done to her son.

'How do they do this to a boy?' Lucinda asked. No one answered. There were no answers.

As the days passed, Tjirwe's back healed but Saul became sicker. He stopped eating and his skin developed a rash. Sick or not, they all had to go to the docks every day. There was no time to stop and attend to a baby. Tjipuka strapped Saul to her back and felt his hot suffering body against her. She spoke to him in a low voice. She begged him to stay with her, but she could feel him slipping away.

On the fifth day, Tjipuka woke early. She reached for Saul and he was no longer hot. His tiny body was cold. She picked her son up and held him, his body already growing stiff. She rocked him but he did not cry. He did not reach up to touch her face; he never would now. Her son was gone.

She wasn't aware that she was screaming until Novengi got up and pulled her away from the dead baby, pulled her outside the tent and held her tightly as the relentless wind battered them.

Lucinda and Tjirwe stayed in the tent preparing Saul for burial. That morning, along with the other dead from the camp, would be a small child. Another body. Another extra piece of work for those who remained.

Tjirwe was well enough to carry Saul's body to the wagon that would carry him back into the desert. They wrapped him in a blanket and Tjirwe laid him carefully inside.

Tjipuka watched her still son. He was the last bit of Ruhapo that she had, the last reason for her to keep fighting, for her to keep living. Their small group had put everything into the small boy. He'd been their hope. In him were all of their dreams. Yet he had been given no real chance to live, always balancing tenuously between the two worlds, and now he was gone, gone to his father. Gone to Maveipi, gone to all of them, wherever they were.

Now, Tjipuka was emptied inside. It was over for her. Her only wish was that her death would come quickly. That was the only hope that she had left.

They left Saul. There were many bodies that morning, nine in total. There was a sickness moving through the camp. A fever with a rash, and then death within a few days. They suspected it was smallpox, but no doctors confirmed it. There were no doctors to confirm it in any case. Tjipuka hoped she would get it soon.

She knew Saul was wheeled away, but she didn't remember it. On the days that followed, sometimes she reached for her son – to see him, to feed him, to rock him to sleep. He was not there, and she reminded herself that he was cold, lying in a mass grave with nine strangers in that hated desert. Gone. Gone forever.

When Tjirwe started work again, he discovered something. Near the place where they were working there was a rubbish dump. When he could, which was rarely, he sneaked off and collected things that might help them. Sometimes mouldy bread, old clothes, bits of rotten meat. He brought wood too, so they could have fire most nights and get relief from the cold.

'Do you think he's in heaven?' Tjirwe asked Tjipuka one evening when he found her alone.

'Yes, if there is a heaven then Saul is there.' She spoke words only, words she felt no commitment to.

'And that heaven, it's for the Germans too, are they there with him?'

'Maybe, I don't know. But they'll be kind there. Heaven is only for kindness.' Tjipuka believed none of it, but she would say it for his sake.

'There's a man, a soldier, he's called Kurtis. He's the one who beat me.' Tjirwe had not spoken about the incident to anyone. 'I would have killed him that day. That would have made me as evil as him … as them. Then I wouldn't go to heaven. I'd not be with my father, with my sisters, with Saul.'

Tjipuka put her hand on his shoulder. She could not help him. She could only listen.

'He's mean. He beat an old man to death, a Nama man. He was old and sick and couldn't lift the sleeper. But Kurtis didn't care. He beat him and laughed as the man begged for his life. I couldn't take any more. I lifted a piece of iron and knocked him off his horse. I beat him on the head. He was bleeding, but he didn't die. They wanted to shoot me, but another soldier stepped in. I heard him say to the soldiers that

Kurtis deserved it. He's gone now, Kurtis. I wonder where they took him. But that day I could have killed him.'

'Yes, and you would have been forgiven. Even his fellow soldiers agreed with you. Kurtis killed a man.'

When Tjirwe turned to Tjipuka, she saw, in his eyes, the little boy he still was. He'd been forced to be a man before he should have been, but he was really just a boy.

'Do you think God took Saul because of me? Because I'm so evil? Because I wanted to kill Kurtis?'

Tjipuka grabbed him up in her arms. She held him tightly and the tears that she had held back for her son flowed for this poor boy.

'No, never. God would never do that. Saul died because he got sick. That's all. You're a good boy, a kind boy. You did nothing wrong. None of us did anything wrong.'

27
Lüderitz, German South-West Africa
August 1905

Every day began with death. The smallpox that had killed Saul and so many others seemed to have moved on, but there was always something new to kill the people. Beaten, exhausted, starved people were easy targets for death.

They worked no matter the weather. Novengi, Lucinda and Tjipuka still worked at the docks. Many of the women were moved to camps closer to the railway line that was pushing into the desert. Tjipuka thought maybe it was better there, away from the sea and the wet, cold nights, but at least they were together.

Tjirwe was moved to the railway camp, though. They heard little bits of news about him, but Lucinda was constantly anxious for her son. With Tjirwe gone, food was scarcer. Tjipuka didn't mind – food just prolonged everything. She wondered about her body, its inherent overpowering will to live. How could it be, when her heart was dead and her mind only wanted it all to end, that she still lived? How could her body be so deceptive?

When Saul died, living became the enemy. She no longer searched for memories to lighten her mind. Instead she pushed her mind to the worst. To Ruhapo dead, eaten by animals. To Mara bleeding into the sand. To Joseph hanging from the tree. To Saul dead next to her, his little body buried somewhere in the desert, cold and alone, lost to her forever.

That day as she marched out of the gate with the others, heading for the docks, one of the guards stopped her. He beckoned her to come to the side. The two guards who were normally there were joined by a tall man. He was so tall he hunched over to try to curtail his towering form. He had blond hair streaked with grey, hanging to his shoulders. Tjipuka suspected his face was older than the rest of him, which still looked strong and able. His face was lined deeply, his mouth slack as if it had given up trying to hide his disappointments. He was German, but not a soldier. She thought he might be a farmer or a shopkeeper.

'Is this the one?' the guard asked.

Tjipuka wondered what she had done now. The rules in the camp were fluid and you often broke them without knowing it. The tall, hunched German man nodded.

'Okay, it's ten marks per month,' the guard said. The tall man handed him sixty marks.

'For six months? Do you think that's wise? They're weak, she might not last, and we can't return your money,' the guard said, looking down at the cash.

The tall man nodded. He waited while the guard wrote out a receipt, took the money and put it in a cloth sack, then handed him the receipt with another paper.

'This is the permit if anyone troubles you. We will expect her back in six months or for you to come and pay again. Do you understand?'

The man nodded. The guard turned to her. 'You go with him now.'

Tjipuka followed the tall man. She saw Novengi and Lucinda down the road. She shouted after them in Otjiherero, 'Me kotoka mapeta', promising she'd be back that night.

The tall man, she found out, was called Ludwig Schmeller. He took her to his horse-drawn cart and helped her into the back. During the short ride to his shop he said little. He wanted her name; he gave her his. He explained, 'You will work at my shop. You must never step away from the shop. They say they'll shoot you if they see you out of the shop.'

As on most days for Tjipuka, none of it mattered.

The shop was not far, on a side street in town. There were no other workers there; she would be expected to help in the shop and in his house. He'd paid for that. He handed her a broom. 'You can sweep first.'

Tjipuka was glad to be out of the sun and the wind. This work was much easier than hauling the big crates from the ships to the docks. She cleaned the shop and stocked the shelves. Customers came and went. Ludwig served them and they ignored her – she was nothing, transparent, of no importance.

At lunch, he emptied a tin of beans on a plate and cut two thick slices of bread that he spread with jam. He put the plate before her. Tjipuka looked at it, but did nothing; she wasn't sure if all of the food was for her. She hadn't seen food like that for a long time.

'Eat,' he said and disappeared out the back door, leaving her in the shop alone.

She wrapped the bread in a bit of cloth and put it carefully in the pocket of her dress. Novengi and Lucinda would be happy for this when she went back to the camp. This job would bring more food for all of them. Tjipuka ate the beans quickly. It was so much food, but she finished it all, then wiped up the plate with her finger. She could not leave anything. She didn't know when she might get food like this again.

After lunch, Ludwig took her to his small house at the back of the shop. He handed her a broom. 'Clean this.' He pointed to a hut to the side. 'And that one.'

The house was very dirty, as if it hadn't been cleaned since it was built. There were dirty clothes and dishes everywhere. Tjipuka decided that Ludwig must live alone here. It took the whole afternoon to clean the house. But she didn't mind. It was work that kept her mind busy, and her stomach was full. She had the gift of food in her pocket. Lucinda had become much thinner since Tjirwe had left. She was always desperate to hear anything about him. She spent the time between bits of news worrying, and this was taking its toll on her. She feared for her hot-headed son and hoped he would take her advice and keep quiet and do his work. She could not bear the thought of him getting another beating, especially when she was not there to look after him. The bread would help her, Tjipuka hoped – it would lighten her mood.

When Tjipuka finished cleaning Ludwig's house, it was already dark. He came in and looked around. 'Thank you, you've done a good job. Time to rest now.'

She waited for him to take her back to the cart, to return her to the camp.

'You can go,' he said.

'Will we go in the cart?' she asked.

'Cart? No.' He pointed at the mud hut. 'You sleep there. You will not go back to the camp.'

She walked out the door to the hut. Inside it was empty except for a mattress on the floor. There was a pillow and a blanket. She couldn't remember the last time her head lain on a pillow. She sat down on the mattress, wishing Novengi could be there. Now Lucinda and Novengi would not have their bread. She wished Ludwig had chosen someone else, someone who cared about living.

She lay down, thinking about Novengi and Lucinda lying in the shelter, the wind howling, the waves bashing. Their stomachs empty. She cried for them and for herself. Now everything would be better for her, but not for them.

That first night she lay on her mattress feeling scared and lonely, and guilty for leaving Novengi behind. How could she be away from Novengi? It was only her and Novengi now. If only she could have got this job when Saul was still alive, maybe he might have been saved – but now it was for nothing. It had all come too late. She didn't want to live now; she ached only for death.

Tjipuka's days in the shop were routine – she cleaned and stocked shelves. Ludwig gave her soap to wash her dress and body. After some time, he taught her to cook for him, stews and German dishes that he liked. She ate what she cooked and gained some weight back.

One day he came to her hut with a suitcase. He stood for a bit and then he set the suitcase down. Looking slightly above Tjipuka's head, he said, 'Here, I think you can wear these.'

He left and Tjipuka opened the suitcase to find four dresses: two quite used, two nearly new. There were two petticoats, underwear and stockings. This was a suitcase packed by a woman going on a trip. But where was that woman now?

Tjipuka was shy to wear the dresses. A few days passed before she put one on, and then only the oldest one, a dress made of thick cotton, sun bleached and worn in places. She was working in the shop early before Ludwig arrived. When he entered, he looked at the dress. For a moment he stood, caught by it. Then he turned and went back out the door, saying nothing.

Sometimes the white people sent their servants to the shop. When they did, Ludwig let Tjipuka serve them. She got to know some of them quite well. She knew where they lived and how much freedom they had. There was one man, an older man, Peter, who was always friendly. He was a Berg Damara. Under other circumstances, before all of this, Peter would not think of speaking to Tjipuka, a Herero from a royal family, but now all of that was gone. Tjipuka liked Peter. He lived near the sea with an old woman, Mrs Joubert, an Afrikaner. Her husband was employed on a whaling boat and rarely around. Mrs Joubert trusted Peter and gave him a lot of freedom. Once Tjipuka knew this, she realised Peter was the exact person she needed.

'Wa penduka, Mama Tjipuka,' Peter said when he entered that day.

He handed her Mrs Joubert's list. Peter couldn't read, but Mrs Joubert told him what was on it and he forgot nothing. The fact that Tjipuka could read and write and do sums was an added benefit for Ludwig. She helped him more and more in the shop, preparing orders for stock, working on accounts. She was bright and picked things up quickly.

Tjipuka looked over the list. She pulled down a five-kilogram bag of sugar and put it in the box for Mrs Joubert. 'Peter, do you ever see the people at the camp … at Shark Island?'

She spoke in Otjiherero. Though she knew Ludwig was not like the other Germans, he was still a German and could not be trusted.

'Yes, I see them walking out there. Sitting on the ground, looking at the sea. Sad, those people, the way they suffer. Sometimes I see them working at the docks. I feel sad you once lived out there.'

'Peter, I wonder if you could do me a favour. I could pay you in some way, I'm not sure how, but I will find some way.'

Peter smiled. 'For a beautiful woman like you, I would walk on the sun.'

'My good friends are in the camp. They need food or they'll die. If I give you something, could you get it to them? Maybe when they're at the docks, offloading. That would be the easiest time I think. But it will be tricky. The soldiers watch everything – it might put you at risk. Maybe it's too much to ask of you …'

'Too much? You don't know me, Tjipuka. I have passed in front of those Schutztruppe so that they didn't even see me. Like a ghost, I am,' he boasted.

'A ghost? A ghost is just what I need.'

Peter smiled. They agreed that the next time Peter came, Tjipuka would have the parcel ready. She would give it to him in his box for Mrs Joubert and on his way home he would make sure Novengi received it. Tjipuka described her dear friend as best she could. She hadn't seen her for some weeks; she hoped the cruelty of the camp hadn't changed her too much. She hoped Peter would find her.

He did. From then on Peter was her messenger. Novengi wrote short notes, using bits of charcoal from the fire, on the wrappers of what Tjipuka had sent. One time, Tjipuka took a pad of paper and a pencil from Ludwig's desk where he did his accounts and put it into the parcel. With the paper and the pencil, Novengi's letters became longer.

Tjipuka was always anxious on the days Peter was meant to come. She lived for Novengi's letters. She rarely wrote about the camp – she seemed to want to ignore its very existence. Instead she wrote about the past. About when they were little girls, the games they used to play, the trouble they got into. She wrote about Kahaka and Ruhapo. She wrote about their weddings, about Saul and Maveipi. Novengi held tightly to the past now; there was nothing in the present she wanted to think about. It was painful for Tjipuka to read about Saul and Ruhapo, about Maveipi and Kahaka. She still felt her body ache when she thought of them dead, dead far from their home and their ancestors. Lost and never to be found again.

Tjipuka never read Novengi's letters straight away when they arrived. She hid them in her pocket to read later. She would sit in her tiny room and read them slowly by the light of her candle. She would laugh and then usually cry. She missed Novengi, but these letters were a link to her, a hand outstretched and touching hers in the night. Novengi was all she had now, and those letters were all that kept her alive.

28

Lüderitz, German South-West Africa
March 1906

'Tjipuka,' said Ludwig, 'please bring me the accounts book.'

She rushed to the back and returned with the red-covered book he used to keep track of his customers' credit. A white woman, Mrs von Hemmler, had come to pay her account. Tjipuka went back to dusting the shelves.

Mrs von Hemmler whispered loud enough for anyone to hear, 'She's quite beautiful for a black.'

Ludwig ignored her comment. 'It's forty-five marks.'

She gave him the money, he wrote a receipt, and she left. When they were alone again Ludwig said to Tjipuka, 'I'm sorry for that.'

Tjipuka looked at him. 'For what?'

'For what she said.'

For Tjipuka, Ludwig was a problem. A complication of emotions. She struggled to know how to think of him. He was mostly just made of sadness, like her. In Germany, he'd been told that German South-West Africa was heaven on earth, that there was money to be made for those willing to work hard. The government had given them many incentives to resettle here. Ludwig and his wife needed something new to live for. Their son, Rudolf, had died of measles at six years old. They thought that, by moving to Africa, so far away from their sorrow, things would be better – but they only got worse.

Now, after seven months had passed, Ludwig and Tjipuka ate their meals together. He didn't see the need for her to serve him at the small table in his house and then disappear to eat outside, sitting on the stoep. So they ate their meals together at the small wooden table in his house, he at one end, she at the other.

One evening he told her about his wife, the owner of Tjipuka's inherited dresses. 'She was much younger than me, my Anna. I took long to marry – I was too shy with women, they said. But Anna was kind and patient with me. I think she loved me, at least eventually. When Rudolf was sick, she took it very hard. She tried every tonic, every pill. She had priests in to pray for him. Nothing worked. He was too sick, too small. God, I think, wanted such a beautiful boy. When he died, my Anna, she nearly went with him. She became like a leaf in autumn, so fragile. I tried everything but I couldn't fix it. She wanted Rudolf back and this I couldn't do. I couldn't bring him back.

'So we left. We got on the boat and came to Africa. The change was already good for her. On the boat she was like herself again. It was easy to think differently because everything was different. I was sure we'd left all of the sadness behind in Germany. But then there was a sickness on the boat. I don't know what. Many got it. First a fever and then stomach aches, terrible stomach aches. Anna took the medicine, but still it was not enough. She died. Just like that, she was also gone. I went up on deck for a moment, I needed air, and when I came back, she was gone. Dying all alone in that small bed on that strange ship. They threw her in the water. All of them that died, they just dropped them in the sea. It's the way of the ship, they said. Sometimes this is what hurts me the most, her at the bottom, lying all alone. I wish it could have been some other way.'

'I'm sorry,' she said. If anyone understood loss it was her; it was all she was made up of now.

'Yes, well … And you?' he said that night, suddenly so talkative, so out of character. 'Do you not have a husband somewhere? Waiting for you to return when this war is over?'

'No,' Tjipuka said. 'They killed him.'

She never told Ludwig about Saul – at least not then. She mostly kept that locked away. And she thought, too, that if she told him, it would hurt him to know that if he had come for her a few weeks earlier, Saul might have been saved. She knew enough of this man to know this would add to the burden he already carried. He'd been kind to her, and she didn't want to make things worse for him. Also, this man was still German, still white. She needed to be careful despite his kindness. She kept her most precious thoughts for herself only. She would not let him in that deep.

One afternoon, she saw Peter coming towards the shop and her mood improved. She hadn't expected him that day, so she rushed to her house to prepare a package. She always had some food there for Novengi, just in case. She had some dried fish, a half jar of jam, some bread. She wrapped it up in a newspaper and put it into the wide pocket of her apron. She quickly finished the letter she'd been writing.

'Good afternoon,' Peter greeted Ludwig.

'Mrs Joubert is well then?' Ludwig asked.

'Yes, sir.'

'Good.' Ludwig disappeared into the storeroom when Tjipuka returned. Peter handed Tjipuka Mrs Joubert's list.

'I didn't expect you today.'

'Yes, it's special things she needs. Visitors from the Cape. And, too, there was a letter.' He said the last bit in Otjiherero.

'Is there a problem?'

'I think so,' Peter said.

Tjipuka quickly packed the items on the list and slipped in her parcel. Peter took the box and slid the letter from Novengi into her hand. She pushed it into her apron pocket.

Peter left, but she could not wait until the evening to read the letter. She needed to know what the problem was.

'I need to start the dinner,' she called to Ludwig in the storeroom. He came out. 'All right,' he said.

She disappeared to the outdoor kitchen, where she put a pot of water on the fire and sat down on the small stool to read Novengi's letter.

My dear Tjipuka,

We have had problems here. I do not want to burden you with such things but I believe you would want to know. I am very sorry to say that Tjirwe is dead. The soldier who beat him returned. We have heard only in bits and pieces but it seems he spotted Tjirwe the first day he came back to the railway site. He went out of his way to make trouble for our Tjirwe. He gave him work he could not perform so he had reason to beat him, and beat him he did. Tjirwe took it like the man that he has been forced to become, until it was too much. He did exactly what this Kurtis man wanted. He turned on him. He grabbed the sjambok from the soldier's hand and the soldier pulled out his gun and shot him.

It has been a terrible shock for Lucinda. I do not think she will last, Tjipuka. Her heart is broken beyond repair and her body will soon follow. Please pray for her, pray she finds the strength to live. I'm not sure how I will continue here all alone.

Please, I tell you this only so that you will know. Do not carry the burden in your heart, my darling. You have enough there already. You are helping us so much with the food you send by dear Peter. Please keep yourself well.

Your loving sister,
Novengi

Tjipuka put the letter in her pocket. She thought of Tjirwe and how he had loved Saul. How he'd tried to teach him to walk. How he'd cried when Saul died. He was going to be a good man, a kind, good man and a caring father, if only they had given him the chance to grow up. She thought of Lucinda and the pain she must be carrying. She let her head fall into her hands and she cried, she didn't know for how long. But she cried until the tears were finished. When she looked up, there stood Ludwig. She didn't know how long he'd been there. How much he had seen.

'You've had sad news?' he asked.

'Do you care?' she snapped.

Ludwig stood in place, looking at her. 'You blame me for everything here that is wrong in your country. You should. My countrymen have done wrong. Much wrong.'

He was hurt, Tjipuka could see that. 'No … I don't blame you. Not really. You're one of them, yes, but you don't want this, I know that. I'm just so very tired of all of this, this sadness, the endless, unrelenting sadness of all of this, of this living.'

He waited. 'There's a problem?'

'Yes, my friend … my friend in the camp.'

'Can I help?'

Tjipuka didn't care any more. She didn't care about hiding the food and the letters. If he beat her or sent her back to the camp, it was fine. She needed to see Novengi and Lucinda.

'Can you take me to the camp? Will they allow it? Just for a short time?'

'Yes,' he said. 'I think I can sort something out.'

Ludwig got the cart and the horses. It was just getting dark as they headed towards Shark Island. The place was separate from the town, like another country. As the wagon neared the camp, the temperature dipped and the wind picked up as though they were entering another land altogether. At the soldiers' camp, Ludwig spoke to the guards in German. Tjipuka saw him hand them some tobacco and a bottle of whiskey, which she hadn't seen him take from the shop. She was surprised to see he understood how to negotiate such interactions – to her he often seemed naive about the ways of the world beyond the shop.

At the camp gate, there were two more guards. Again Ludwig spoke to them for some time. They laughed together. Ludwig gave them another bottle of whiskey and a pouch of tobacco. He gave them some money too, and then he came back to the wagon.

'They'll let you in. But not for long. I'll wait here.' He handed her a bag. There were blankets and food inside; she wondered when he had organised that.

'You're a good man, Ludwig.'

Tjipuka ran through the open gate, rushing through the shelters to the spot where they had all stayed. She stopped when she got there. A woman stooped at the fire. Her dress was worn thin. On her shoulders there were holes, her sharp bones poking through. Her face was skeletal; the skin lay in folds, battered from the sun and wind, the lines of loss etched as if that was all this woman had ever known. A familiar face, but different too. This was not her brave, fearless Novengi – it was someone else, an old, tired woman. Tjipuka could see that Novengi had lost all hope. She couldn't stop the cry that escaped her.

Novengi looked up. 'Is it you?'

'It is me.'

They stood looking at each other. There was a solidness between them they couldn't get past, like strangers meeting. Tjipuka was filled with guilt, guilt that she was living with Ludwig while Novengi was left here, left in this place of death and suffering.

'You look so beautiful, nearly like yourself,' Novengi said. 'You look as if nothing has happened.'

It was a condemnation – at least that was how Tjipuka heard it. 'I'm sorry. I … it's terrible and so unfair. I should refuse to go back. I need to stay here with you.'

'No! Never say that! I don't want you here. The only thing that lets me survive is knowing you are there. That you are safe. That you will live.' She stepped away from Tjipuka.

'But I don't want to live, not without you.'

'You must live. You promised me that we will have a big farm with many cattle. You must live and I will live too and one day we'll be together. Happy and healthy and together again,' Novengi said. 'Don't take it away from me. That thought allows me to get through each hour, each day.'

Tjipuka pulled Novengi's thin body into her arms. She clung to her. She never wanted to be apart from her again. Novengi embraced her back, but without strength.

Tjipuka pulled out a blanket from the bag Ludwig had given her and wrapped it around her friend's thin shoulders. She wrapped her up against the cold; it was nothing, but it was all she could do.

'Where's Lucinda?'

'She's inside.'

Tjipuka ducked into the dark shelter. If she'd thought Novengi was thin and wasted, Lucinda was even worse. She breathed with effort.

Tjipuka sat next to her, taking the woman's hand in hers. 'Lucinda?'

'Is it you, Tjipuka? Do you know our boy has died? That they have finally killed him?' She began to wail, a low groan that shook her emaciated body and used up its small reserves of energy.

'Yes, I know, I know about this terrible sadness they have brought onto us. You must rest, though. I brought more food. You must eat. You need to get better. We'll soon be through with all of this. You remember the farm we spoke about? We'll go there, you and Novengi and me. We'll be happy. We'll keep cows again, and drink milk. We'll find a way to be happy again. We must just get through all of this. You must live, Tjirwe would want that. You must live for him, Lucinda.'

Tjipuka left the tent. Despite her words, she knew Lucinda would not last much longer, a few hours, maybe a day. She had learned how to recognise death when it had its hold on a person. She went to Novengi.

They sat quietly at the fire holding hands. They both knew Lucinda would not survive. 'I can't stay,' Tjipuka said, after a while. 'The man, he's waiting. How will you manage?'

Novengi smiled, and in there was a hint of the person Tjipuka knew. 'I'll be fine. Don't worry. This place won't break me. We have plans, you and I. We're going to have that farm. When this is over, I'll be waiting for you. We'll go home together. I promise I'll live for you. I promise, on the other side of all of this, we'll be together. Do you make the same promise to me?'

'You know that I do.'

Tjipuka held her. She knew Ludwig was waiting and she didn't want to abuse his kindness, but she couldn't let go just yet. 'I will send more with Peter. You must eat everything. Please, you must take care of yourself,' she begged her.

Tjipuka walked away without looking back, willing her legs to press forward. She climbed into the cart. Ludwig asked, 'Is everything all right?'

Tjipuka nodded. 'Thank you,' she said.

He flicked the reins and they headed home.

29

Lüderitz, German South-West Africa
March 1906

The days passed in a blur of routine. Tjipuka swept floors, cooked meals, hid away food for Novengi, waited for Peter, read and cherished Novengi's letters. This was life now; it was how it was. Tjipuka began to accept, and she began to forget, and this she was most afraid of.

As time passed, Tjipuka didn't notice that the memories of Ruhapo and Saul, and the sadness that covered her, slowly shrank. The sadness did not grip her as if she was living in its bondage. It came and went, and in between she lived. When she remembered, she felt guilt for the times she didn't ache from missing them. She would spend the day imagining Ruhapo's body, bloody and torn, in the bush at Ohamakari. She would see him unburied. Imagine animals chewing him, carrying off pieces. The worms and flies finishing what was left of his beautiful, strong body. Now it was just a spot of sand, maybe darker, that no one knew meant a person had died there. She forced herself to see everything, to feel the ache of the loss anew.

She looked at mind pictures of Saul's small body, covered in rash. Limp and finished. She saw Tjirwe placing his tiny corpse in the wagon with the other dead bodies. She reminded herself that she would never know where they took him, where they buried him. Her son was lost in the desert.

She felt guilty that she must do that, that she must search for the pain and put it back in its rightful place, that she had to remember that her husband and son were dead. It was wrong to forget the sadness, to laugh at Peter's jokes, to enjoy listening to one of Ludwig's stories. To eat well, to sleep soundly, to hear birdsong, to turn her cheek to a cool breeze and welcome it. It was wrong for her to live while they died, while Novengi suffered at the camp. But she did. She lived, despite her inner protests.

She was always in the shop before Ludwig. It was still her way to wake before the sun. She made tea and sat on the stoep to watch the day begin. Then she swept her house and the small bit of yard in front of it and opened the shop. By the time Ludwig arrived, the shop was tidy and ready.

'Good morning, Tjipuka,' he said when he arrived. He was never talkative, but in the morning even less so, speaking only when customers forced him to. Tjipuka knew this and tried to attend to as many customers as would allow. Most didn't mind, but a few would not be served by a black woman. Tjipuka knew them by now so she never tried. She made herself busy elsewhere and let Ludwig attend to them.

Tjipuka rarely left the yard that contained the shop and the houses. She did not ask to go to Novengi again. Ludwig made it clear that they had taken a very big risk that evening. The guards he had bribed could turn on him at any time. They could tell the authorities. He might lose the right to have her help at the shop. He could go to prison himself, and then what would they do? He did not say it out loud, but he didn't want her to go back to Shark Island.

He told her it was against the terms of the agreement he had with the government for her to leave the shop premises. She knew this was not true. Peter told her that many of the prisoners from Shark Island who worked for companies moved around Lüderitz. But even Peter admitted it was often difficult for the prisoners, especially women. Lüderitz was a rough place. It was mostly men – men who had arrived from the war in the south, new settlers from Germany, miners heading inland to find their fortunes. The women were few. Occasionally a group of white women would arrive, sent from Germany, wives for men they'd never met. There were a few white women at the bar, who would assist the men with their needs for a price. But mostly the men were rough and would grab what they wanted. A passing black wom an was not safe. She would have no chance to file a case against a white man. The men knew this, so they were free to do what they liked. Ludwig told her it was forbidden for her to walk around Lüderitz, but she knew he was lying. He was trying to keep her safe.

Oddly enough, Tjipuka used her free time to sew, something she'd always despised. She learned to make her own dresses, which she never had to do before. She made a dress for Novengi from material Ludwig had given her to make a dress for herself. She cut carefully and managed to make two dresses out of it. She sent Novengi's at the bottom of Mrs Joubert's groceries. She wondered if it would fit properly. She wondered what it looked like on her.

Between customers and other work in the shop, she began working on a quilt using old bits of material and offcuts. She'd never made a quilt before – it was an ambitious project, but she enjoyed the challenge. A young German woman, Marietta, one of the regular customers, loved quilting and often gave Tjipuka pointers on how to improve. Two weeks earlier, she'd come in with a large sack of leftover material for her.

'Here, I thought these might help. I have so much. I'll never use it all.'

Tjipuka went through the sack. There were some lovely pieces in there, as well as a complete roll of lace. 'And this?' Tjipuka said, holding the lace up. 'Have you forgotten it?'

'No, you keep it. My mother sends me new rolls with every shipment.'

'Thank you.'

'You might use the lace as a border. I see you're nearly done with that one,' Marietta suggested.

Tjipuka spread the quilt out in front of her to have a look. Marietta was right, it was nearly finished. She imagined the border of lace and smiled. 'Yes, it will make it very nice.'

Marietta often lingered in the shop, talking about this and that with Tjipuka. She rarely spoke to Ludwig; she seemed scared of him. She was young, not yet twenty, Tjipuka suspected. She'd been sent to marry here, in one of the shipments from Germany. Tjipuka saw Marietta's husband only once. He was old, older than Ludwig, and very dirty. He owned an import company in town and, though a businessman, wore the same caked dungarees every day. He smelled horrible. Tjipuka thought that if she were Marietta she would leave him. There were many men who would marry her and pay off the money her husband had used to bring her to German South-West Africa. She didn't need to stay with him. She was white and she had choices, but she seemed blind to them, afraid to make a move, in a prison as secure as any other.

Tjipuka held the quilt and the lace out to Marietta. 'Can you show me how it's attached?'

Marietta took the quilt from her and explained how the lace could be added. After about an hour, she looked up at the clock. 'Oh, I need to go,' she said, gathering together her parcels. 'Tjipuka, let me know how you manage.'

It was a slow day in the shop, and by the time they closed, the quilt was almost finished. Tjipuka took it to her house and then went to cook dinner for her and Ludwig. They sat at the table and ate quietly. Ludwig spoke about a shipment that might arrive the next day. Tjipuka said how nice it was of Marietta to give her the sack of cloth.

She cleaned up the table and washed the dishes at the outside tap, then stacked them in the cupboards inside and went to her house. She finished the last bit of the quilt and spread it out to look at her work. She was pleased with it. Though the pattern was not perfect, the lace made it look smartly finished. She folded it carefully and carried it out the door.

She knocked on Ludwig's door. She never came to his house at night – once dinner was over and cleaned up, she felt she had no right to enter. So she knocked and waited.

He opened the door with his reading glasses perched on his nose. 'Tjipuka?' he asked, an edge of concern in his voice. 'Are you all right?'

'Yes. I finished the quilt.'

'That's nice.' He stood awkwardly, not knowing what he was meant to do. He was like that, not good with any human interactions that were not routine.

Tjipuka pushed the quilt towards him. 'It's yours … I want you to have it.'

'All right.' He stood looking at her, still not sure what to do. He made no effort to take it from her hands.

'Shall I put it on your bed?' Tjipuka suggested.

He moved aside. The lamp near the chair was on and a book was hanging over the arm. She walked in and crossed the main room. She opened the door to his bedroom. It was dark, but she knew her way around and soon her eyes adjusted. She spread the quilt out over the bed. It was a little long. Ludwig came into the room with a lamp and set it on the high dresser in the corner. They both stood looking at the quilt.

'It's lovely. It's very kind of you to give me such a beautiful thing. You've worked so hard on it.'

'You've been good to me. Besides, your bed was so bare.' She looked up at him and smiled. She had been hoping to pay him back in some way for all he had done for her.

Ludwig's face changed. 'Tjipuka, you're a very kind woman. You are good and kind. And intelligent. I don't think everything is right that's happening to you. You don't deserve to be in the camp, or even here. It's wrong.'

Ludwig made the world very confusing for her. It was much easier to hate. To hate in a solid block with no exceptions. To think of the Germans as evil, not human. But Ludwig was German and he was not evil. He was just a man trying to get through his life without harming others. A person trying to find some happiness, just like her.

'I like you very much,' Ludwig tried. 'I know you think you have no choices, here in this place ... but I cannot do that. I will not. I know it's not right. Not like the others. But I'm thankful for this quilt ... and for you. I'm happy now that you live here, that you help me. I hope you know this. You've made my life good.'

'You saved me. You're letting me save my friend Novengi. You're a good man, Ludwig.'

He took her hand, slowly, as if he feared she would snatch it back. He brought it to his lips and kissed it. It was so reverent, a kiss of worship. The kindness of it caught Tjipuka by surprise. Tears filled her eyes. He reached forward and wiped away one that had slipped out and was running down her cheek. She held his hand against her face. She'd forgotten how good tenderness felt.

He pulled her to him and pressed his lips to hers. Then he stopped and pushed her away, suddenly embarrassed.

'I'm wrong. I'm sorry. Please, Tjipuka, I'm sorry. I won't do that. I promise. I don't want to be like that. I'm wrong.'

'No,' Tjipuka said. 'You're not wrong.'

She moved close to him and wrapped her arms around his neck. She kissed him. She would not think now. She only wanted to feel. To be free of the world. To be lost in her physical needs, in his. To live only in that room where nothing was judged and everything was right. Where two broken people tried to find relief, if only for a few moments.

He scooped her up in his big arms and carried her to his bed. On the quilt she had made him, they made an awkward, too-conscious kind of love. Neither thought of the implications, of the past they carried without choice, the future that would weigh heavily on them. They thought only of that moment and, for both of them, that moment was everything.

30

Lüderitz, German South-West Africa
August 1907

'Watch everything, I'll be back tomorrow,' Ludwig said as he left.

'Everything will be fine. Don't worry.' Tjipuka handed him a pail with his food inside. He climbed into the wagon and headed down the road. As she watched him leave, she realised she would miss him when he was gone, a thought that surprised her. She went into the shop, pulled up the blinds and propped the door open with a brick. Then she opened the accounts books to finish the bookkeeping from the day before.

'I see your master has gone.'

She looked up and there was Peter.

'Yes, until tomorrow.' She reached her hand out for his list.

He didn't hand it to her. 'You could leave.'

The words hit her. She could leave. Was it true that she'd never even considered that? This was not the first time Ludwig had left her alone, but she'd never once thought *I could leave*. Why? Was she not a prisoner? Had the guard not left his post? What prisoner doesn't dream of escaping? What had happened to her?

She thought about Ludwig. Was he her guard? Yes, but he had also become her life. They never spoke about what they did in the night, they never said, 'We are like husband and wife' – but they were. Except no one could know. She could never tell Peter. She knew what he would think of her. She knew what everyone would think of her.

'I can't ... Novengi ... What about Novengi? I can't leave her.'

Peter raised his eyebrows. 'Is it really about Novengi?'

'What do you mean?' she said. 'You think you know everything, but you know nothing!'

'I know that your master is not just your master.'

She covered her ears. She would not listen to this. Peter could not know. 'Shut up! You know nothing.'

He yanked her hands from her ears. 'Don't you see? You have lost everything. You lost your husband, your son, and now you have lost your dignity, your self-respect. You can't even see yourself as a free woman. You're a slave in your mind. You're a prisoner in your mind. You *can* go. I'll take care of Novengi. You need to go.'

'You are no better. You could run. Any day you could run, but you don't.' She tore her hands away from him. 'Why do you come here and say such things? Who are you to judge? Who?'

Peter looked at her, his face solemn. 'I'm the one to judge, because I know you. I know you because I am who you will become. I can't even imagine freedom, even in my dreams. I'm old now, and where would I run to? I was a slave to the Nama, to the Herero before, now I'm a slave to the whites. What difference does it make who owns me? I'm a slave in my mind even when I'm all alone. But you, you know freedom. How do you stay in chains when you know freedom?'

She slumped onto the stool behind the counter. He was right and she knew this. But what did she have? Everything was gone. She only had Novengi – and Ludwig. She didn't love him, she reminded herself. She couldn't, he was one of them; no matter what, he was one of them. But she cared for him; there was relief with him. Brief moments of kindness. She had nothing else, so their time together appeared larger than it should. Life, reduced to such a sliver, offered only morsels, but those morsels were cherished. It was all a crazy trick of the mind, a mechanism for survival.

'I'm going to wait for Novengi. They talk of closing all of the camps … the war is over, they say. I'm going to leave this place with Novengi.' She was grappling for reasons not to go and it made her sick to hear herself.

'They'll never close Shark Island. They need the workers. They'll not close it until the railway line is complete and that will be more than a year. Will you wait until then? You must take your chance when it's offered. Today a chance is being offered. When Novengi is free, I'll tell her where you've gone. But today you must go.'

Peter enraged her, but who was she really angry at?

The day passed. Customers came and went. In between Tjipuka sewed in the corner, mending Ludwig's shirts. She was becoming a good seamstress. Some of the customers brought their mending jobs to her and paid her for them. Ludwig let her keep the money. It was quite a bit already. She thought how it would help her and Novengi to start their farm. They'd buy their first cattle with the money.

At closing time, she locked the front door and pulled down the blinds. She counted the money and filled in the accounts book. When she was finished, she sat in the dark shop. She looked around. So would this be her life forever? What would happen if Shark Island closed? Would Ludwig allow her to leave with Novengi? *Would he?* She knew the answer and that decided it.

She stood up. She took off the metal tag they'd told her always to wear at Shark Island. She took it off and left it on the counter – a free woman did not have a number, she had a name. She took all of the money from the day's sales and put it in her pocket. She collected her few belongings from her room, and the money she'd saved from sewing. Then she packed food and water and walked out the gate.

As quickly as possible, she left the main road and headed east into the desert. The desert she realised she knew now. She'd been so scared of it the first time, but now she found that she welcomed it. She would follow the cattle trails; she knew how to do that now. They would lead her to watering spots. She would walk east until she got to Bechuana-land. And this time she would make it.

At first she was scared. She'd never been all alone in the desert like this. She'd always been with Novengi. But she tried to remember how she was when she was a girl, when she was too naive to consider that anything could harm her, before she knew the truth of things. Instead of being afraid, she thought how she used to see the open places, the bush and the mountains, as places of freedom, not places of fear.

By the second day, she felt light with her plan. She'd not known the walls of her cell had been so oppressive. She could not get enough of the open space ahead of her. She slept under the stars and imagined the wide expanse of the universe. The wide world was so open and excit-ing, full of a million possibilities. She could travel it all, she thought. She could just keep moving forever. The world was endless and she was free to see and feel it all.

The cage that had held her had been in place before Ludwig, before the scattering, she realised. Maybe she would buy a horse and ride to the Cape, or to the Nile River or to the huge Lake Victoria. Maybe she would build a house in the valley Ruhapo made for her. She would search for it and find the lake and the waterfall and build a house in one of the tall trees, surrounded by butterflies and bees. Novengi would find her there, living in the trees like a flying thing. Anything was possible now.

On the fourth night, as a light breeze blew across the sand, she woke up with a start. Two men stood over her with guns. 'Get up,' one said.

The other one tied her hands behind her back and threw her up into the wagon. They collected her things and threw them into the wagon too. She lay still, not fighting. She knew where she was going; it was Ludwig's wagon. He had sent them for her. Her freedom had come to an end.

They took her back to Lüderitz. They took her back to the shop, back to Ludwig. Back to her prison.

When they arrived, Ludwig paid the men and they left. Tjipuka stood looking at him. His face, normally soft with sadness, was suddenly hard.

'I thought you were different,' he said. 'Lie down.'

She lay on the bare concrete floor of the shop without a word. She felt the first blow as it hit her back, but then her mind closed down. As Ludwig slammed the sjambok down on her back, she waited. She neither screamed nor fought it. He hit her once and then twice. Then he stopped. She sat up and watched him. He sat on the chair, his arms limp at his sides, the sjambok fallen to the floor. She feared she might be sick – the pain on her back pulsed like a burning fire – but she held herself firm.

'Why?' he said after some time. 'I thought we were fine. I thought you were happy, that you liked this place. Why would you escape? I have been good to you. Why run away from me?'

How could he not understand? She was in chains and always would be if she stayed with him.

She said nothing. She stood up and walked to her room, ignoring the pain. Once there she fell to the bed, and the world turned dark and cold and very, very small again.

31
Lüderitz, German South-West Africa
August 1907

They never went back to how it was before her escape. There were no more discussions. There was no trust between them – Ludwig watched her all the time. They still had sex, but it was different. It was only in her room, never in his bedroom with the quilt any more. He would enter her room without knocking, asserting who owned it, who owned everything. He would get undressed and get into the bed without a word. He would enter her until he was satisfied, and then he would dress and disappear. There was no kindness. It was a physical release, nothing more.

He began counting everything. It was becoming difficult to find food to send to Novengi. Often all she could give Peter were leftover table scraps, sometimes days old. She ate less so that Novengi might have more. But what Ludwig didn't know was that the more he made the shop a prison, the more she wanted to get away, the more she dreamed of her nights alone under the stars, the massive world calling to her. Next time she would be smarter. Next time she would not be caught.

One evening, at dinner, Ludwig said, 'I need to go. I have a friend, he has some elephant tusks for me. I can make big money from those. But it's a long trip, over the border. You'll have to come with me – I can't trust you here alone.'

Tjipuka nodded. She barely spoke to him any more.

On the day set aside for travelling, they packed the wagon and closed the shop. They would be gone for nearly a month. Tjipuka was finally going to Bechuanaland, but not the way she had thought she would. She would watch carefully. The first opening, she would make her escape. Her heart beat with excitement – she knew she was going to be free soon.

'I'll try again,' she told Peter in Otjiherero. 'If I don't return, know I was successful. Know I'm in Bechuanaland, I'm free and I'm happy.'

'I'll pray that you're successful. I'll pray every day. Tjipuka, I know that your time of sadness is over. Your future is there. You'll make a new life. You'll find much happiness there. You'll finally be free again.'

'And Novengi? Will you tell Novengi?' she asked.

'Yes, I'll tell her. If you don't return, I'll tell her you're in Bechuanaland. When they set her free, she'll come to you. I'll tell her she must go and find you in that place.'

They left Lüderitz and its cold, wet air, and entered the dry, hot Namib. They were heading to Tjipuka's freedom, she could feel it. She took the new air of freedom into her lungs and let it move to all parts of her body. She wanted to remind herself that she was not born to be a slave, born to cower. She was born to be free. She watched carefully for her opportunity. There would be a chance, and she would take it, and this time no one would stop her.

Tsau, Bechuanaland

32

September 1907

Each day they travelled eastward, each night they stopped and set up camp. During the day, Ludwig watched Tjipuka. At night, he bound them together with leg irons, one on his leg, one on hers. Though it seemed impossible with his vigilance, she was certain she would not return to Lüderitz.

Finally they were near the border. She knew about this area; they were near Gobabis, the place where Ruhapo had grown up. The grass was high, though it was only the beginning of the rainy season. It looked as if the rains had been good so far.

They passed farms named Paradies and Der Himmel auf Erden. Large areas, once range for the herds of cattle owned by the Herero, were now farms owned by single German families. There were fields ploughed with maize, potatoes and beans. There were herds of cattle fenced in by barbed wire. Not the long-horned red cattle that the Herero loved, but other breeds. The bulky grey Brahmin, the black-and-white Holstein.

This land had been for Ruhapo and his father and the Herero who had lived there, but that was only a story now. A tale to tell at the fire.

All of it was gone and likely never to return. The land now belonged to the family stories of the Germans who lived there.

'We'll cross the border tomorrow,' Ludwig said. 'It was not easy for me to get permission. I had to sign many papers, pay a lot of money. They don't want you people leaving the country.'

'You could have left me if it was so difficult,' she said. She was tired of holding her words in her mouth.

'And you run again? I'd rather take you with me, even if it's with so many difficulties.'

They camped that night. Ludwig shot a springbok. Tjipuka cooked some of it and the rest she prepared for drying on the wagon, to be eaten when meat was scarce.

'This is good. You've learned to cook almost as well as my wife,' Ludwig said.

'So? Is that your plan? To make me into another wife? Another Anna? A black Anna?' She knew her words bit him. Ludwig looked at the fire and remained silent. 'I can never be your wife. You must take that from your mind. I'm your slave, nothing more. Anything I do, I do because I have no choice. You're my master, I'm your slave, held captive by you.'

She got up and headed for the tent. He grabbed her arm. 'You're lying. I know you're lying. What about the quilt? You didn't think of me that way always. You liked me then. You lie to punish me. But it's not true. I know that.'

She looked at him. He was so vulnerable just then – she could have slashed him open with her words, but she didn't. Instead she retreated. He let go and she turned to the tent. Once inside, she lay on her mat. She shook from emotions too strong to understand. She closed her eyes; she tried to close her mind too. She didn't want to think these feelings through. Just let them be, she told herself. Just let them be.

They crossed into Bechuanaland just as the sun set. For all of the dreams she'd had about what her place of refuge would look like, the country looked very similar to Hereroland. It was only starting to green up, still brown and dusty from winter. There were scattered low thorn trees and tall dry grass.

'Who's the woman?' the Bechuanaland policeman said, pointing at Tjipuka.

'She's my servant. I have permission.' Ludwig took out papers from his satchel and shoved them at the man. 'We'll only go and come back. It's business.'

The white British border officer came over to the wagon to see what the border policeman was doing.

'Good evening, sir,' he said to Ludwig.

'Good evening.'

He stared at Tjipuka, who sat on the long seat next to Ludwig. She knew what he thought: she should be at the back with the goods, not up front next to her master. She looked him in the face; he was nothing to her. He would not force her to the place where he wanted her. She would not lower her eyes, not any more.

'So you come from the coast?'

'Yes.' Ludwig was uncomfortable speaking in English.

'You'll be sure you take her back with you. We've had enough of your kaffirs this side.'

'Yes, sir,' Ludwig said.

They drove through the makeshift border and turned north as the sun set. After a while, they stopped at a watering hole. 'We'll camp here,' Ludwig said.

He outspanned the horses and led them to the water. Tjipuka made a fire and unpacked the tent and what they needed for the night. Though this place looked similar to Hereroland, it felt different. They'd passed many people on the way, passed through small settlements, and in all cases the people were black. The settlements were traditional, no cement-and-brick buildings, just mud huts built in clusters, each surrounded by a low mud wall, the ground around swept clean.

The only white person she saw was the border officer. The black people ran this country. She saw them in their fields, planting, herding their animals. If the British were here in this place, she thought, they were all in one place, or barely here at all. She wondered if the people here were aware of how lucky they were to not have the whites clamouring for all they had – for their cattle, their land, their people.

'I'll see what I can find for dinner,' Ludwig said.

Ludwig spoke only when he needed to now. As the trip had progressed, he'd moved further and further from her. He'd been hurt by her words the night before. But he did not go far from the wagon in search of food – he needed to keep an eye on her. She watched him move carefully in the bush. Two shots and he was back with a hare.

She made tea while Ludwig skinned and gutted the hare. He made a spit and put it through the animal and placed it on the fire. Tjipuka handed him his tea and he sat on the stool next to her. Every few minutes he turned the spit. Darkness fell. It was a cloudy night so the stars were missing. The moon had not yet risen and outside the ring of light from the fire there was nothing but solid black.

'My son used to like rabbit,' Ludwig said.

'You hardly ever speak about him.'

'Yes, but I'm always thinking about him.'

Tjipuka understood this. Saul lived constantly in her mind too. 'Did he ever hunt with you?'

'He was young still. Anna wouldn't let him. She'd agreed that when he was eight he could go with me, but that never happened.'

They sat quietly. Tjipuka heard movement in the bush. She told herself it was cattle. She heard the deep rumble of a lion far off. She inched closer to the fire. Ludwig touched his gun to remember where he had laid it.

'I wonder what kind of man he was going to be, my Rudolf. This is what I wonder most of the time. Was he going to be good? Or weak? Or too soft? It's all gone now, never to be known.'

Ludwig picked at the fire with a stick, speaking low, almost to himself. The solid dark outside the circle of firelight created a safe space, where what came before did not exist. Tjipuka felt it too.

'I'm sure he was going to be good,' Tjipuka said, speaking of both Rudolf and Saul.

'Yes, I think he was too. He was so brave and good when he was sick, hardly complained at all. He once told his mother not to worry, he would be better soon. That's a sign of a boy with a good heart. Don't you think?'

'Yes, I do.'

The lion roared, now closer. Ludwig turned his head to find the direction the sound came from.

'Will you go home to Germany?' she asked.

He sat quietly. Moments passed and he turned the hare sizzling on the fire. 'I don't know. Maybe. What's home? Nothing is there really.'

'But nothing's here for you either.'

Ludwig looked at her, his eyes soft with emotion. 'You're here.'

'No. I'm not.' She pushed an ember back in place with the point of her shoe. The intimacy the darkness had allowed disappeared with her words.

'Yes, I suppose you're right.'

He got up and walked into the bush. His gun sat at the fire still. She could pick it up. She could wait for him and shoot him dead, take everything. The wagon was loaded with things to trade at the place where they were going. She would be rich to start her new life.

She looked at the gun. Did she really want freedom? It was right there, she told herself. She reached forward, but instead of taking the gun, she turned the hare.

She knew what stopped her. Despite all her efforts to feel otherwise, she cared about Ludwig. She wondered if she would be able to leave him when she finally got her chance. She'd promised Peter she would not return. She could take the gun and run into the bush. But she wouldn't. She knew she was no longer mentally a slave, but she knew too that she could not run. Not tonight at least.

Then what future did she have? To stay with Ludwig and live a secret life with him? No one would allow a white husband and a black wife. She had seen such things – on all sides the couple was looked down upon. No one accepted them.

And what about the children of such unions? They were not wanted anywhere. They would not be protected by the ancestors. They could not go to the sacred fire; they could not drink the sacred milk. How would they live? Who would guide them? They were lost children.

Tjipuka heard the lion again. Was it coming nearer? Where was Ludwig? She could no longer hear him – he must have walked far. But he knew this place, so she hoped he would take care.

She lay down at the fire and waited for him. She soon fell asleep and dreamed about Saul. He was in heaven, playing with a thin, blond-haired boy. She knew it was Rudolf. They were running and jumping and rolling in the deep grass. In heaven it was like that, she thought. She woke up happy.

Ludwig was sitting next to her. 'You said a name in your sleep. You said the name Saul.'

'Did I?' Tjipuka sat up. 'Saul is my son. He died in the camp. They were together, he and Rudolf, in my dream. Do you think it can be that way? Do you think they're together, happy, in heaven?'

'Maybe. I don't know. I'm not sure I believe in all of that any more. God and heaven. I think maybe it was a story they told us so we could fall asleep at night.' He moved the hare to the side of the fire. 'It's done. Do you want to eat?'

She sat up and watched him slice the meat off the bones. He handed her a plate and they ate in silence.

'There was a lion … I was afraid for you,' she said.

'They sound closer than they are. I've travelled this place before. There're many animals. Elephants too. Buffalo are the worst. They're very dangerous.' He stopped eating. 'I understand this place a bit. I'm not foolish. I know you're staying with me because you must, not because you want to. That place, Lüderitz … in fact the whole country there, it's difficult. I know we can't be married properly. But here, maybe it's different here. I've seen couples here. It's not like there. We could stay here. I could find land, make a new shop. Be a farmer.' His face was so hopeful. 'What do we have, you and me? We're alone now. We know what this life can do. It's vicious and cruel. But you and I, sometimes … at least before … sometimes before, we had kindness together, and that's good. It's enough, kindness.'

'I have Novengi.'

Tjipuka was afraid of his words. She wanted to run away from them. The words sounded so comforting, so easy to fall into. She could choose that life, she knew she could, but she shouldn't. It would be a settling for something less than she should. She knew now that, in life, the choices were not few but could be endless if a person wanted, if a person was brave enough. She'd learned that alone in the desert. She knew it now and wasn't sure she could accept a compromised life, no matter how easy it was.

'We could go back. I could pay for Novengi. Once we have her, we could take everything and come here. All of us.' There was desperation in his voice and she was afraid for him. He was laying himself too bare for her, he was too hopeful. For the first time, she thought he might not survive when she left him. He would disappear back into himself, the way she'd found him those first days.

She was not sure if she nodded. Or if she spoke. She was not sure if she agreed to anything – she suspected she had in some way, maybe out of pity, maybe out of fear. Maybe out of kindness. Ludwig went to her. He kissed her the way he had before she had run away. He pulled her onto his lap. He held her tightly and he rocked her in his arms. She felt safe there, and safe was what she wanted that night.

The moon had risen, half hidden by a cloud; the land glowed blue around them, the air smelled of cooked hare and dust, and a lion roared in the distance.

33

September 1907

They had been travelling through Bechuanaland since morning and Tjipuka was dusty and tired. As they entered the village, there was a big camel thorn tree to the right, encircled by a large wall of thick branches stuck into the ground to form an enclosure. She guessed it was a kraal of some sort. A Herero woman walked along the road with a baby tied to her back. Tjipuka greeted her and she spoke back in Otjiherero. Hearing her language spoken so far from home thrilled Tjipuka's heart. The words seemed to confirm something in her.

'What's the name of this place?' Tjipuka asked Ludwig.

'Tsau. This is where we'll meet the man with the elephant tusks.'

Tsau was where Samuel Maharero was, and the other chiefs. All of them had come here, the survivors who followed him. And now she was here too. It seemed right to have finally arrived.

Ludwig stopped the ox wagon at the odd kraal with the camel thorn tree.

'You wait here. I must speak with the chief, let him know we're here. I need permission to stay, to trade here.' He went inside.

The woman walking along the road caught up to them. Tjipuka

climbed down from the wagon. She walked to her and the woman stopped.

'My name's Tjipuka, Tjipuka Ruhapo. We're here from Lüderitz.'

The woman's face changed. 'You're from Okahandja?'

'Yes! Yes. Do you know me? My people?' Tjipuka could not hide her happiness.

'Yes,' she said. 'I'm Kakumbe from Omaruru. Are you coming to stay here with us?'

'I … I don't know. I'm with a German, he's paid for me.' The woman looked at the metal badge attached to Tjipuka's dress with her number, 8868. 'I am a prisoner of war at Shark Island.'

'You're not a prisoner here. In the land of the Batawana, you're not a prisoner.'

They spoke some more, until Ludwig came out of the mud hut, followed by a short, dark man.

'Dumela, Mma,' he said to Tjipuka. She nodded at him, not understanding the language but sensing it was a greeting. At the wagon, Ludwig gave the man two bags of tobacco.

'Ke a leboga,' he said and pointed to a place under a canopy of trees at the edge of the village. 'You can set up camp there – the river's not far.'

Tjipuka climbed back into the wagon. Ludwig looked at her. 'You're smiling.'

'I like this place.'

Ludwig told her to stay at the camp with the wagon. He had to go and find the man he was looking for, who might not be in the village – he might have to ride out to him. She should wait. Because they seemed closer now, he trusted she would do as he said.

Before he left, they went to the nearby general dealer for a few supplies. He bought her fabric for a dress as a parting gift. He was trying his best to make up for his behaviour since she'd run away. But Tjipuka preferred him mean; she was too vulnerable to his kindness.

34

September 1907

For Riette, the five years she'd been in Tsau had passed quickly. It had been tough work establishing herself, setting up her shop, gaining the trust of the people of the area. She'd been lucky to arrive when she did. Kgosi Sekgoma Letsholathebe had welcomed new arrivals then. His acceptance gave her a certain stature that helped the people accept her too. Now things were not as easy for newcomers. The village had changed lately. Kgosi Sekgoma Letsholathebe had been arrested in Gaborone and he was now in prison. Riette found that hard to accept – a man who had been so kind and helpful to her, sitting in a colonial prison.

It felt as if this village on the edge of the Okavango Delta had always been her home. She found a calmness here that helped her find peace in herself. Above all, there was no one here who knew her before, who knew her secrets, knew her pains. Here she was just Mma Venter, the odd, widowed, white Afrikaner woman who ran the general dealer.

She rarely saw other white people. Occasionally a British colonial official might pass by to see the kgosi or to collect taxes. Stanley Williams, the man from Mafeking, brought her new stock and bought any ivory or cattle her customers might have sold to her. He cared more about money than any gossip he might hear about Riette; it was not his concern. Riette liked that about him.

She was almost sure she was happy in Tsau. She had a few friends among the people of the village, but mostly she kept to herself. Occasionally she got the chance to put her nursing training into practice. She helped with difficult deliveries, and people came to her for medicines for various aches and pains. But she liked her small, tidy life. It was free of the boundaries that had boxed her in for most of her years, and she was willing to pay just about anything for that, even a bit of loneliness.

The bell above the door rang, and Riette looked up from her sewing and her thoughts. She was surprised to see a tall, hunched white man. He was neither handsome nor ugly. Riette wondered what he was doing in Tsau.

'Can I help you?' she said.

'I need sugar and flour if you have any.' He spoke in an awkward Afrikaans. She thought he might be German.

Riette got to work. 'I have some dried waterbuck meat if you'd like,' she offered.

He nodded. He eyed some bright-red linen fabric behind the counter. 'And, and give me some of that … enough for a dress.' So he had a woman with him.

The bell above the door rang again, and both she and the man looked there. It was a Herero woman, Riette thought, but not one she was familiar with. She was tall, like her people, dark, with clear skin. But she was quiet in her movements; without the bell they would not have known she was there. She spoke to the man in German.

The man turned to Riette, who had finished cutting the cloth and was folding it. 'And some coffee, please.'

The man took the cloth and handed it to the Herero woman. She rubbed it on her face and smiled at him.

'She is Tjipuka,' the man said. 'Your chief is letting us camp across the way. I must go into the bush for some days. You can keep watch for her maybe?'

225

Riette came around the counter to look out the window again. She saw the covered wagon and the tent near by. She turned to the woman and held out her hand. 'Tjipuka, I am Mma Venter.'

She spoke first in Setswana, which this woman did not know. Then she tried English and the woman replied. 'I'm happy to meet you, madam.'

'When your master is gone, if you have problems, come to me. I'll help you. I live here in a house behind the shop.'

Tjipuka nodded and looked at the tall German. Riette knew 'master' was not the correct word for the German man in relation to this Herero woman. Anyone could see that. It was the polite word.

She got the coffee and packaged up the purchases. Riette hoped Tjipuka wouldn't have trouble once the German left. A woman like this Herero, in the position that she was in, could have problems. Riette would not be the only one to see that the German was more than a master to her.

Riette saw the German ride off later that day. In between customers, she sat at the window to sew in the better light and to keep an eye on Tjipuka. After a while, a Herero woman stopped by the camp. She must have heard about Tjipuka. Later in the day, Riette watched as the same Herero woman returned, but with a group of men, Herero men. For a moment, she was scared for Tjipuka. Had they heard she was here with the German man?

Just before Riette closed the shop, Tjipuka came back. Riette was busy restocking shelves and missed the sound of the bell. She turned and Tjipuka was standing quietly, waiting.

'Oh, there you are,' Riette said.

'Did I startle you?'

'No, not really. Is anything wrong?'

'No.'

'No one is troubling you? I saw some of the Herero there.'

'Yes. It seems I might know them. We've been scattered … our people, we've lost each other.'

'Yes, I know about the war. I know some of the people here, their stories.'

'I wanted a tin of condensed milk. He should have bought it earlier,' Tjipuka said.

Riette took the tin down from the shelf and handed it to Tjipuka. She wanted to speak, to say what she was feeling about this woman. To warn her of the dangers she faced, dangers Riette knew too well. How different they were from each other on the surface – too different to cross that space. She wanted to say something, but she couldn't. She couldn't see any way to say those intimate words to this stranger.

35

September 1907

After Ludwig left, Mama Kakumbe came back with some other Herero, a small group of men, to meet Tjipuka. They spoke for only a short time and suddenly Mama Kakumbe said, 'We need to go, but we will be back.'

Tjipuka thought this was odd. It was as if Mama Kakumbe was bringing people to check her out. They asked the same questions she had already asked Tjipuka. What is your name? Where are you from? Tjipuka answered them again.

'We'll come back later,' Mama Kakumbe repeated as they left.

Tjipuka watched them go and then she tidied up the camp. She went to the shop for some milk she had forgotten and then to the river for water. The river was wide. She spotted elephants on the far side. Some people were passing in a low, dugout boat: a man, a woman and three children. The man pushed it with a tall pole while standing. They greeted her in their language, and she struggled to greet them back.

She walked back to the camp with the bucket of water balanced on her head. She saw people at the camp, waiting. As she neared, she saw it was Mama Kakumbe again. She was with some men. She was with a certain man, a familiar-looking man.

Tjipuka stopped when she was near enough to see clearly. The bucket fell to the ground with a loud clatter, the water spilling on her. But she did not move closer. She was too scared to move closer. She fell to her knees.

Mama Kakumbe bent down to where she knelt on the ground. She took Tjipuka's arm and helped her to her feet. She spoke in a soft voice.

'It's all right. You are fine. Everything is going to be fine. I have someone who needs to meet you, someone who has been waiting a very long time for your return.'

Tjipuka managed to walk with the help of Mama Kakumbe. She felt her body shaking. As they walked towards the man, Mama Kakumbe whispered in Tjipuka's ear, 'Everything is all right. You will be fine now. Do not be afraid.'

He was tall, just as she remembered. He stood with his arms at his sides, his long fingers stretched out along his legs. He looked at her. It was his face, she was sure of that. His body too. He stood silently. Despite everything her mind told her, her eyes told her the truth.

It was him. He was alive. It was Ruhapo.

'Wa penduka, Mama,' the man said in Ruhapo's voice.

She ran to him, and he took her in his strong arms. Miracles did happen; people did come back from the dead. Her prayers had been answered. Wails echoed through the trees into the village, bringing people out of their huts.

Ruhapo was alive and Tjipuka had finally found him.

It was her, just as Mama Kakumbe had said – his wife, his Tjipuka returned. She looked untouched by the war; she was the Tjipuka of his memories.

'You're not dead,' he said.

Her eyes glistened with tears. 'You're not dead either.'

'And Saul? Where is Saul?' he asked. She shook her head, and from where his heart had soared it fell again.

He took her hand and led her away from the others. They needed time alone to fill in the spaces between them, the three long years apart. He turned to Mama Kakumbe. 'I'll find you at home.'

The group left and Ruhapo led his wife into the tent she shared with the German who'd brought her; he tried his best to forget that.

'I can't believe you are here … Did someone tell you I was in Tsau?' he asked.

'No, it's the ancestors who led me here; I knew nothing. I only knew I would do everything in my power to escape. I didn't know I was escaping to you.'

He held her face in his hands. He kissed her gently. It was his wife, he told himself. It was Tjipuka. It was her; it was only the time apart that made him forget how she felt, how she smelled. It was only the time that made her appear like a stranger. They would find each other again.

After all that had happened, he had thought he was the cursed one. He had done so much wrong. He had led men to killing, led his people to be slaughtered. He had killed with pleasure, like a bloodthirsty monster, not like a human. He was sure that was why he had been sent to Tsau all alone, as penance for all he had done. But now the ancestors were blessing him. He would not let them down again.

'He tried so hard to live. I gave him everything I could, but it was too much. When the sickness came to the camp, he was too weak. He couldn't fight it.' Tjipuka held Ruhapo's hands in hers. They sat face to face while she told him how their son had died. She tried to be strong, to speak in a level way, to somehow hold the burden of his death inside her to save Ruhapo from the worst of it.

'But you, you look fine. As if you didn't suffer at all. Why could you not save our son as you saved yourself?' He stood and paced around the small tent.

Tjipuka tried to find a way to explain, while Ruhapo's words slashed at her heart. 'It was not like that … Ludwig saved me from the camp after Saul died.'

'Ludwig? You call that poisonous man Ludwig? He is a German pig, nothing more.'

Tjipuka accepted everything Ruhapo said. She thought the same way most of the time. Why had she not been able to save her son? It was wrong that she should live and he should die, that she should be strong and healthy when others suffered so much, all because of a German. She accepted everything Ruhapo said, even as painful as it was to hear.

Ruhapo held his face in his hands; his anger and sadness were too much. When he looked up, he must have seen the effect of his words on his wife's face. He went to her and held her tightly. 'I'm sorry. Tjipuka, I was wrong to say such things. I've been so bitter and angry for so long I don't know how to be any other way. I need time to adjust, to learn how to love again. Please forgive me.'

Tjipuka knew she had found Ruhapo – he was somewhere in this man before her. Three years, and they were finally together again. It was a miracle, a miracle they both needed to adjust to.

'Of course I forgive you. I love you, I can forgive you anything.'

It was two days before Ludwig returned with the man selling the elephant tusks. For those two days Ruhapo stayed with Tjipuka in the tent she had shared with Ludwig.

When Ludwig arrived, Ruhapo was gone. He had gone to fetch Katjimune at the cattlepost. Katjimune was a headman and Ruhapo wanted someone in authority present when he told the German that his wife would remain in Tsau.

'Is everything fine?' Ludwig asked when he got back.

'Yes,' she said.

'Is this your woman then?' said the man with Ludwig. He was a light-skinned man, Nama, rough and rude. Tjipuka instantly disliked him.

'Yes,' Ludwig said, to Tjipuka's surprise. She understood now that he had already taken up his dream as reality. He was living his new life where Tjipuka was his wife. Tjipuka realised it would make everything more difficult.

'Yes,' the Nama said, looking her over. 'She's a nice one. These Herero women are beautiful in their way, better than the others. They say they come from the Nubians up north. You picked a good one.'

Ludwig turned away and the Nama man moved close to her and ran his hand over her buttocks. She slapped him. When Ludwig turned back, neither of them said a thing. There would soon be enough trouble, Tjipuka thought. This was of no consequence.

The Nama man carried two large elephant tusks to the back of the wagon. He and Ludwig talked, negotiating a price. He wouldn't accept goods. He wanted only cash and gold. As they talked at the back of the wagon, Ruhapo, Katjimune and a small group of Herero, about twenty in all, walked up to the camp. They greeted Tjipuka. Ludwig and the Nama man came out from behind the wagon.

Ludwig looked at the group. 'What is this now?'

Katjimune came to the front of the group. 'Perhaps we might sit down.'

'No. Speak. I'm in the middle of something now,' Ludwig said. 'I'm busy. Tell me what you want.'

Ruhapo came to the front. He took Tjipuka's hand. 'This woman is my wife.'

Ludwig looked at Tjipuka. 'No. That can't be. No … she's not your wife. Her husband is dead. You are lying.'

'I thought that, Ludwig,' Tjipuka interrupted. 'I thought Ruhapo was dead. They told me that. But they lied. This is Ruhapo – he's my legal husband. He's alive. He was living here all along.'

Ludwig stepped back. He pulled a stool from beside the fire and sat on it. 'Your husband is here? He has been here all along?'

'Yes. I didn't know, but he was here, waiting for me.'

'I think you can see, she can't go back with you,' Katjimune said.

Ludwig said nothing. He looked at Tjipuka. 'So you want to stay here? With him?'

'Yes.' She went to Ludwig and knelt in front of him and spoke softly. 'Please, please allow this. You're a good man, I know this. What if you had another chance with Anna? What if she reappeared? Think of that. Please, Ludwig, please do what's right.'

Katjimune stepped forward. 'I can vouch for this man. Ruhapo is the husband to this woman. He thought she was dead like the others. If not he would still have been out looking for her.'

Ludwig stood and turned away from them all.

'Go then. Leave. Take your things and leave,' he roared, without turning back to them.

Ruhapo pulled Tjipuka up from where she knelt, more roughly than he needed to. 'Why do you kneel for a man like that? For a German?' he spat at her in Otjiherero.

'I was begging him to let me stay. I was doing it for us.'

'There was no need to beg. He's lucky I don't slice his neck open right here. We're many, and he's one. We could cut him into pieces for the hyenas – a German is no better than food for hyenas in any case. Why beg him for anything? I'm showing him mercy. He should be begging me; he should be at my feet begging me for mercy after his insults.'

Ruhapo led her away from the camp and the others followed.

Ruhapo took her to Katjimune's compound, where he'd been given a mud hut. Once there, they performed the ritual to bring her home. They slaughtered a cow to welcome Tjipuka back, to tell the ancestors that their lost daughter had been found. The traditional ceremony made Tjipuka feel that indeed she had arrived home, finally.

Ruhapo worked for some Batawana, taking care of their cattle. The next day when Ruhapo left for work, Tjipuka walked into the village. She found Ludwig hitching the oxen to the wagon, preparing to go.

'You're leaving,' Tjipuka said.

Ludwig looked up at her, but then went back to what he was doing. 'Yes, I'm finished here.'

'Will you be all right crossing the border without me?'

'You've made a lot of trouble for me. But I'll pay them, give them some things, normally that works.' The anger in his voice was gone, replaced with resignation.

'So you'll go back to Lüderitz?'

'Where else?'

She handed him a small purse. It was the money she'd raised from sewing. 'Can you give this to Peter?'

He looked at it. 'You keep it. I'll give him money.'

He took a cloth bag from his pocket and handed it to her.

She opened it. Inside were five gold coins and a diamond ring. She looked at him, confused.

'You worked for me for a long time. You need to be paid. I don't keep slaves.'

'And the ring?'

'It was Anna's. I wanted you to have it – that was my plan in bringing it. I'll not need it again.'

'Thank you for this,' Tjipuka said. 'Please … I shouldn't ask for anything else … but Novengi …'

'I will see to Novengi. I know how much you care for her. I was angry yesterday, but you must be with your husband, I know that now. It's the right thing. You've been kind to me, always kind, even when I didn't deserve it. I can't say the same and I feel bad about that. I'm sorry. I owe you at least that. I'll take care of Novengi.'

Tjipuka took his hands in hers. 'No, never feel bad. You saved me. I would have died there. When Saul died, I wanted the camp to kill me too. I prayed for death and you saved me. I would have never lived to come here, to find Ruhapo again.'

He said nothing more. He climbed up onto the wagon and flicked the reins. She stood on the long, straight dirt road out of the village and watched him until he disappeared into the dust.

36

January 1908

Ruhapo woke and dressed silently. Tjipuka went out of the hut and returned, bringing him milk. She handed it to him without a word. He drank it and then said, 'I must go.' He disappeared into the new day, still dark and cold, still clinging to the night.

She watched him leave. She knew he hated having to work for someone else. He was proud, and being told what to do by another wore on him. Each time he swallowed it, it ate away a bit more at him, but it also gave him more resolve, more determination to be free.

Since Tjipuka had been found, Ruhapo had begun to make plans again. He dreamed now of being free from Mogalakwe, of no longer having to work for anyone except himself. But he would need enough cattle and small stock so that he and Tjipuka could survive. He was close. He had eleven cattle, and two cows were pregnant. Fifteen healthy cows and a few goats and sheep would get them started. In Ruhapo's hands the herd would quickly increase.

Tjipuka now helped in the fields with Mma Mogalakwe. At the end of the ploughing season, Mma Mogalakwe had promised Tjipuka three bags of sorghum as payment for her work. Tjipuka would trade them for four goats. She'd made the deal with her friend, Mma Venter, the owner of the shop in town. Tjipuka sold omaze uozondombe, the butter she made from sour milk, to Mma Venter too. From that money she'd bought two goats already, and one was pregnant.

Ruhapo promised they would break away from the Mogalakwes before the dry season came. He wanted to be free by the time their child was born. Tjipuka was now four months pregnant. Before the rains stopped, he wanted his own cattlepost, their own home to start their new life, to raise their child. When the baby was born, he wanted to be a free, independent man.

Tjipuka hoped that once Ruhapo was free, things would improve. She hoped that freedom would change things between them, that once the baby in her womb arrived, they would be happy again, just as they'd been before. Free and happy.

She tied her headscarf in place and glanced at herself in the piece of broken mirror she'd fixed to the wall of their mud hut. She was still beautiful, even after everything, but now it was of no meaning. Maybe it was even a curse – she sometimes wondered about that. But in some ways, she knew it had allowed her to survive. Survival was a good thing, she was almost sure of that now. Sometimes survival was the only thing; it was the last thing in any case.

The sun was already creeping up the sky, and the bite of the noonday heat was in the air. She found Mama Zozo, Katjimune's first wife, resting at the fire, while MmaLesedi, Katjimune's fourth wife, started the tea.

'Wa penduka, Tjipuka,' Mama Zozo said.

Though she was late to the fields, Tjipuka went to them. Mama Zozo was old and had been sick ever since Tjipuka arrived in Tsau. Tjipuka could see that today was not a good day. She had become very thin, her skin stretched over her cheekbones, her complexion pale grey.

'How are you this morning, Mama?' Tjipuka asked, sitting down next to her, taking her hand.

'Oh, my child, my day to meet the ancestors will be soon.' She chewed a stick that she used to clean her teeth.

'Wa penduka, MmaLesedi,' Tjipuka called to the younger woman at the fire.

She left the fire and came to sit near them. She carried a chipped enamel cup with warm milk and handed it to the older woman. MmaLesedi was more like a daughter to Mama Zozo than a junior wife. Mama Zozo had only one son, now married and living in his own homestead. MmaLesedi was the one who cared for the old woman.

Mama Zozo shook her head; she didn't want the milk. She ate very little nowadays.

'You must drink this,' MmaLesedi said forcefully.

She was a tall, strong woman, middle-aged now, though youthful in her energy. Tjipuka liked her. She did not gossip like the other women. She spoke what was in her mind, she didn't whisper in corners. The women in the village, the Herero and Mbanderu women, shunned Tjipuka. They spoke about her in secret until she was present, then they greeted her like snakes. They thought they knew everything about her; they thought this gave them the right to judge her. They knew nothing.

But Mama Zozo and MmaLesedi were not like that. Though they had not been there for the war and what followed, they knew it had been difficult. People had to make choices from only evil options. Mama Zozo and MmaLesedi did not judge; they took Tjipuka as she was.

Mama Zozo took the cup and sipped from it slowly, while MmaLesedi sat next to Tjipuka on a thin wooden bench. 'How is the baby?'

'He's awake.' Tjipuka took MmaLesedi's hand and placed it on her stomach. They waited until the baby kicked back at her hand.

'Yes, the baby's strong.' MmaLesedi looked at Mama Zozo, who was trying to set the cup down in the dirt. Mama Zozo stopped when she saw she was being watched, and put it to her lips again and sipped. It was better to do what MmaLesedi wanted – she was very determined when she set her mind in a certain direction. 'And Ruhapo?'

'He's fine. He's gone already.'

'That man is caught in a cage. Like a bull caught in a cage.' MmaLesedi shook her head. 'But it's only in his mind.'

Tjipuka listened to a dove cooing. She liked the watery sound of a dove. She searched for the bird in the trees behind the fire where he sat with his partner, cooing and nodding his head, hoping his partner would give in to his love advances. Tjipuka said nothing in reply to MmaLesedi's words. They both knew she was right.

'I must go.'

Tjipuka liked to be at the fields first, before Mma Mogalakwe and her daughters. She stood and MmaLesedi stood too.

'Let me walk with you a bit.' She turned back to Mama Zozo. 'Don't dump that milk out, Old Woman. The ancestors punish waste.'

Mama Zozo clicked her tongue in annoyance at this cheeky junior wife, but took another sip of the milk. Tjipuka and MmaLesedi walked towards the Mogalakwes' fields.

'It's a good year. The harvest will be good,' she said. Tjipuka nodded. 'I hear that you and Ruhapo will leave Katjimune's after the harvest, that you'll make your own homestead.'

'Yes, that's what Ruhapo wants.'

They walked in silence for a while. 'Ruhapo must find a way to make peace with the past. He's troubled by everything, never settled, so full of anger. This isn't good. I hear it. And I see it. I know that he takes his troubles out on you, and I'm afraid for that. I'm afraid for when you're away – alone in your own home, in a place where no one can help you.'

Tjipuka could see that it had taken a lot for MmaLesedi to be so forthcoming, to speak of private things between a husband and his wife. She liked MmaLesedi, but still she must be loyal to Ruhapo.

'It's not like that, MmaLesedi. You're seeing things that are not there. He just wants to be free of the Mogalakwes. When he's free, we'll be fine. Everything will be fine. All of this … it will stop. Our new child will arrive and our life will be like before, before everything … before the scattering. Ruhapo will remember how we were, how he was, and everything will be fine again.'

MmaLesedi said nothing else. She neither denied nor acknowledged what Tjipuka had said.

'I must go back. That stubborn old lady will have dumped the milk – I know her and her ways.'

She turned and walked back and Tjipuka continued to the fields. She wondered if everyone believed that *this* Ruhapo, the one that they saw, was the real one. She wanted to tell them he was not. She wished she could show them how he really was. If MmaLesedi knew how loving and kind the real Ruhapo was, before everything, she would believe what Tjipuka said. She would believe that everything would be fine once they had their own home and their own work. Ruhapo would remember himself then. All the layers of bitterness and sadness would fall away. They would be again as they were meant to be.

She walked out to the fields. The sorghum was nearly ready; the harvest would be good, just as MmaLesedi had said. Mma Mogalakwe would be pleased. This crop was doing well because of Tjipuka. She worked hard – the field was free of weeds, and she didn't allow a single bird to land. She chased them off with the fierceness of survival. The success of this crop would be her success too.

Sometimes she thought of the old Tjipuka, the chief's daughter who would find such work as planting and tending crops below her status. Planting sorghum was no work for a Herero woman: those beneath them, like the Berg Damara, planted crops, not her. But none of that meant anything any more.

She saw the Mogalakwe daughters, Kagisanyo and Marang, in the field already and she walked to them.

'Dumelang!' she shouted. They were still at a distance so she waved to them.

Kagisanyo, the youngest, came running up to her. 'Is the baby moving today?' she asked. She was fascinated by it all. Tjipuka took her hand and placed it on her stomach.

'I don't feel anything.'

'Wait. Babies require patience.'

They stood quietly. A breeze came up and Tjipuka hoped it would stay. It would help with the heat.

'There! I felt it! She's busy today.' Kagisanyo smiled and Tjipuka saw something that reminded her a little of Maveipi. A wave of grief came over her and she looked away. She looked westward, the direction where Novengi was, Novengi, who she was sure she would see again – sure in the only way sureness existed now for her, contingent on other things, qualified by what she could not control.

Tjipuka picked up her hoe. 'We'd better get to work or your mother will come after both of us with a switch.'

Tjipuka bent and slammed the hoe into the sun-baked ground, turning over the soil and displacing the weeds. She would finish half the field on her own today. The girls helped, but they were slow and they often stopped and talked. If Mma Mogalakwe saw she had worked hard maybe she would be more generous. The plan to break free was still a secret. The Mogalakwes could not know, since they would not want to lose her and Ruhapo. But they had to suspect it would happen one day. The Herero were nobody's servants. This was all temporary. No one should see it as a permanent situation.

The sun was up properly now, with only the odd cloud to give relief. She looked out into the distance. She could see just the edge of the river. This country, Bechuanaland, was different from their home in Hereroland, but similar too, with its temperamental rains, its hot summers with violent thunderstorms, cold dry winters. Its blistering days and cool, gentle nights.

She rubbed her stomach. It was still a while before she would meet her child. Five more months of this anxiousness would be difficult to bear. But she could do it. The past three years had shown her that she could bear anything. This baby felt different from Saul, her dear Saul. Every day, even after so much time, she ached for him; she knew she always would. Such a good baby, so brave against all of the suffering he went through.

This baby already seemed different. Tjipuka had been sick most of the pregnancy. Her feet were swollen, and the baby liked to move, to press against her back so it ached.

Saul was happy growing inside her; it was as if he could have stayed in her womb forever. He arrived in the world easily, with no noise, his eyes open and curious, like his father's. This baby had already shown her he would be his own person; he would not be coming into the world to replace anyone. She thought that would be better, a blank, clean slate.

She cleared her mind of all of her worries and got back to work. She had an entire day ahead of her and she had every intention of finishing the work she'd set out to do.

37
February 1908

'This is nice,' Mma Venter said, taking a bit of butter in her mouth. 'I'll give you two shillings, all right?'

'That's fine.' Tjipuka occasionally negotiated a better rate, but two shillings was good enough today.

'So how's that baby?' Mma Venter asked. She liked to hear about the baby growing inside Tjipuka.

Mma Venter had run to Bechuanaland to get away from war, just as Tjipuka had. She never explained clearly what had happened, only bits and pieces. Tjipuka knew she had worked as a nurse in the past. She knew that Mma Venter's husband had been a Boer fighter, a guerrilla fighter in the bush.

But the British caught him and sent him far away where he died. She knew, too, that Mma Venter had stayed in a camp in the south for some time.

'The baby is good today, Mma Venter.'

'Can I feel?' She came around the high counter. She liked to check, to feel where the baby was, how it was progressing. She had hands for babies. She could move them to where they belonged. Many women came to her for this; many babies were saved by her hands. Tjipuka stood still and let Mma Venter rub her hands over her stomach.

'Yes, she's good. She's going just right.'

'Why do you say *she?*' Tjipuka asked.

'Why? You don't want a girl?' Mma Venter closed her eyes and thought for a moment. She did this when she needed a moment to find the truth. 'I think I know why. But you mustn't be like that. Children die, new ones come. Don't make this little soul inside of you carry so much even before she's born. Let your son free now.'

She rested her hand on Tjipuka's shoulder. Though Mma Venter was not so much older than her, ten years at most, Tjipuka saw her as a kind of mother. Inside, she fought against leaning into her, giving in to her. How lovely it would be to be held by her, and to allow all her worries and pain to flow out, even just for a moment. To set down her burden, for a single moment only. Although Tjipuka wished she could do this, she knew it would open everything. All would come pouring out and she was not sure she could survive that.

She thought of her own mother. A tall, proud, cold woman. She cared for Tjipuka, but kept a distance. She was the first wife of a chief – three other wives made up the family. She could not show weakness, or the hierarchy she strictly enforced would come toppling down. Emotion was weakness. If Tjipuka wanted hugs and kisses when she was a child, it was not her mother she went to but her father. He was the soft-hearted one and Tjipuka was the youngest, his favourite. How she wished she still had her father to run to. She knew nothing about what had happened to them during the scattering; she suspected that, like almost everyone, they were dead.

Mma Venter was softening her. She moved away so the older woman's hand fell. She must not let softness in now; she must not succumb to kindness. It would be her downfall. Like her mother, Tjipuka must be strong, and strength required her not to succumb to the emotions that raged inside her. To ignore what had happened, to keep moving forward hour by hour, day by day. Eventually, maybe – once she was some distance away from the events – she could begin to start feeling again. She had thought her broken emotions were because Ruhapo and Saul were gone, but now Ruhapo was back. Shouldn't she be at least partly restored?

'It's not what you think. I know my son is gone. It's not that.' Tjipu-ka spoke with hard words. Distancing words. 'This baby is important, that's all. A girl or boy – it doesn't matter. I just wondered why you always said *she*.'

'Ah, yes. All right. That's better then.' Mma Venter moved back behind the counter, physically acknowledging the distance Tjipuka wanted to maintain.

She took out her book. She kept a book for the butter Tjipuka brought her. When the money was enough for Tjipuka to buy another goat, she gave her the cash and tore out the page. Mma Venter knew that she and Ruhapo were trying to build up their cattle and small livestock, which would bring them some independence. She understood independence herself. She respected it and she helped Tjipuka in any way she could.

Tjipuka felt bad for having spoken so harshly. She knew Mma Venter was a good woman; she didn't deserve to be spoken to in such a way.

'I … you know some of what troubles me,' Tjipuka said carefully. She did not want to cross a line. She felt that line inside of her, imaginary but solid. She defended that line like a soldier. 'It's a heavy weight in my heart, this waiting. So much will be decided by the outcome.'

Mma Venter nodded her head. 'I think I know. I think I do. But things were how things were. You had no choices. Women in war are just like toys, pawns for the soldiers to barter with. Your husband must know this too. What is to happen will. Only then you'll see what you'll do. Problems always find a way to their solution. You'll find a way to the end, no matter what happens.'

'Yes … but … this baby scares me. War has changed everyone, not just me. My husband, my Ruhapo, he's changed too. He's not who he was, no matter how much I want him to be. Maybe he'll come back, but he hasn't yet, and I can't expect him to accept everything.'

Tjipuka wouldn't speak the words she feared most. Once spoken, they would become hard and immovable – they would become true.

Mma Venter set the book down.

'Don't worry about things you cannot change. Wait. We'll wait. When it's time for the baby, you come to me, no one else. We'll see what to do then. But for now, we wait. Worrying about things you can't change helps nothing. Believe me, I know this. It's not good for the baby, or for you.'

Mma Venter's words settled Tjipuka. She felt better for now. She left the small shop and walked through the tiny settlement of Tsau, smelling the fishy scent of the nearby Delta. She passed the buildings for the Batawana chief, Kgosi Mathiba. Mud blocks with a corrugated-iron roof. She passed the massive camel thorn that shaded what she knew now was the kgotla. She stepped first into, then out of, its cool shade.

She thought of that first day she arrived in Tsau. She'd been so excited to see another Herero woman. She thought she'd found a refuge in this village. Since then she'd come to see that Tsau was not a place of safety. She could never be completely safe here or anywhere. What she feared most was inside of her.

She walked and with each step she pushed her fears down, back to where she could manage them. Mma Venter would help her. It would all be fine. One way or another, they would find a way to get through it.

38

February 1908

Ruhapo pushed her back onto the bed, fierce and lost in his need. He wanted her; he couldn't control that. He wanted his wife, the woman he knew before, and he suspected it was in their bed where he might find her again.

She was dirty now – this could not be ignored, though they both tried. They never spoke about it, but he knew. He loved her and hated her. He forgave her and punished her. She'd had no choice, but he blamed her anyway.

He pushed into her, he must. There was an uncontrollable fury inside him. Perhaps the truth was there, perhaps the peace they both needed. He could not stand what he was doing to her, but he had to be with her and this was the only way. It was not loving or gentle or right. It was brutal and vicious. He wanted to make love to her and, at the same time, he wanted to hurt her for what she had done to him, to them.

Though Ruhapo tried, he could not forget that *he* had been there too. Maybe others, maybe many, she would not say. He did not ask. He didn't want to know, but not knowing was killing him. He wanted to know every detail, yet he asked no questions to get the answers he knew he could not bear. He didn't want to hear the truth. He hoped his imagination was worse than reality.

When he touched her he wondered, did he touch there too? When he moved in a certain way he thought, does it remind her of him? He could not be free to love his wife because his wife was gone. A stranger lay in his bed. A stranger he loved but couldn't love without dying each time. A stranger who had betrayed him in the deepest way.

When he finished, when he knew it had changed nothing, he held her with icy arms that offered no refuge. He held her and wished she might cry into his chest.

If she cried, some things might be righted. She didn't, though. She held him and it seemed like love. He kissed her and that seemed like love too. For now that was all they had, the thin wavering appearance of love covering a darkness neither would admit they saw.

39
February 1908

Tjipuka woke up and sat straight in the bed, the dream still fresh and vivid. Her mind betrayed her whenever she wasn't vigilant. She lay still and let the dream fade away. She held her hand on her stomach. The baby was awake – she held what she thought was the heel of his foot. He was strong and big for his age already. She was happy about this because she knew he would need to be very strong. He should arrive prepared.

She heard Ruhapo up already, out with the cattle. She dressed quickly, threw a shawl around her shoulders and headed towards the kraal.

Today they wouldn't go to the Mogalakwes because there was a wedding in the village. Two of the Mbanderu families would be celebrating, and the Mogalakwes had allowed them the day off to attend.

It was still dark but Tjipuka saw the outline of Ruhapo in the kraal. He stood looking out over the bush, as if waiting for someone. She often found him like that, caught in an in-between place, waiting to move forward or backward, waiting for someone to arrive. She was careful to make a noise as she walked up to him; she had no wish to surprise him. He didn't like being surprised.

'Has she given birth?'

They'd been waiting for one of their cows to calve. The new one would bring the cattle to twelve. Every birth was a step towards freedom.

Ruhapo turned and looked at her without speaking. She entered the kraal and stood near to him. She wanted to put her arms around her husband, to feel him pressed against her, but she didn't. They were not that couple any more. It used to be that they needed always to touch: a hand on a shoulder, a finger hooked around the other's finger. Touch now only meant sex. And sex did not mean love. Sex was a search for lost things.

Ruhapo smiled at her and for a moment he was there completely, and a breath caught in her throat. She had forgotten how much she ached to see that smile. Or perhaps she had not forgotten, perhaps she'd pushed it far down and covered it with every spare thing. She had found many ways to adapt.

'She has given birth. It's a female.'

They pushed through the herd to the other side, and there was the new mother with her calf, already standing and nursing. Tjipuka smiled up at Ruhapo. This was good. The new calf was solid red. In the past, it might have been kept carefully, either to join the sacred cattle or to be used for bride price. For most of their people, those days were gone, but both Tjipuka and Ruhapo knew this; they knew this calf was special. Tjipuka ran her hand over the still-wet hide of the calf. The cow looked at her, Tjipuka thought with a look of pride. She knew she had done well for them.

'A fine calf,' Tjipuka said.

'Yes.'

They stood together watching mother and child. The sky lightened but still they stood. They should get to the wedding to help with preparations, but they stayed fixed.

'Do you remember the ox I brought to your father?' Ruhapo asked.

She was thinking of the same thing. 'It shone in the sun like gold glitters. The hide was so red and the horns so perfect. People came out of their houses to touch it, to make sure it was real.'

'I rubbed it with fat for days. Even the horns. I didn't want to be turned back, I wanted you as my wife. I wouldn't be turned back and I knew your father's brothers, they wanted someone special for you. They would look for anything to turn me back, so I made sure the ox was perfect.' Ruhapo smiled, looking out into the bush, the new day's sun on his face.

'And the wedding … it was so perfect. Everything was so perfect.' Sadness crept into Tjipuka's voice. She remembered Novengi by her side. Helping her with everything, making sure all was right. She thought of baby Maveipi, just walking then. She remembered everyone who was there, everyone who was now lost. They were so young and foolish then. They thought they had the right to be happy, that it was an absolute, not a gift given only for a moment. They thought things would always be as they were; it seemed impossible to think otherwise. Now it seemed impossible to think she had ever believed that.

'Yes.' Ruhapo's voice was hard again. The voice she knew to be his now. He was gone again, her Ruhapo. But she was not ready to leave the past. Not yet.

'We were happy then?' she said, like a question. She needed the right answer from him, the answer that told her it hadn't all been a mirage, a dream.

He looked at her. The light was dim but she saw pain in his eyes. It was too much for him to remember. Loss and sadness are bearable, but remembering happiness, in the middle of everything, can crush a person.

'Yes … yes, we were.'

He left the kraal and walked out, out into the bush. Tjipuka slumped to the ground. She crouched among the legs of the cattle. She closed her eyes and rocked and waited for her mind to forget all of that. She picked details, painful details: Kahaka hanging from a wire, Saul quiet and dead in her arms, Novengi standing with the bitter, cold sea wind pressing her thin dress against her skeletal body. She picked each image apart to interrogate every angle, every shade of misery. She embraced the pain; it was what she had grown used to. The pain comforted her and soon she recovered from those brutal glimpses of happiness.

40

February 1908

'They are doing well,' Rre Mogalakwe said, looking over Ruhapo's cattle in their kraal. 'I wish mine did as well.'

Ruhapo held his tongue – he knew the implication. He knew that Mogalakwe was trying to say Ruhapo did not do his job properly with Mogalakwe's cattle. This was a lie. He kept those cattle as he kept his own. They'd prospered under his care and Mogalakwe knew it. It would have been unwise for Ruhapo to do otherwise, since the worst among them would be the ones Mogalakwe would give him in payment for his services. He grazed and watered all the cattle together. There was no difference in the care he'd given them.

'How many do you have now?' Mogalakwe asked. It was a rude question to ask a man, how many cattle he owned; it undermined him. Mogalakwe didn't see Ruhapo as an equal. He was a servant, Mogalakwe the master. There was no respect.

'They're a few now,' Ruhapo said. If Mogalakwe really wanted to know he could count for himself; they were twelve, not a number too large to count. He wanted only to humiliate Ruhapo, and Ruhapo would not allow that.

'I hear you intend to set up your own place before the child is born.'

Ruhapo gripped the rough pole of the kraal. Why did this man want to trouble him today? He was in no mood for such play. Mogalakwe was a small man, brittle and thin. He was not more than five years older than Ruhapo, but Ruhapo towered over him, strong and straight. The size and strength of Ruhapo might have been enough to keep another man quiet, but not Mogalakwe. He could not see it. For him, he was the bigger man, the stronger man, the man with all the power.

'How long is it now?' he tried again.

'Four months and our child will be born.'

'Yes, *your* child.'

Ruhapo moved into the kraal and bent to inspect a brand that had not healed well. He tried to control himself. Beating this man would ruin everything.

Who was Mogalakwe to question anything? To smile as if he knew something? Ruhapo's life was not up for him to judge. But he was aware that the people in the village all knew their story, Tjipuka's story. Still, he was furious that they speculated, that they wondered about his child – that they felt they had the right to do so.

Ruhapo busied himself so as to hide his hands that ached to strike out.

Mogalakwe continued. He was not a man who noticed things, insensitive to the people around him. He didn't know how his words were affecting Ruhapo; he didn't know how close he was to physical harm. He could not feel the air between them sizzling with anger.

'Four months is a short time to set up a cattlepost. Besides, I doubt Kgosi Mathiba will be willing to give Mbanderu land. He wishes you would all go back to your home now. He's not Kgosi Letsholathebe. Your friend is rotting in prison in Gaborone. That one favoured you foreigners, even above us, his own people. Kgosi Mathiba doesn't. You'll not find it easy.'

'I am not Mbanderu, I'm Herero.'

'I don't think that matters. It's all the same to him. And besides, you're friends with Katjimune and the other Mbanderu – Kgosi Mathiba will see no difference. Have you asked for land yet?'

'Yes,' Ruhapo grudgingly admitted. 'I believe he's speaking with his advisors.'

'I doubt it,' Mogalakwe said. Ruhapo thought Mogalakwe knew something but was not saying. He must be free of this man. He would not be a servant to anyone when his son was born. He would not allow his son to see him under such a useless, tiresome man. If Kgosi Mathiba did not give him land, he would ask for a portion from Katjimune. He'd offered before. Or he would move off, somewhere else. Maybe he could get land from the Bamangwato south of Tsau. Kgosi Khama was a kind man, it was said, and he appreciated the animal husbandry skills of the Herero. Ruhapo didn't need to stay in the Batawana area. He could move away. But, either way, he would be free. This he was sure about. Mogalakwe would not stop him.

41

February 1908

In her sleep, Tjipuka heard Marang, at first as part of her dream world, and then slowly the sound rose up to reality. She was shouting and running. In her half-sleep mind Tjipuka heard her singing, 'Dinonyane! Dinonyane di tletse mo tshimong! Dinonyane di tletse mo tshimong!'

In moments, Tjipuka was awake and the panic of the words filled her. She shook Ruhapo. 'Come. We must go.'

She and Ruhapo ran to the fields in the grey dawn. Mma Mogalakwe and Kagisanyo were already there. The sorghum was nearly ready to be harvested – this was the worst time for the birds to have come, but they had come nevertheless. The sky was dark with them. There were hundreds, thousands.

Quelea birds covered the plants. Tjipuka heard the sound of crunching as she and Ruhapo neared the fields.

Rre Mogalakwe arrived and shot his gun in the air. The birds flew up for a few seconds, landed again and continued eating. For them it was a game, nothing more. The field was covered with them, like a writhing brown blanket. The sorghum stalks bent with their weight. Their squawks filled the air.

The people ran up and down the rows shouting, but the birds knew they could do little. They flew up and around them until they'd moved on and then settled back on the plants. This was their field now and they would only go when they were ready.

Mma Mogalakwe let her arms fall at her sides. 'It's over. There's nothing we can do. It's done. They'll get everything.'

She stood and watched all of her crop, all of her work, disappearing. It would be a very lean, dry season for them.

Tjipuka could not accept defeat. She ran up and down the rows, shouting and flapping her shawl at the birds. The birds looked at her with their black bead-eyes, knowing they were the victors. But she could not allow it; there had to be a way to save the crop. This crop was her life. This was her way to freedom. It meant a new life for her baby and for Ruhapo. It meant Ruhapo would no longer be humiliated as a servant to someone else. He would be free. He would be free and maybe he would come back to her from that dead place where he was stuck. This crop meant she would get her stolen life back, the one lost on Ohamakari.

She could not let it go so easily.

She ran up and down, barefoot, shouting at the birds. Her head was uncovered, her long hair wild, standing around her head like the crown of a mad queen. Kagisanyo and Marang stood with their parents, watching her. She ran and shouted. Furious, she beat at the birds. One fell to the ground and she attacked it. She stamped on its head, over and over; she ground its broken body into the soil. Her bare foot was stained with its blood, but she could not stop. It would pay for what it had done to her.

She stood up and used her shawl to knock another bird to the ground. Again she stamped on it. She would kill them one by one if she had to. There were thousands, but she would succeed. She was crying but didn't realise it – she couldn't hear her own screams. Her feet were not enough; she fell to the ground and began tearing at the dead birds. Ripping out feathers, pulling off feet. She pulled the beak off one and threw it viciously into the field, shouting to the other birds.

Her face was smeared with dirt and blood. She was wild, shouting and crying and screaming at the birds. They would not win. Not this time. They would not take everything again. She would kill them – *this time.*

Ruhapo knelt down next to her. He gently held her hands. At last she stopped moving and fell silent. The birds were squawking around her, and the sound of sorghum being stripped from the plants filled the morning air as if such sounds were commonplace.

'It's over,' he said, just above a whisper. 'We'll be fine.'

She fell. It was a distance, a long, breathtaking distance. She broke through the icy wall and fell, but she was not afraid, even though she was not sure where the bottom was. Not then, not in that moment. She let herself fall.

She fell and he caught her; he was there.

Though he was far away, eventually he arrived and caught her. And it felt good. She let go for a moment. She set her burden down. She laid herself bare in his arms and he protected her. Time stopped and they knelt in the field of birds and she was finally with Ruhapo again.

42

February 1908

Riette was preparing her list for new stock. When the bell on the door rang, she looked up and saw it was Tjipuka, whom she'd grown quite fond of.

'I'm sorry about the fields,' Riette said. 'I heard the birds got many people's crops.'

'Yes ... well. Sometimes I wonder if we're not bewitched. Bad luck can't seem to leave us alone. I thought finally we were clear of it.'

There was little Riette could say to that, so she changed the subject. 'Tjipuka, I could use someone to help me here in the shop, around the house too. Maybe you could work here until the baby is born.'

'Really? That would be such a help. I've felt so useless. Now only Ruhapo works and I sit and do nothing. Can I start now?'

'Yes, yes. Start now. Here.' Riette handed her a cloth. 'You can clean there on the lower shelves. Leave the high ones. I'll do the high ones. Not good for a pregnant woman to climb up there.'

Tjipuka took the cloth, and Riette already felt happier for the company. They worked all day, mostly in companionable silence. At lunchtime, Riette made tea and brought big chunks of home-made bread spread with the marula jam she made from the fruit that fell from her tree in the backyard. They locked the shop and sat outside at the wooden table placed in the shade in front of her little cement house.

'Here, eat. You must eat, there's someone depending on you.'

'Thank you for this,' Tjipuka said. 'You're very good to take care of me like this. You'd be a good mother. Did you ever want to have children?'

Riette thought about Martie and Annemie. She thought about the dream children she'd had with John Reilly, and the loss of them all descended upon her. 'I had children once. I guess they weren't really mine, but I loved them. They were my husband's children. They died in the camp.'

The block of that common grief between them kept them silent for a while. 'What was that camp like, the one they put you in, the Germans?' Riette asked.

'It was nothing. It was not a camp really,' Tjipuka began. 'We were just told to go and live on the rocks, behind the barbed wire. They were rocks pushed out into the sea, a long thin piece of land pushed out into the sea. The sea is a cold place, the wind from the sea is so wet and so cold. I never knew anything like that before.'

'Our camp was not as bad, I think. Not compared to what you say. We had shelters at least, tents.' Riette leaned forward and took Tjipuka's hand. 'I'm sorry for it all. I'm sorry for what you've gone through.'

'And me you.'

'Did you have friends in the camp?' Riette thought how much easier it was with Annemie and John. If she'd been alone, it would have been much worse.

'Yes. I had some friends. One died there, her son too. But my friend Novengi survived.' Tjipuka said it like a fact. 'Novengi and I have been friends since we were little girls. She was with me through all of it. In the desert … well … through most of it anyway.'

'That helped, I think.'

'Yes, it helped. Novengi's very strong. The strongest and bravest person I know.' Tjipuka looked down at her hand. 'I shouldn't be sad. I'll see her again. I know I'll see Novengi again.'

Riette reached forward and patted Tjipuka's arm. Silence sat between them for some moments. 'But how did you live with no houses?' Riette asked.

'We made something – people always find a way. It wasn't as bad as it seems. I wasn't there long, only a few months. Then Ludwig paid for me to work at his shop. Then it was a bit better.'

'The German? That man who brought you here, he was good then?' Riette asked. She wanted to hear that things were not as bad as they sounded.

Tjipuka drank her tea. Riette wondered why she needed to know this man was good. What was good? No one was good close up, and no one was bad, not completely, she thought.

'Yes ... he was good, I suppose,' Tjipuka said after some time. 'In his way he was good.'

Ruhapo was with their cattle when Tjipuka arrived home. It was nearly dark and she'd been gone since morning. She entered the kraal. He didn't turn to her. He ran his hand over the back of one of the cows. Down the whole way to the start of the tail, and then he moved his hand to its neck and then down again. Over and over. He didn't turn to Tjipuka, but she knew he'd heard her arrive. She was always sure to make noise so as not to startle him.

'Where have you been?' He spoke in an even voice, looking out into the bush away from her. His hand still ran mechanically up and down the cow. 'The women in the compound say you've been gone the entire day.'

'I was at Mma Venter's. She's given me a job.'

He turned. His eyes were wild and his breath hard. 'You're lying.'

'No, I'm not.'

'You've gone to him.'

She knew who he meant. He thought she had gone to Ludwig. How could she have gone to Ludwig? He was back in Lüderitz. He was far away, no part of her life. She knew rational talk would not calm Ruhapo, but she tried anyway.

'No. It's not like that. He's gone. He's gone back. You know he went back. I got a job. At Mma Venter. You can come and she'll tell you. I was with her the entire day.'

Ruhapo came towards her slowly. She stepped back but was soon up against the thick, rough branches that made up the kraal. Before she could move, his hand came out like a knife and slashed across her face. The force was massive. She fell, her hands squished into the cow dung, her knees cut from the rough ground.

'You're a whore. Why did you do it to me? Why? After all I suffered for you, after all I was forced to do, to see. Why did you do it to me?'

She lay in the mud and looked up at him. She said nothing. She knew what he was asking, but she didn't answer him. No answer would ever ease his pain.

He turned and left her lying there.

Tjipuka got up and went to the river. Though it was dusk and the hippos might be leaving the water, the time that they were the most dangerous, she didn't care. She walked into the river, her dress billowing around her. She cupped water in her hands and gently poured it over her painful face. She lay down in the shallow water, the stony bottom against her back. A crocodile swam some distance away. She willed it to come to her. She wanted to feel its powerful jaws grab her leg. She wanted to feel herself being pulled under the water. She would not fight. She would let it pull her deep into the water, pull her head under until all of the air in her was finished, and then take her to its cave, somewhere deep in the lake. There she would stay until it was ready to eat her. She thought about this like the dream of a child, a wished-for event that might finally give her peace. But the crocodile swam away from her.

Fearfully, she put her hand on her stomach. She was frightened the fall in the kraal had harmed the baby, but he was there. He had survived. She rubbed her stomach. He was of her. He was a survivor. 'Everything will be fine,' she lied. 'Everything is going to be just fine.'

43

February 1908

Ruhapo found her in the river, in the shallow water. Her head rested on the stones that covered the bottom and her long hair flowed out around her head like an angel's halo. At first he thought she was dead, but then he saw her hand rubbing her belly, caressing her child, whispering quietly to him.

He sat in the water next to her, but did not touch her. He looked out over the wrinkles of moonlight that covered the river.

'I'm sorry. I don't know what's wrong with me,' he whispered, almost to himself. 'I don't know why I hurt you. When it starts I can't seem to stop it.'

He looked at her. Her eye was swollen; even in the moonlight he could see a darkening on her cheek where his hand had hit. It was as if an animal lived inside him. He thought of going to a traditional doctor, but he didn't want any of them to know how he behaved. How he beat his wife, the woman he'd longed for all those months. The woman he'd searched the desert for. The woman he'd begged the ancestors to bring back to him. Then they did and this was how he repaid them. He could not go to a traditional doctor and tell him the kind of man he was now.

He didn't want them to know how weak he was. The doctor would be able to look inside his soul and see the truth and see the evil that he was made of now. He would see all the things he had seen and all the things he had done.

Everything was like a dust storm – wild and overwhelming. He didn't know the person who'd done this to Tjipuka, but it was him. It was who he was now. He had to accept that this was who he was now. A weak man, an unpredictable animal. A man with no control over anything.

He needed to forget the past, forget everything that had happened to bring him to this state. He needed to concentrate on his life now, on Tjipuka, on their child who would soon be born. He needed to be strong.

He scooped her from the water and pulled her onto his lap. He held her, but she lay prostrate in his arms. She was gone, away somewhere else. He held her and rocked back and forth.

The tears came at last; they pushed through him. He screamed out into the darkness. The groans of pain, the sound of weeping, the ugliness that he was filled with – the night air collected all of it. The night is huge and accommodating. It has space for such things. He gave everything to it, at least all that he could. The night could run smooth hands over wild emotions and rub salve into open wounds. It could offer forgiveness that the fragile people could not, that the harsh daylight could never.

Time passed and the emotions stopped. The night had made everything clean; nothing was left inside, for now. The only sound was the moonlit waves hitting against the shore. And finally Tjipuka's arms held him and, for a moment, in the hands of the benevolent night, they found each other again.

44

February 1908

When Tjipuka walked into the shop, Mma Venter gasped.

'What has happened?' She ran her hand gently over the large purple bruise on Tjipuka's cheek. 'What has happened to you?'

Tjipuka pulled away. She didn't want to talk about any of it. She wanted to forget it all. What could she say anyway? *My husband beat me like this.* How could she say this out loud? She'd fought her way through worse to get here. Now was she to die at the hands of her own husband?

She was full of anger. Anger at him and anger at herself.

'I'm fine. It's nothing.'

She grabbed the broom and began to sweep. Mma Venter took her firmly by the shoulders.

'It's fine if you won't protect yourself. I can't force you to do that. But I must check the baby. I won't leave the baby to be harmed.'

Mma Venter led Tjipuka to her house. The tin roof cracked in the hot sun. Mma Venter was not a person who filled her house with many things. There were two upright cushioned chairs in the sitting room. There was a wooden table with four straight-backed wooden chairs.

In the bedroom, a bed, wooden, with a hard cotton mattress, two side tables and a tall imposing wardrobe.

'Take your dress and petticoat off and lie down.'

Mma Venter took a horn-shaped object made of wood from the wardrobe and turned back to Tjipuka just as she pulled her petticoat over her head.

'Lie down on the bed.'

Mma Venter placed the horn on Tjipuka's stomach. She moved it to several places, listening for sounds of the baby. She looked at Tjipuka but her eyes said nothing. She moved the horn under the mound, at the bottom of Tjipuka's stomach, then lifted it.

'She's there. Her heart is strong. She's fine,' she said in a relieved voice.

Mma Venter applied liniment to the scratches on Tjipuka's arms and legs. Then she applied a different ointment to the bruises, one ground up with leaves. She was careful and thorough and did not allow Tjipuka to refuse, though she tried.

When she'd finished, Tjipuka sat up on the side of the bed.

'You mustn't allow this again,' Mma Venter said. 'You must fight him, fight back.'

'I can't fight him.'

'Yes, you can. There are many things you can do even if he's bigger than you. You must fight him. It's not only for you, it's for the baby too.'

How could she explain to this woman? How could she tell her that this man was not who he seemed to be? If he beat her, he was beating himself. He was fighting himself. He was trying to find his way out, trying to find a way to get to her. He was only trying to find a way through it all. She couldn't blame him for that because he was doing it for them. She was to blame as well. She knew the things that she'd had to do to survive had killed a part of him. Mma Venter meant well, she wanted to help, but she could never understand.

'Yes,' Tjipuka lied. 'Next time I will fight him.'

That evening, Riette sat at the table in her house and pulled the lamp closer. Stanley Williams had arrived during the day with new stock. He'd also brought a letter from Abigail Woods. With all of the trouble with Tjipuka and the stock from Stanley to attend to, she only now had a chance to read the letter.

Dear Riette,

I hope this letter finds you well. I'm happy to hear your life is peaceful there. Stanley has assured me that you are not lying to me. I know you well and know that you might lie to me to protect me from the truth, but Stanley assures me that is not the case.

I have received a letter from John Reilly. I had thought perhaps I should not mention it to you, that it might open up old wounds, but I've decided otherwise. He speaks fondly of you. Despite how things ended, I do believe he loved you. He was given difficult choices. You should know at least he is well. He and his wife are expecting their third child. But he asked me to please pass on his best wishes to you.

My dear Riette, I hope you are really well. I hope you have found some peace there so far away. Know that I think of you constantly and if you should decide to return, you always have a home with us.

Love,
Abigail

Riette folded the letter. Time was so deceptive. She had been in Tsau for six years and yet she was always at the camp, always on the koppie with John. She swam in the dam with Annemie. She worked in the hospital in Kimberley. Everything was always happening at the same time.

Running away had worked for her. She was safe in her tiny house, in her shop. But Tsau was a lonely place for her sometimes. She was forever an outsider because of her white skin. It was only recently, with Tjipuka, that she felt any real closeness. She wondered if it would continue after the baby was born. Tjipuka would stop working in the shop. If all went as she hoped, the baby might be the key that finally allowed her husband to accept her as she was now. If she left the shop, Riette knew she would miss her.

But loneliness was not the worst thing. She filled it with her memories, and that was not a bad thing either. She sometimes imagined that she'd been pregnant when she left John. She dreamed about her and John's child, a girl, she thought. A happy, carefree girl. She would have been something more concrete than memories. Riette tried not to be sad that this child didn't exist outside her dreams.

She carried the lamp to her bedroom and took off her clothes and placed them in the wardrobe. She pulled her nightgown over her head and pushed back the bedclothes. Then she placed the letter in the drawer of the bedside table and blew out the lamp.

In the dark it was easier to see John's face. He leaned over her and kissed her deeply, tenderly. She felt the kiss throughout her body and she let it move freely. She held him to her and he was solid and safe and she was there. She was just there and it was good enough.

45

March 1908

'The money is enough for a sheep or a goat. Should I give it to you now or wait?' Mma Venter asked.

'Do you know anyone selling?'

'The quelea birds ate many fields; people need money. I think you'll find a good price. If you like, I could give you an advance, then you can buy two. You can negotiate for two and you'll get an even better price. Try Mma Gaone. She has some very nice sheep.'

'Yes, I'll do that later today. I'll go to Mma Gaone.'

They heard a wagon outside, and Mma Venter looked out the door. 'It's Mr du Preez. I suppose he's delivering the lumber I asked for and a few other things.' She sighed heavily. 'I see he brought his wife.'

Tjipuka watched Mma Venter from the doorway. She greeted them both. 'Goeie môre.'

Mr du Preez gave a terse greeting and got down from the wagon to begin offloading the stock.

The woman, the wife, ignored the greeting and walked out towards the bush without a word to anyone. Mma Venter watched her, but said nothing and began offloading the wagon with Mr du Preez. Tjipuka went out to help but Mma Venter stopped her. 'No, this is too much for you. Watch the shop.'

When they'd finished, the woman seemed to know and reappeared from the bush. She climbed onto the wagon without a word, her eyes straight ahead, and they were off. Mma Venter came back into the shop. Tjipuka could see that her mood had changed, but they had stock to unpack so they got to work in silence.

They unpacked the crates and began stocking the shelves. Mma Venter held up some yellow wool she'd pulled out from among the crates.

'Look. I ordered this for the baby. I'm going to knit a small blanket. It took a long time to arrive though, I must knit quickly.' She handed it to Tjipuka.

Tjipuka reached out for the wool, which was a fine weave, and held it to her face. 'It's lovely. The baby will be sleeping with feathers.'

She put the wool to the side and they continued stocking the shelves. They talked of nothing. Mma Venter repeated a recipe for biscuits that Tjipuka wanted to know. Then they lapsed into silence.

'What was wrong with that woman? Du Preez's woman? Why didn't she greet you? It was as if she was angry. Do you know her?' Tjipuka asked, at last.

'No, I don't know her, but they all seem to know me, they all seem to judge me.'

'Judge? You?'

Mma Venter sat back from where she was kneeling. 'It has to do with the camp, about how I left.'

'What do you mean?'

Mma Venter stood up, rubbing her knees. She sat down in a chair. Tjipuka wished she hadn't asked. She'd thought it was nothing, a story like any other, but Mma Venter's face was serious, strained, readying itself for painful words.

'I worked in the hospital in the camp. I became friends with an Irish man there. To them it made me a traitor. Some people saw that as a betrayal of whatever cause they were fighting for. But it wasn't my fight. Maybe it was my husband's fight, or my father's – but not mine.'

'What happened to the Irish man?'

'John Reilly?' Mma Venter looked down at her hands, which now held a tin of condensed milk. She rolled it back and forth. 'He was a good man. He tried his best. For a while we made each other happy, and that's important. Now I wonder if it was not the happiest time of my life. I don't know. He helped me escape the camp. He's my hero for that. There was just too much against it all … I think our lives are not always our own. John went home to his people and I eventually came to Tsau.'

Tjipuka continued placing the tins in tidy rows on the shelves. Beans next to beans. Syrup next to syrup. 'And you? Don't you miss your people?' Tjipuka asked.

'Who are my people? My parents were harsh, strict, distant people, angry I didn't find a husband sooner and leave their house, stop eating their food. My husband was a stranger. The women in the camps hated me in the end. How are they my people? No, I don't miss them. I had a brother I missed for a long time after he died. I miss John sometimes. I miss Annemie, one of my husband's daughters. But they're gone. I don't miss anyone else really.'

Tjipuka reached out for Mma Venter's hand. She squeezed it and they continued stocking the shelves.

'We're so similar, you and I. Can it be so?' Tjipuka said. Was it wrong to say such a thing? That a black person and a white person could be the same, more similar to each other than to any of their own race, their own people?

Mma Venter stood up. 'I think so. I saw it that first day you arrived with Ludwig.'

She walked to the back of the shop carrying a crate. The conversation had upset her. Tjipuka sat on her stool for a moment, stroking the yellow wool. She thought of Mma Venter escaping through the bush, through the hills, over the rivers, to get away from everything that she found familiar because the familiar was painful and needed to be forgotten. Only the unknown had the safety and comfort she needed. Tjipuka understood that.

She wondered what had gone on between Mma Venter and John Reilly. From her eyes when she spoke about him, she suspected Mma Venter had loved him, that she had loved the enemy. Tjipuka wondered if she had as well. Had she also loved the enemy? But was John Reilly the enemy? Was Ludwig? For people like Mrs du Preez, everything was easily understood, with stark divides between right and wrong, because they knew nothing. It was the understanding, the knowing, that brought the difficulties. It was the closeness, where right and wrong could no longer be seen clearly – that was where the real truth was and where the answers were difficult, often impossible, to find.

46

March 1908

Tjipuka, at the cooking fire, waited for Ruhapo to come to her. He sat down on the wooden chair next to her, inside the kitchen made of reeds. She shifted the three-legged pot on the fire.

He was quiet for a moment, watching her. 'I got the land for the cattlepost,' he said. 'It's near the lake so water will not be a problem.'

'Good, very good news.' It was another relief, another step towards things being right.

He took her hands in his. 'Tjipuka, it'll be better now. You'll see. We'll move all of our animals there. Everything will be better. Shall we build a hut there?'

'If you think so,' she said. 'Yes, I think it's a good idea.'

'We'll keep our house here, but we can build a house there too. So we can be near the cattle. There are lions. We can't afford to lose a cow to a lion, not now. But it's very good land. We'll do well there.'

His voice filled with excitement. He liked planning and dreaming, and he had things to plan and dream about now. He had been waiting for this day, for his independence day. Everything would come right now.

'We'll make a new life there. We'll forget about everything. It will be better, you'll see. The past won't matter any more.'

She looked at him. She wanted to believe him. A new place. A new life – no longer servants, but masters of their own futures. Though she knew that meant a lot, she also knew it would not wipe their memories away; it would not change the two of them back to how they were. Even so, she tried to hope.

They sat quietly for a while. 'When I thought you were dead, I didn't care if I stayed working for Mogalakwe forever. It didn't matter. Everything changed when I saw you that day, though. I got another chance. We got another chance.'

Tjipuka looked at Ruhapo. He had not spoken about this before. She wanted to listen to every word. She wanted to hear his true heart.

'Tjipuka, I know the child may not be mine. And I know you had no choice in any of it. You thought I was dead. I try to think that you were like me, you were feeling what I was feeling. Nothing mattered any more. I think that's how it was when you thought I was dead, wasn't it?'

She nodded her head.

'Yes, I knew it. I try my hardest to remember that. Then anger takes over. I feel like I'm to blame, I'm to blame for everything. That time in Okahandja before it all, I was so certain a war with the Germans would be the end of it and that we would all have our lives back. I was young and stupid and so wrong. We were all wrong. It was the beginning of everything. If I hadn't been so certain I was right, Saul would be alive, you wouldn't have had to go through all that you did. You would have been with me, where I could have protected you. You wanted to leave. Do you remember? You said we should leave before the war started. But I wouldn't. I thought I knew something, that I was needed for everything to go as it should. But instead I let you down.' Ruhapo looked around the compound and then back at Tjipuka. 'It's all because of me. But that's over now. All of that can disappear, be forgotten.'

He was holding her hands and looking at her. 'I promise you, it won't matter. If the child is his or mine, it will not matter. I promise you. I'll take the child as my own. The child will be ours. This child is ours.'

He pulled Tjipuka to him and held her. She wanted so much to believe him. He wanted to take the burden from her but, no matter how much he wished for it, he couldn't. He thought he was telling her the truth, but she knew he was lying. Not deliberately, but he was lying. She wished she could accept that it was all over, gone, as if it had never happened – but that was a fairy tale, and she'd never been a girl who believed in fairy tales.

47
May 1908

Ruhapo decided to build the kraal and hut on a small hill away from the lake. Good rainy seasons would see the lake flood and they wanted to be safe. The men came and put up the poles and the rafters, and the women built the mud walls and a small lolwapa at the front. The thatching would start the next day. Though the hut was at the cattlepost, Tjipuka and Ruhapo would live there, at least for now. They didn't want to take any chances with the few cattle they had. It would be their new home, away from everyone, only for them.

'It's good. We'll move the animals tomorrow.' Ruhapo looked over his small patch of land. 'I think this land is better than what we had in Okahandja – there's more pasture. It won't take long to build up our herd.'

Ruhapo sat down on the floor of the lolwapa next to Tjipuka, leaning against the short wall, his legs shot out in front of him. 'Have you told Mma Venter you'll leave the job?'

'Not yet. I thought maybe I should wait until the baby's born. It's not long now. I think I'll get at least two sheep with the last money. That'll help.'

'Yes.' Ruhapo looked out down the hill to the lake. 'You're a good wife. I couldn't have done this alone.'

'Are you ready to eat?'

Tjipuka gave him a plate with bread and slices of biltong she'd packed from the village. 'Mma Venter says Kgosi Mathiba gave you this land because he was frightened. He believes the Mbanderu are witches. He says they've poisoned the camel thorn tree at the kgotla.'

'He's a silly man, scared and superstitious. Always afraid Sekgoma's supporters are organising to kill him. I don't care about his reasons. Let him think what he likes. All I care about is that I got the land. I thought Mogalakwe was going to block me. It seems he changed his mind.'

'No, he tried, but the chief wouldn't listen. That's what they're saying in the village.'

'It doesn't matter. I can't hold it against him. If I were Mogalakwe I would have tried to keep me as well. He's a very wealthy man because of me.'

They sat looking out at the lake. It was the end of the wet season and the lake was full. The water from the Delta would continue to flow into it, filling it for many months after the rains stopped. It was water from far away that filled the lakes of the Delta, water from the north, that flowed over many places, free and unhindered, collecting here. It seemed right that their new home would be in such a place.

They finished eating and sat silently. Things were better already between them. The tension had eased. Ruhapo stood and held out his hand to her. She took it and he pulled her to her feet. They walked to the lake and looked out over its calm surface. Tjipuka heard the mad cry of a fish eagle and looked up in time to see it swoop down leisurely to the water's surface and snatch a fat fish in its claws.

Ruhapo turned to her. He pulled her dress over her head. She felt awkward with her big stomach, but he bent down and kissed it. He slipped out of his clothes and led her to the river. She was hot from the day's work and the cool water felt like magic on her skin.

He pulled her in deeper and held her to him. 'This reminds me of that day ...'

He began but didn't finish. He didn't need to. They both remembered. The day at the hidden waterfall, the one he made just for her. She held him around his neck and he kissed her. She realised that it had been a long time since he'd kissed her like that. She kissed him back and wrapped her legs around him.

'I do still love you,' he said like a plea. 'I love you as I always did.'

'I love you too,' she said.

They wanted to stamp that, proclaim it – to mark this moment, in case it became lost again.

Tjipuka lay back in the water and pushed herself up into the sun. The coolness on her back and the hot sun on her stomach felt good. With her legs still wrapped around Ruhapo's waist, she felt light. Her mind was free of its burdens, and she closed her eyes. She wanted to be only in that moment, nowhere else. She stopped her mind from moving to the past or to the future. She felt only the water lap against her. She felt only Ruhapo's strong hands on her buttocks. The heat of the sun warmed her all the way through. This will be our life now, she told herself.

They slept on a reed mat inside the new mud hut, the roof wide open so they were watched by the clear night sky, littered with stars. The stars Tjipuka used to resent for shining. But the way her heart was open now, it was easy to forgive even the traitorous stars. She watched them back and ran her hand along Ruhapo's side where he slept, snoring lightly.

She could feel the baby rolling over. She held her stomach. 'Sleep little one, sleep. All is well tonight.'

48

May 1908

She woke up confused. She'd been dreaming about Okahandja, about the time just after Saul was born. He was such a good baby, always content. He rarely cried and Ruhapo worried about that.

'What kind of fighter will he be?' he asked.

'Maybe he won't be a fighter. Maybe he'll be a peacemaker.'

'My sons must be fighters, they must be brave warriors.' He looked down at Saul. He poked at him to wake him up.

'Stop that. He's sleeping. You know he's my son too.'

'Perhaps,' Ruhapo said, not wanting to give in just yet.

Awake now, she looked up through the roofless hut at the open sky and remembered where she was. Saul was gone. No one would know who was right. Was he to be a peacemaker? A warrior? They never got to find out.

She sat up and realised Ruhapo was gone. The baby repositioned himself. Maybe this one intends to be a warrior, she thought – though she suspected that that was not the child Ruhapo wished for any more.

She took a bucket and headed towards the lake, where she washed her face and collected water to take back to the hut. In the distance she saw two hippos. There were many in the lake and in the Delta. But these hippos were calm, resting in the water after a night of grazing on land. They did not want to harm her.

As she climbed the hill to their house, she saw Ruhapo returning with someone. Drawing nearer, she saw it was Tjizumo, Ruhapo's regiment member and friend, the one who'd helped him get to Tsau. She was surprised to see him because he had left with Samuel Maharero for the Transvaal the year before. He was a keen supporter of Maharero and there had been no question of him staying behind. Tjipuka wondered what had gone wrong to bring him back to Tsau.

'Wa penduka, Tjizumo,' she said.

'Are you well, Mama Tjipuka?' he asked. He'd aged in that short time. His voice was rough, as if a cough was caught along his throat. He was bent like an old man. Standing next to one another, the two men looked like father and son, not age-mates.

'I'm well. I was about to make tea. Will you join us? I'm sorry we have no chairs – we're still moving, as you can see.'

'That's fine.'

Ruhapo sat on the wall of the lolwapa and Tjizumo joined him. 'So you're back now? To stay?' Ruhapo asked him.

'I'm not sure. The Transvaal was bad. The men are dying every day underground in those mines. The work is too much, and there's little food and hardly any money. Omuhona was lied to and now he's stuck. I doubt he'll stay much longer either.'

'So you'll wait for him?' Ruhapo asked.

'He won't come back here, not to the land of the Batawana. Not after they disrespected him like that. Sekgoma Letsholathebe made treaties that he didn't keep. He promised if the Herero had problems he would help them and then, when Omuhona asked for that help, he pretended he had never said it. Samuel Maharero is a proud man. If he moves, he will only move to where they recognise him as the paramount chief of the Herero. I'll wait here for now until things are decided. My mother's uncle has a compound in Tsau. I'm staying with him.'

Tjipuka brought the tea. She poured and handed the two cups to the men. She sat on the floor of the lolwapa and listened.

'I think Samuel Maharero is thinking of returning to Hereroland,' Tjizumo said. The war is over. The Germans have set the people free. All of the camps have been closed now, and the people need their leader that side.'

Ruhapo shook his head. 'The Germans won't allow him to return. They might lie and say yes, but they'll kill him once he sets foot on their land.'

'Are all the camps closed then?' Tjipuka asked.

'Yes, the people are free.'

'Free to leave?'

'Yes. I suspect some will come here, looking for the people they lost in the war. It will take time, but things will be like before.'

Tjizumo spoke so hopefully, but Tjipuka knew things would never be like before. She hoped it was true that the people were free to leave, to come to Tsau if they wanted. Did Novengi know where to find her? Would she be able to come looking? If she could, Tjipuka knew she would.

'No one will be free there while the Germans are in control of the country,' Ruhapo said. 'They say the new laws don't allow a black person to own a cow, not even a goat. They must only work as servants under the whites. Is that freedom? Not any kind I know. There's no way the Germans will let the Herero leave. They need their labour. They'll go from being prisoners in the camps to being prisoners on the farms and in the mines.'

Tjipuka and Tjizumo kept quiet. Ruhapo stood, leaving his tea untouched. 'I need to go to the village,' he said. 'I need to collect something.'

He walked down the hill towards the village, with Tjizumo following him. Tjipuka hoped Tjizumo would know enough to stop talking about Hereroland and Maharero, about the Germans. Ruhapo's anger was not limited to her.

Even so, Tjipuka was excited about what she'd heard. Somewhere

Novengi was free. Finally free. Since Ludwig had left Tjipuka in Tsau, eight months ago, she'd not had any contact with him. She thought of him sometimes, wondered how he was, but she didn't want to risk anything by sending him a letter. Everything was too tenuous between her and Ruhapo. But now things were better and she needed to know about Novengi. She needed Novengi to know where she was, and her only link was through Ludwig. There would be no way to get a letter to Peter, but to Ludwig she could.

She dug in her bag, pulled out a notebook and a pencil, carefully tore out one of the pages and began to write.

Dear Ludwig,

I hope that you travelled safely back to Lüderitz. I never got to thank you for the generosity you showed by allowing me to stay here with my husband. We are forever in your debt.

I have heard that the camp at Shark Island is closed. Do you know anything about my sister Novengi? Please, if you know where she is, can you tell her I am in Tsau? I still have the money you gave me. I could send it to her so that she could come to me if you can find her.

I know you have done so much for me already, I have no right to ask anything else of you, but I have no one else to turn to.

Yours truly,
Tjipuka

She read over the letter and put it in her bag. She would send it through Mma Venter and use that return address too. Ruhapo needn't know about it. She was hopeful that Ludwig would help her and that he would get the letter to Novengi and help her get to Tsau.

The sun was climbing up the sky, so Tjipuka collected the enga and went to cut thatch for the roof. She could not climb the ladder to thatch now that she was so close to delivering, but she would prepare everything for when Ruhapo returned. She hoped he would come with help. It would be better to have the roof done before night.

She worked the whole day, only stopping for water and a bit of food at lunch. She felt good and wanted to work while she could. She knew this child in her womb was temperamental, and lately when he was upset he made sure she suffered with him.

Evening came and still Ruhapo had not returned. She lay on the mat and covered herself with the blanket; with the night sky clear above her, she fell asleep.

Sometime in the night she heard shouting. She woke up and saw the lamp on. Their things were spread all over the hut. For a moment, she thought thieves had broken in, but then she saw Ruhapo standing above her. To her surprise, she could smell alcohol. He didn't usually drink. She suspected the talk with Tjizumo had upset him. Something was wrong, but her sleepy mind could not sort things out.

'What is this?' He threw the letter at her.

She was confused at first, and then she remembered. How had he found it? It meant he'd searched through everything.

'So now that it's all over, you want to go back to your German lover? Is that it?'

Tjipuka stood up. She felt vulnerable lying at his feet on the ground – at least standing she had a better chance.

'It's not like that. I wrote to him so I could find Novengi ... You read the letter. She's all alone there. I want him to tell her where I am.'

'You're a whore! A German whore. I saw what some women did. They gave themselves to those animals so that they could avoid the suffering. But did I ever think my own wife could be one of them? I thought you had no choice, that you were forced. I see now that was never the case. You chose him to save yourself, leaving Novengi in the camp to die!'

The words cut at her. He came towards her with the letter in his hand, and he pushed it in her face.

'Do you know what these people did? They raped old women and stabbed them through their private parts afterwards. They put knives through babies' stomachs, cut off the men's penises. And you lay with this man. His bastard grows in you!'

He reached to hit her and she stepped back. He came at her. He grabbed her hair, turned her around and pushed her face into the rough mud wall.

'Please, Ruhapo. You're hurting me, you're hurting the baby.'

He leaned hard against her, her body pressed against the wall. She begged but he heard nothing. His anger rang too loudly in his ears. His monsters were in control now; her husband, what was left of him, was gone.

'You let him touch you. Why? And now you thank him for it! You thank him for enslaving you? For raping you?'

He was roaring. He let her go and she fell to the floor. Then he turned back and grabbed her. He dragged her by the arm and pulled her down the hill towards the lake. She stumbled and fell, and he pulled her to her feet again. At the lake, he dragged her into the water. He dunked her and then began scrubbing her all over with a rough rock – her arms, her legs, her face. He was wild action, nothing more.

'I'll get rid of him! I'll get rid of him. I'll clean him from you once and for all.'

He was lost. He didn't see her. He saw only the pictures in his mind that haunted him, that would never let him alone. Holding her tightly, he scrubbed at her skin, rubbing the rough stone over her body. The water darkened as the scrapes on her skin began to bleed.

She didn't fight him. He was right. She had sinned. She knew the truth of what had happened. She had left Novengi to die so she could live. She'd chosen to be with Ludwig. She'd told Ruhapo lies, she'd told Mma Venter lies, but she knew the truth, and it was much worse than Ruhapo thought. She knew that she too was the enemy.

She left him to his job. Maybe he could scrape and scrape and finally she would be free, free of it all, free of the guilt. Finally she would be clean. It was one thing to be raped, to carry a child from that rape in your womb, but what did it mean when you willingly entered the enemy's bed? The enemy that destroyed your people? That killed your son? That imprisoned the friend you loved more than a sister? What did it mean when you *chose* the enemy?

Ruhapo was right; she was evil and needed to be cleaned of her sins. Yes, she thought. Let him clean me. Let him finally make me clean.

Ruhapo stopped. He dropped the stone. He walked away from the lake and into the moonlight's shadows, and was gone.

She dragged her body to the edge. She could hear hippos grunting nearby, but she didn't care. She was so very tired of this life. Every time she thought the suffering was over, it reared its head again. It was relentless and would not let her go. She was tired now. She wanted release.

She stung in the places where he'd scrubbed. She could feel the cold on her skin. Her body shook. She didn't know how long she lay there but at last she stood, carefully testing her legs, and walked out of the shallows. Slowly she made her way back to the hut. Ruhapo was not there and she was glad for that. She could not hear his apologies or his silence. She did not want to see him. She wasn't angry. She was not even afraid of him. She just wanted him not there.

She lay on the mat. Where were Tjipuka and Ruhapo, the people they'd once been? She'd hoped they lurked like ghosts waiting to take repossession of their bodies. She had been so sure that eventually they would both be found and they'd be whole again.

Now she knew that would never happen. Nothing could bring them back. Nothing. Not a new house, not a new life. Not a new child. They were broken beyond repair and their old selves had disappeared into the ether. The blood, the cruelty, the loss, the mistakes – it had all killed those people they once knew.

She tried to see herself and Ruhapo as they might have been if everything had not happened, and she could picture nothing. Everything had stopped. They were not there, no matter where she looked. The possibility of going back to the path they had been following had been lost. Too much had happened. Hard work in a new place would not bring them back. Forgetting it all would not bring them back.

Now she knew – she must accept everything only as it was now. He was this man. He was this man who hated her. Who saw her as the enemy. Worse than that – the whore to the enemy. She was the woman she was now, made of everything she had done. No wish, no hope would change that.

She could not lie to herself any more. She could no longer justify anything – she'd made her choices, some within confined spaces, but she'd made her choices, and now she was here. She could undo nothing and neither could Ruhapo. He wanted to, and she suspected that was where his anger emanated from. He was still fighting the truth. He wanted to deny what was. But a person can only do that for so long.

She wished she had died at Ohamakari or at Shark Island. Then her story would be a simple one. The heroic Herero woman sacrificing her life for the revolution. Now she was neither heroic nor cowardly. She was not dead, nor was she properly alive.

When, eventually, she fell asleep, it was a fitful sleep. She was with Novengi, but then Novengi was dead. She and Ruhapo were making love and then Saul's dead body lay between them. Ludwig saved her and then cut her up and fed her to the circling sharks in the cold, wild sea. It was chaotic and frightening, and she jumped awake.

The sun was nearly over the wall of the roofless hut. She moved carefully since her skin was tender, patched with places where it had been scraped away. The blanket she lay on was dotted with blood. She stood up, painfully, and felt dizzy. Reaching for the wall to steady herself, she felt she might be sick. She walked along the wall, inching towards the door. Outside she retched, nothing more than water, since she couldn't remember the last time she ate. When she straightened herself, a deep pain pushed through her body. She held her heavy stomach, then felt something wet. She looked down. Blood was dripping down her legs. She felt for the baby, but he didn't move. Something was wrong. She must get to Mma Venter in the village, a mile or more away.

She took her bag with everything of value to her inside and then picked a tall branch from the firewood near the hut. Using it as a walking stick, she headed to the village. She needed to save her child.

49
May 1908

How Tjipuka made it all the way to the village, she could not say. On the way she made peace with the fact that the baby was dead. Blood dripped down her legs, leaving a spotted trail behind her. Her stomach was still. She didn't blame Ruhapo. Maybe it was better if the baby were dead. It was not fair to bring a child into their home filled with broken people.

Mma Venter was in the shop when she arrived. Tjipuka held the door frame for support; she could not take another step. She barely had the strength to say, 'Help me.'

'Oh no! My god, what has he done to you? What has he done?'

Mma Venter went to Tjipuka and helped her into her house and to her bedroom. 'Here, lie here.'

She pushed the blankets back off the bed, then rushed out and came back with a bucket of warm water and a bottle of antiseptic. She took out the wooden horn she used to hear the baby and put it carefully on Tjipuka's stomach. She moved it around, first near the top, then towards the bottom. Her face looked worried.

She tried again and then she stopped and she looked up. 'She's alive. She's alive, but only just. We need to get her out.'

Mma Venter disappeared. Tjipuka heard her going through cupboards, through her big chest where she kept her herbs and medicines. Tjipuka held her hand on her stomach. For the first time, she didn't care who the baby's father was – it didn't matter. What mattered was that she was the baby's mother. This child would be strong and proud and resilient. Nothing would come before her that she could not withstand. And Tjipuka knew, she knew now that Mma Venter had always been right. This baby was a girl.

Mma Venter came back with a cup of brown-green tea. 'Drink this. It will get everything going. You drink it and we wait – by evening the pains will start. Until then you'll rest and prepare yourself.'

Tjipuka drank the bitter tea and lay back on the pillows. Mma Venter got to work cleaning the many scrapes around Tjipuka's body. The whole time Mma Venter spoke, half to herself and half to Tjipuka.

'Always selfish, these men. How does he do something like this when you carry a baby? I don't care what has happened. It has all happened. It is always happening. It will happen again. Over and over they do it. Men fight, men make war that destroys everything, and women carry the wounds, they clean it up. They rub it away, and they go on. On and on. And yet men pound their chests and say we are the winners. What? What? What do they win? They win the right to say they are animals, and killers. That's not a win. And women keep going. Head down, they move forward. They bind the wounds. They stroke the foreheads. They bear the children – and they bury them. And this man blames you? He should blame himself. Himself and his kind. War is for men. It's always for men. They have a dark place where war grows. They set it free with a patriotic song and a flag; they speak of how right it is – though it's all wrong. He beats you from that place. He kills others from that place. And then he closes it up and puts on nice clothes and pretends he's upstanding and good. But it's there, always there. He sees it as separate, but it's him. And it will always come again.

'But women, we don't know that part. We don't have it. We know it only from its actions. How does he do this to the woman he loves? I don't understand, I can never understand. I won't … I won't understand. Men made all of this and yet women, women carry the wreckage.'

Tjipuka listened to Mma Venter's angry words. Was it really Ruhapo and Ludwig and all of the men who were the ones to blame? What about Peter? What about Joseph? Were they to blame? Did they also have this dark place? Tjipuka didn't think so. She listened to Mma Venter's angry words, which she spoke like a chant. Tjipuka could not accept all that Mma Venter said. She was angry. Just like Tjipuka, she had withstood the burden of war. She'd tried to find a way to understand it and this was her way. Tjipuka could not judge that.

She no longer felt scared to see her baby. She was not fearful for what the baby could mean. She didn't care about any of that any more. She agreed with Mma Venter now. Perhaps in a way she loved Ludwig. He was not a bad man. He made mistakes. He was only who he was. He was all that came before him, he was everything around him. He was who he was. Just as Ruhapo was who he was. Each trying to make sense of things. Each trying to see how to get through this life. She blamed no one. And she did not blame herself now. It was the same for her.

She didn't blame this child. This child would live. She would be born and, if Tjipuka had her way, she would carry no expectations on her shoulders, no burdens, no guilt, no history. She would not have questions to answer. Tjipuka would not allow that. She had had enough. She would not allow any more. Everything must stop now.

Mma Venter was still ranting about men and war as she washed the blood away, and Tjipuka drifted off to sleep.

The pains came just as the day ended. Tjipuka knew life preferred to begin and end in the night. She walked outside to watch the sun disappear below the horizon. The heat of the day went with the sun and the coolness of night arrived. The spicy smell of wild sage filled the air. A grey hornbill whistled in a tree near the house. In the next yard, she heard a child laughing. A dog barked in the distance. Cooking fires were starting. A woman sang.

Mma Venter came up next to her. They stood quietly, listening to the day ending. Tjipuka gripped her arm as a pain pushed through her body in its long and winding way. First stepping softly, then roaring, then slipping off in a slow crawl. She steadied her legs as it retreated. She knew it would not be gone for long.

'I think I'll go in,' she said, and Mma Venter followed her.

Tjipuka lay on the bed. Mma Venter gave her water. Then she went away and came back with two bowls of warm yellow custard. She handed one to Tjipuka.

'You must build up your strength. We don't know how long this one will take to arrive.'

Mma Venter sat down on a chair near the bed, facing the open window. Tjipuka set the custard dish to the side. Another pain was moving through her body. She didn't make a sound. She closed her eyes and let it make its way through; she did not fight it, it was what would bring her child to her. She welcomed it.

'Even though it was wrong, I hoped I would get pregnant by John Reilly,' Mma Venter said. 'He was such a kind, lovely man.'

'And have you heard from your John Reilly?' Tjipuka asked.

'He's back with the wife he belongs to. I hope he's well. He was soft hearted, those kinds don't take easily to war. Sometimes they don't survive inside even if they survive outside.'

Tjipuka stood up. She could take the pains better standing. They were coming faster. She leaned against the window. It was night now. A sliver of a moon, like a bit of a fingernail, hung above. Stars littered the sky.

'I think some men don't have that place, that dark place you believe in. Don't you think John Reilly was free of it?'

'Maybe. On my good days, I think yes. On my bad days, I think no. Today's a maybe day.' Mma Venter laughed. Tjipuka joined her, it felt good. 'How are you doing? The pains are coming faster now, eh?'

'Yes, I think this baby will arrive soon.'

Tjipuka went back to the bed. Mma Venter got her wooden horn. She placed it on Tjipuka's stomach.

'Yes, there she is. She's back now. Her heart is strong. She knows she is going to meet her mother soon.' She put her hands on Tjipuka's stomach to check the baby's position. She pressed carefully. 'She is ready to meet us.'

The time passed. Mma Venter read to Tjipuka from a book about a man, a traveller in the Transvaal, and his dog called Jock, *Jock of the Bushveld*. Tjipuka was reminded of Joseph and how he used to read to them, a happy time in a chain of sadness. She closed her eyes and pictured the man with his dog, Jock, facing down an elephant ready to attack them.

Before midnight her water broke and everything sped up. Mma Venter brought a basin of warm water with fragrant herbs floating in it. The lamp's flame made shadows dance on the wall and Tjipuka concentrated on them as she felt the urge to push. Mma Venter told her it was time. Three times she pushed and the baby arrived with a loud scream. Mma Venter tied the cord off with two pieces of boiled cotton and cut the middle with a pair of scissors.

Tjipuka lay back and watched as Mma Venter carefully washed her daughter. The entire time, the baby screamed in protest.

'She's not quiet like her mother, this one,' Mma Venter said. 'She's here to make a big noise.'

'It's better like that,' Tjipuka said.

Mma Venter handed her the baby swaddled in a thick blanket. Once in Tjipuka's arms her daughter finally became silent. She had a bright-red, heart-shaped mouth. Her eyes were wide open, looking at this new world of hers. Her skin was a shade darker than white, her eyes blue, her hair curly and light brown.

Tjipuka touched her daughter's hair, then she held her child to her chest and wept. She cried for all of the loss. For all of the people gone, all of the hopes dashed, all of the love denied. She cried for Ludwig, who would never know his beautiful daughter. She cried for Maveipi and Saul. She cried for the brave Mara and Tjirwe. And for Joseph and Kahaka and Lucinda. It all poured from her. She cried for Ruhapo – and she cried for herself.

Mma Venter watched but did nothing. No one could change anything of what had already passed.

50
May 1908

'Is my wife here?'

Tjipuka heard Ruhapo at the front of the house. She was in Mma Venter's bed, nursing her daughter.

Mma Venter's voice was hard. 'No, she's not here.'

'They say you have her here.'

'They lie. She came here after you nearly killed her, yes. I helped her and she left. She's gone now. If she has any sense, she'll be far from you. She'll run far away and never return.'

'She's carrying my child. She's my wife and she's carrying my child. You shouldn't say such things.' Tjipuka could hear in his voice that he wanted to be fierce, but was restraining himself.

'There are many things we should not do, but we do them, don't we? You should not take your wife into the river and scrape her skin off. But you do it.' Mma Venter was a warrior too, Ruhapo would be taught that.

'I was angry. I was … I was not in my right mind.'

'And next time? Next time when you're not in your right mind? Will you kill her? Kill her child?'

Ruhapo didn't reply. Tjipuka heard the door slam. Then she heard a horse being ridden away at speed.

Mma Venter came into the bedroom. 'He's gone. But he'll come back. I think he knows I was lying.'

'Yes, well ...' Tjipuka didn't want to think about that now.

'Tjipuka, I need to go to the other side of the village. I must collect the bread for the shop from Mma Refilwe. Will you be all right by yourself?'

'Yes, we'll be fine.'

Tjipuka heard the front door close. She looked down at her daughter – she was so beautiful. For two days, they'd been together, getting to know each other. She hadn't had the courage yet to think beyond the walls of that room, but she knew decisions needed to be made, and she thought it was the right time.

She laid her daughter in the middle of the bed. She was sleeping, her long lashes resting on her powder cheeks. Tjipuka got up carefully. She must be quick. She packed some food. She had her money, her sewing money, the gold coins and the diamond ring. The time had never been right to tell Ruhapo about what she had been given. She was glad about that now.

She wrote a quick note for Mma Venter. This baby needed a mother who would not see her own mistakes and losses each time she looked into her daughter's face. Mma Venter would love the little girl freely and without judgement, as all children deserved to be loved. Tjipuka knew that leaving her child would be difficult, but she had done it before. She had left Saul behind in that cold desert. She could do it again. If nothing else, everything had taught her that she could withstand even the most difficult circumstances. Even this.

She wrote another note to Ruhapo.

Dear Ruhapo,

We tried our best. I love you and I want you to be happy and I know you cannot do that with me. It is not my fault. And it is not your fault. You must forget me. And, please, I beg of you, forget my daughter.

Pretend you never knew she existed between us. Let her live her life only. Let her live in happiness, not be pulled down by our burdens and mistakes. Let her live free.

Forever your loving wife,
Tjipuka

She folded the letter and placed it on the table.

The wind would take her, she thought. The night-time stars would show her where her happiness lived. She would be free. Free of everything. When she stepped away from this place, it would disappear. She told herself it would be gone, wiped away. It would all live somewhere, continue somewhere, but she would never be able to find it again. It was better that way.

And she would be wiped clean too. The blood, the cruelty, the evil, the mistakes, the guilt – all gone, left behind. Forgotten.

She kissed her daughter carefully so as not to wake her. She picked up her bags and strapped them to her back. She placed Anna's diamond ring on the table next to the bed. Then she walked out of the door, closing it carefully behind her, and disappeared back into the desert.

Acknowledgements

I'd like to thank my early readers of the manuscript in its various forms. They are: Peter Midgley, Jenny Robson, Moses Ndiriva Kandjou, Lizzy Attree and Wame Molefhe. It truly does take a village. Ke a leboga le kamoso.

I also must thank the academics who wrote books and papers that I read in order to have the background knowledge to write Tjipuka's story. So much of the history of southern Africa is unwritten, and it is through your work of discovery that it will survive. Thank you. These publications include, among others, 'Oral Tradition and Identity: The Herero in Botswana' and *The History of Herero Settlement in Botswana* by Kristen Alnaes, 'The Okavango Delta Peoples of Botswana' by John Bock and Sarah E. Johnson, *Herero Heroes. The Revolt of the Hereros (Perspectives on Southern Africa)* by Jon M. Bridgman, *'The angel of death has descended violently among them': Concentration Camps and Prisoners-of-War in Namibia, 1904–08* by C.W. Erichsen, '"I Was Afraid of Samuel, Therefore I Came to Sekgoma": Herero Refugees and Patronage Politics in Ngamiland, Bechuanaland Protectorate, 1890–1914' and 'The Great General of the Kaiser' by Jan-Bart Gewald, 'Double Descent and Its Correlates among the Herero of Ngamiland' by Gordon D. Gibson, 'Herero Households' by Henry Harpending and Renee Pennington, 'War, flight, asylum: A brief history of the Ovambanderu of Ngamiland, Botswana, 1896–1961' by Kaendee ua Kandapaera, 'The History of the Herero in Mahalapye, Central District: 1922–1984' by Boammaruri Bahumi Kebonang, *The Politics of Separation: The Case of the Ovaherero of Ngamiland* by George Uaisana Manase, *Herero Ecology: The Literary Impact* by Rajmund Ohly, *Words Cannot Be Found – German Colonial Rule in Namibia: An Annotated Reprint of the 1918 Blue Book* by Jeremy Silvester and Jan-Bart Gewald, and 'The Entry of the Herero into Botswana' by Frank Robert Vivelo.

By the same author

Thato Lekoko: Superhero, 2015
The Second Worst Thing, 2013
Signed, The Secret Keeper, 2013
In the Spirit of McPhineas Lata and Other Stories, 2012
Love in the Shadows, 2012
Anything for Money, 2011
Signed, Hopelessly in Love, 2011
Mr Not Quite Good Enough, 2011
Can He Be The One?, 2010
Curse of the Gold Coins, 2010
Kwaito Love, 2010
Lorato and Her Wire Car, 2009
Birthday Wishes and Other Stories, 2009
Mmele and the Magic Bones, 2009
No One is Alone and Other Stories, 2009 (co-authored)
The Ram and Other Stories, 2009 (co-authored)
He Brings a Message and Other Stories, 2009 (co-authored)
Murder for Profit, 2008
The Fatal Payout, 2005